GRAND STREET 71

Danger

GRAND STREET 71

Danger

Grand Street (ISSN 0734-5496; ISBN 1-885490-22-4) is published by Grand Street Press
(a project of the New York Foundation for the Arts, Inc., a not-for-profit corporation),
214 Sullivan Street, Suite 6C, New York, NY 10012. Tel: (212) 533-2944, Fax: (212) 533-2737.
Contributions and gifts to Grand Street Press are tax-deductible to the extent allowed
by law.

Grand Street 71— Spring 2003. Copyright © 2003 by the New York Foundation for the Arts,
Inc., Grand Street Press. All rights reserved. Reproduction, whether in whole or in part,
without permission is strictly prohibited. Second-class bound printed matter postage paid
at Trenton, NJ, and additional mailing offices. Postmaster: Please send address changes to
Grand Street Magazine, 214 Sullivan Street, Suite 6C, New York, NY 10012. Subscriptions
are $25 a year (two issues). Foreign subscriptions (including Canada) are $35 a year, and
institutional orders are $30 a year, payable in U.S. funds. Single-copy price is $15 ($24 in
Canada). For subscription inquiries, please call (877) 533-2944.

Grand Street is printed by Finlay Printing in Bloomfield, CT. It is distributed to the trade
by D.A.P./Distributed Art Publishers, 155 Avenue of the Americas, New York, NY 10013; and
Ingram Periodicals, 1240 Heil Quaker Blvd., La Vergne, TN 37086. It is distributed to news-
stands only by Bernhard DeBoer, Inc., 113 E. Centre Street, Nutley, NJ 07110; and Ubiquity
Distributors, 607 Degraw Street, Brooklyn, NY 11217. Grand Street is distributed in Australia
and New Zealand by Peribo Pty, Ltd., 58 Beaumont Road, Mount Kuring-Gai, NSW 2080,
Australia; and in the United Kingdom by Central Books, 99 Wallis Road, London, E9 5LN.

GRAND STREET

EDITOR
Jean Stein

MANAGING EDITOR
Radhika Jones

ART EDITOR
Walter Hopps

ASSISTANT EDITOR
Michael Mraz

ASSOCIATE ART EDITOR
Anne Doran

POETRY EDITOR
James Lasdun

ASSOCIATE POETRY EDITOR
Justin Ginnetti

CREATIVE DIRECTOR (PRINT)
J. Abbott Miller, Pentagram

DESIGN (PRINT)
Jeremy Hoffman, Pentagram

WEBSITE DESIGN
Faruk Ulay

COPY EDITOR
Nell McClister

INTERNS
Leyla Ertegun, Aaron Hawn, Kelly Virzi

ADVISORY EDITORS
Edward W. Said, Charles Merewether

CONTRIBUTING EDITORS
George Andreou, Mary Blume, Dominique Bourgois, Natasha Parry Brook, Frances Coady, Mike Davis, Colin de Land (from 1995 to 2003), Barbara Epler, Kennedy Fraser, Stephen Graham, Nikolaus Hansen, John Heilpern, Dennis Hopper, Jane Kramer, Brigitte Lacombe, Alane Mason, Peter Mayer, Michael Naumann, Meghan O'Rourke, Erik Rieselbach, Robin Robertson, Fiona Shaw, Daniel Slager, Robert Storr, Michi Strausfeld, Deborah Treisman, Katrina vanden Heuvel, Wendy vanden Heuvel, Deborah Warner, John Waters, Drenka Willen

FOUNDING CONTRIBUTING EDITOR
Andrew Kopkind (1935–1994)

PUBLISHERS
Jean Stein & Torsten Wiesel

VISIT OUR WEBSITE AT www.grandstreet.com

from The Man Who Walks

ALAN WARNER

The Nephew came into woke-ness of vibrated daylight knowing there was Fed sniffed round outside Man Who Walks' house. Do they Feds never learn, man? They always have their walkie-talkies turned up to squawk assistance, yet they're never done yap-yapping between themselves; specially these backland Feds: cannot shut their cake holes for a moment: never so much as thirty seconds' radio silence; you can hear that distinctive static voice buzzle furlongs away.

Once on his feet in the cellar, stood in cool shadow, the Nephew only had to wait and Fed might climb in that busted scullery window. When he heard glass tinkle into the sink, the whisper, "Up, Stalker; hup, boy," it was enough. Enter your own property and that's them sent the dogs in on you! he thought. He shouldered his backpack, plonked bar stool under, opened the coal hatch to a collapse downward of painfully bright light, and hunckled himself up. Outside he scoped both ways, let coal cellar door close quiet, then he hit out in a disembarkation hunch for a first line of tree cover, as if off a barely touched-down chopper.

Even when well and truly along the slope lines shielding him, there was no sign of mutt nor master. The Fed would be inside the rooms, yielding to the novelty of his radio transmitter, reporting a clean sweep. The Nephew

Eduardo Paolozzi, Head, 1964–84.

hoped the Fed went straight down the cellar hatch and broke his neck, and the Nephew threw himself to his stomach, crawled last fifteen feet over stony ridges of moorland. Sure as fate: a sleek, souped-up Fed Mondeo was parked on their old caravan pitch at the passing place they were always lecturing his Old Dear it was illegal to park in; a gash sunlight off its windscreen; the Nephew turned his head both ways to take in the cathedrals of blue above; it was going into being a real scorcher of a day. Sure enough, the Nephew had seen the signs: cuckoos singing at dawn, swans flying north, and in the rivers the eels turning up their silver or golden undersides or the minnows and perch leaping and the frog's skin, normally blacker among the rotted grass, had been blushing up into mustard and green.

There was no soul around but he waited a jiff, just in case a second Fed was away in trees for a slash or pulling off the gander's head, fantasizing about Juliet Bravo handcuffed to a bed, but that car was unoccupied. Even spotted now, the Nephew knew he could outrun any dog upslope, toward rail embankment, and scramble the drainage tunnel. Do the dog there, in the . . . confines. Do it clean with the hunting knife. Drag its gutted sack for trains to sweep away.

The Nephew glanced back toward Man Who Walks' house; sashayed to that police car, reached out and opened driver's door as his hair went static. He looked: ersatz leather, if no the real thing, and all state-the-art electronics, radar guns, no-expense-spared-taxpayers equipment. Not that the Nephew paid tax; no need to let your imagination completely run riot! But just then he saw a most amazing outrage: top the dashboard a sort of miniaturized video monitor was relaying the moving picture sequence right there an then—inside-swerving infrared down through Man Who Walks' papier-mâché tunnels, right there on that wee screen, view scoping left, then right, the Nephew saw massive mitt of a human hand flutter near and he realized: it was a camera strapped to a collar atop that stupid dog's head, like as used in bomb or terrorist situations! Made him seethe, such equipment in this territory, like the time, just when the pub's come out, the hydro went down with a power cut, no juice was going to them new CCTV cameras in main street: those Dose brothers put in every shop window and looted just for sheer spite, brassières clipped round their oilskins!

There was a dirty sheet of hardboard where the tar macadam turns to moss and ancient moor begins, so he scoped round. Over by thistle clusters was an example. Using the hardboard he cooried in and slid it on:

semi-fresh cow shit, usual glittering array of summer flies and vermilion-tinted bluebottles tense with activity on its crusted top, holed by beetles. Insects scattered with the under-easing of the board. As judged, like a slobbery French omelette, lower portions were green runnings. Looking over his shoulder the Nephew returned to that open police car door, checked the giveaway monitor, then let cow shit smear from the board and plomp heavy onto the driver's leather seat. Smeared it round a bit, allowing some cakelets to fall onto a fitted-carpet floor in by brakes and accelerators.

The Nephew tossed that board, wound down yon window to get some flies in and, knowing sound will carry a mile here in the morning foothills, softly clicked closed police car's door. Reglancing at that monitor (the Fed dog was climbing stairs) off the Nephew swerved, uphill following moor grass doups and swells, case he'd to hit deck, but the Nephew was way in those birch leaves before there was sight of any soul.

Whole scents of this earth was rised up out of it into the Nephew's face, the sun blanching these grasslands. Splashed round his eyes; on the springy moss by a wee stream, rinsed his mouth, lips close to the rock, and spat out, but there was no time for dilly-dally. He'd put down far too many roots already this side of a loch that it was time to get over . . . across. Course he daren't use the old cantilever and away north, not now. Be a sitting duck on its five-hundred-yard dash with no escape but bailing out over that side: hundred-foot drop to rapids below. He shivered.

He crossed the embankment without a glance up the deer cutting and tumbled down through beehives where he'd beaten upon his old friend Hacker those years ago, then fell into thistle ranks behind guest houses, rehopped back of the tin-roofed holiday home and hesitated by a rowan in the garden to get a clear crossing over the road and hither anon he was back down on the bright shoreline, squinted against silvers, grays, and blacks and the top slicks of current on the moving loch mass, coiling and turning like severed worms; he was headed for Hacker's boathouse through plague-clouds of gnats until he was cooried among fecund verdure, pale undersides of bramble leaves swaying close to his cheek, so he turned aside, trying to jalouse how to cross a loch, when he spotted that outline he'd missed in the night's darknesses when it had been black as the earl of hell's waistcoat. There was a bulk in among wild thornbush just off the pale shore stones.

The Nephew didn't want to come out onto open shore yet, so he just tossed a pebble at yonder bulk: looked like something long, plastic-seeming, wrapped in hessian. Stone missed, so he under-lobbed another, like a grenade, and it hit that wrapped thing which made a fiberglassy echo dunk. He crawled forward and tugged at that wrapping. Right enough, it was a long, faded orange canoe, wrapped in rotted sack and blue, sun-bleached fertilizer bags that'd been violently slashed open to increase size. The canoe'd been pulled in under thornbush, right-way-up, but fertilizer bags had stopped it filling with rain. Though a dip where the opening was had a layer of rotted autumn leaves so's it'd lay there since winter past—at least. A paddle was slid inside. The Nephew stood, stooped and dragged that canoe backward, into deeper overgrowths, like a just-shot corpse, he thought, and this movement stripped it of its coverings. The canoe was aswirl in graffiti, couple big quotes in spray paint, smaller quotations most wrote in those silver magic markers:

And I turned myself to behold wisdom, and madness, and folly: for what can the man do that cometh after the king? Even that which hath been already done.

He was no dafty nincompoop or dopey-docus. Ecclesiastes, only gumption in Bibles, he thought, and he could mind whole sections himself because he still had that little pocket Bible that had once belonged to a very, very naughty young woman and it excited him to read it, especially the lines she had underlined in her untutored hand, knowing all the most lustful things that woman had done! There was Romans 8:22, Isaiah 54:3, and much of Ecclesiastes. I sought in my heart to give myself unto wine, yet acquainting my heart and to lay hold on folly. I got me servants and maidens, and had servants born in my house and whatsoever mine eyes desired I kept not from them. As it happeneth to the fool so it happeneth even to me: and why was I then more wise? And how dieth the wise man? as the fool.

Questions, questions, but the Nephew licked his lips at this, for he had most niggling wee suspicion, was not this the entire story of Man Who Walks and his pursuits of him? Were he and the Foreman any better than the Man Who Walks, the fool? You can do the midnight rosary with as many servant girls as you want, but you will never know all the excessive pleasures of past kings and concubines, this is the lament of the sybarites, chasing dreams— seeking ones as yet undreamt and, in the end, fool, imitator of the king, king himself: we all will perish unremembered. Nothing new under the sun on account of all that has gone before, is one conclusion of these musings or, as Sam Beckett, Nobel Prize for Literature 1969, put it, "And for other reasons better not wasted on cunts like you."

Whole bloody canoe was scrawled with these creepy Bible quotations, but the Nephew tried to put mere thoughts and fears of dark waters out there to one side. Such bright morning took dominion and he made himself ready for crossing.

He sat to tug off his combat trousers over boots in case they got all mankyized in that canoe bottom, stood, slipped the mobile in his lumberjack shirt pocket, and dropped down his jacket. He opened his backpack to check his hunting knife and that's when he saw yon bin-liner he'd crammed in as a pillow the night before, still there and all forgot about. He yanked it out. Opened the bin-liner and he thought it was reams and reams of cine-film, a 16 mm ribbon of dreams that was coming out. Whole thing stuffed with it, but then he saw it was actual typewriter ribbon, miles and miles of the stuff; maybe a report one those boffins was writing up on the Man Who Walks, so he crammed it all back in, but he couldn't fit combats and jacket too, so he spraffed them up back of that pointy-ended canoe.

He took the paddle square in two hands and practiced a wee bit, stood there in his shirt and bockers and, guessing there was nothing for it, shouldered on the backpack and pulled the canoe down to water's edge.

He'd never been long enough at the high school to've done this carry-on, the old canoe rolls with helmet banging off bottom of a pee-filled shallow end, but he'd watched the mugs do it one winter's day through the steamed-up outside window of the new swimming pool in his truancy phase. Phases.

There was a lot of creepy popper seaweed close inshore, so it was going to be awkward to gain deep water. None for it but to push the canoe ahead, splash out, bow pointed to opposite shores. Not far at all, he kept thinking; then, using the paddle on rocks under water, he managed to lift sodden boots an snug hisself in, arse soaked right away on the canoe bottom that he thought he'd need to be laving out so much muckwater. He leaned over to one side, took up his paddle and, lo and behold, he was sat steady in a canoe on fearful loch water, squinting at the fast-moving currents ahead, seeing it was rushed west, at a fair old rate of knots, but preferable to being taken upstream to rapids under that old cantilever! If he did coup, he'd be carried outward, but the long, slung sandbar by the old seaplane base would be something he could kick in for. There was nae choice; he set forth.

The Nephew began to paddle and his canoe moved over the loch surface surprisingly quick, out past seaweed slops in the shallows and in and among those currents. He'd imagined force of the black water frothing against sides of the biblical canoe but, by angling the paddle blades down, he could easy counter its sweep and he turned his head round, seeing how far he'd already come in the orange canoe. In a crazy flush of confidence he even considered rounding the sand bar and paddling up to the beach over the clear water and across the wreck of the *Breda* herself, for landfall, walking down to the old station and cutting off Man Who Walks there and then, maybe carry this bloody canoe, balanced on his head! Steady now, old mate, the Nephew thought.

He was well out on that firth, seeing the village off to his right from a new angle over the straits. He couldn't have been far off halfways across—sun all way above. Ahead, the peninsula mountains with the superquarry buried deep in them like a skelf; behind, Ben More, clear as a huge, mad projection on the wall of horizon. So eerily quiet out there, deep under him silence, then a peeping bird hugging the glassy surface made past, saw it dip a wing to miss, pass behind . . . the stern. Far across the perfect polished floor of water, against his squint he could see the wee ferry *Flora MacDonald*, a thirty-footer with a putt-putting Evinrude: full-house, it was towing an unpowered rowing boat heavy with anorak-clad touristos rocking in its lively wake.

The Nephew sang:

> Michael, row the boat ashore
> Hallelujah,
> The river's deep and wide
> Hallelujah
> There's milk and honey on the other side
> Halle-oo-oo-jah.

What he thought was a lobster creel buoy was a sky-pointed seal's nose, its fiber-optic whiskers showing water drops he was so close. Maybe he could come to love the sea, one those late conversions in life he'd often read about!

The seal sunk for cover as the mobile phone shrilly rang "Rule Britannia" in his breast pocket. Damn and blast! He parried the paddle across, hanging on with the right hand, and picked out that phone with the left; the canoe began to drift to bad places as he thumbed up the button.

"Caught me at a poor time here. Delicate ops."

"Are ya with a whoor, boy?"

"A gray seal, phone you back."

"AH YAH!" The Nephew yanked the phone away from his ear.

There was the most intense, jabbing pain on his left leg, then another, so he fiercely jerked, kicked up splashes at the canoe side, thought himself having a heart attack.

"Oh fiddlesticks," he grimaced. "Ouch, oh, OUCH!"

A little voice in his hand trembled, calling, "Whaass matter, laddie . . .?"

He tried drop-pocketing yon mobile in his shirt but another sting on his bare leg! Phone missed, bounced once on fiberglass and slithered down the canoe flank with a neat plop into that sea, extinguishing all the Foreman's protests, for the moment at least.

He had to try to stand and get away from those pains and, as he lifted his torso clear of the canoe, he saw his bare thighs and lower legs were crawling with clung masses of yellow-jacketed wasps! The canoe wobbled down to the left, in a sinking sway as if the top could be breached by the suddenly clear loch water. The Nephew yelled aloud and tried to balance other way as more wasps came fury-buzzing upward from the opened hole in the canoe body. He swiped out at his thigh, got stung on the hand, and dropped the paddle. Down in the canoe bottom with a little muddy water he could see a bust-open half of a whole wasp's nest shoogling from one side to another as he balanced; nest must have been built in there all summer, yacuntya, he thought, looked round, wide-eyed, middle of fucking black lochs under faultless skies. Choice was clear: drown or stung to death—got a last piercing just below his balls and chose: the Nephew leaned, went over with his feet still in that biblical canoe.

Underwater the Nephew kept eyes tight shut, not wanting to see savage serrations and wicked arêtes of a sunken mountain range below, the Foreman's phone bubbling his voice, sinking past scallop meadows and cliff-edge lobster villages, the headless seal's body at surface above. What he felt then, his eyes shut against the salt, believing this was his end, was not fear to be in his worst of feasible scenarios; not fear but huge sense of solidarity with the historical drowned, like that foster-daughter, and a deep spurt of detestation and violence for that animal fool Man Who Walks, his blood Uncle who he clearly hadn't tortured nearly enough.

His face slid out on an oily surface among patches of floated drowned wasps on their backs, wasps' little legs like girl eyelashes held to yonder sky. He spat and spun cause already that capsized canoe had drifted over him and away. What was keeping him floated was his backpack, strapped to his shoulders, so he spun it off cause the buoyancy was forcing his face forward. He could see it was air trapped inside the bin-liner of typewriter ribbon was all that was keeping him up, so, holding it out in front of him with both arms, he began to kick and mush furiously toward that sand bar.

In moments he realized he was actually going to make it to the shore, the current not nearly carrying him as violently as he feared, but his feet were deep cold within his boots and he was fearful of any rock crops with their kelpy sheetings, but, unspectacularly, he came to first levels of seaweed float; found he was already in his own depth.

Drooked, the Nephew had to declare he stuttered through the waves and limped out the loch that morning, onto stone and shattered construction debris of the northern shores, only in boots, clinging shirt and underwear, he shivered and emptied water out his backpack looking for a quiet spot to sneak up onto the trusty old A828 and north.

Numbing cold and salt must act antiseptic, because as soon as he left the waters his legs started to sting away like nobody's business as if he'd eased under his skin with a razor and lifted a strip up, the way Jennifer Faulkner says it felt when he coaxed her to carve his name in her arm. So he just lay among whins down by the road, listening to their seed pods pop in the direct sunlight and the little trickling sound of their thrown spores falling through adjacent bushes. He was getting his puff back, grinning at leg pain, then chuckling, hearing vehicles whizzing past, north. He squeezed the shirt best he could and pink water from its cheap dye came out. His legs were killing with stungness. What he needed wasn't just a pair of breeks, he thought, but some blonde bint in suit and Porsche to take him north for a kiss per kilometer. Or better still, a safe house or bolt-hole himself. Stood with boxer shorts tugged that bit lower below the long shirt, and his big boots, he'd might just pass for some ridiculous Australian backpacker with normal shorts and here he began to think, in his moment of weakness (as, he must confess, he had done after imagining the Hole's anointed fingers, fixing the toilet seat), of Paulette Mahon, who lived a few mile up the road at Boomtown and who might, if he played his cards right, provide a safe house for recovery, and trousers!

So the Nephew lay there, near stung to death and half drowned, shirt spread out on whin-bush spikes, head on the squelchy bag of typewriter ribbon, thought of his young twenties, snout-faced Paulette's lispy vocabulary from a tongue-piercing she once swallowed. Paulette, with a burgundy and aqua tattoo of a weeping willow's downshower at the *very* bottom of her spine and those legs! She was using a tin of his shaving foam a week during his residency! Only let him bide two weeks, then posted him forward a package of oily socks:

"You forgot your socks," wrote in a surprisingly precise hand!

Paulette spent so long in bed, her nail varnish matched her pajamas. Paulette, mostly languid in a long, drained bath, always tuned to Aluminumville FM, playing "Riders on the Storm," "His brain is squirming like a toad," her rendered half-decent through the always-open bathroom door, archipelagoes of clung bubble bath on the strategic points all along her somehow tannedness, devouring cannabis resin through a pipe made from a Coca-Cola can. In the mornings, he had the brief privilege to learn, she only ever seemed to have one dream, about a chocolate malt ball being lodged in her belly button.

First thing Paulette ever said to the Nephew, at a crowded wedding table that he'd gatecrashed, was, "Women stand stiller than men in the Ladies toilets, doing their make-up in the mirror," she said, "you become so still that the movement-sensitive monitor puts the light out on you and you smudge your makeup; it thinks there's nobody in there. Gives me the maximum creeps, makes me feel I don't exist," she shivered.

"You know, I very much identify with your experience of existential dread there. I've felt a very similar feeling, I believe, when I've noticed, late at night, the low swaying bow of a tree setting off a movement-sensitive lamp outside a property."

Ah, the poetry of love!

In those days Paulette's only nourishment ever seeming: sperm, Asti Spumante and forever nibbling on a snap-brittle stalk of unboiled spaghetti. Her famous flight to London on modeling trial for a swimsuit catalogue and picked up by some rich man on the train, her shouting from a pulled-down Hackney taxi window at King's Cross to first London prostitute she'd ever seen, "I love your shoes, they're beautiful, where'd you get em?" After a week or so you imagine the rich boy realized he could not handle Paulette in her wildly scandalous girlhood, but when she came back here she'd a bobby-dazzler wardrobe of silk she was forever having dry-cleaned, so these wee blue number labels were always attached to her cuffs with a tiny safety pin. The Nephew thought, Oh Paulette! Sadness of wild spirits broke by their own excess which only kings should know.

Now she's part-time at the Sea Life Center in a skin-tight wetsuit, kneeled in the Rock Pool Environment holding out starfish to wee kids, hitched to probably some ordinary boy who likes his football, but he'd definitely heard worked shifts offshore. Two wee daughters that look just like her, the Nephew'd heard, when he cautiously inquired round the pubs, and mortgaged to the hilt on the new scheme at Boomtown, just a few mile up the road. What if that hubby was two week offshore? But the Nephew couldn't turn up looking like this . . . had to get a pair of trousers, at any rate, before calling on Paulette, yacuntya!?

He jumped to his feet and got that warmed, damp shirt over his shoulders. He chose his thumbing pitch on the long straight so's he could identify Fed cars at some distance. A white taxi going south made him duck briefly. Forty-seven northbound vehicles, private, heavy goods, utility and public service, passed him, most markedly accelerating. He hardly bothered thumbing latest reg, all company-car chancers. He could read no meanings from resultant registration plates, nothing at all; no combination of number plates communicated to him usual informations, nor did number plates spell out Man Who Walks or Paulette! That concatenation of letters and numerals seemed meaningless. When wee he used to demarcate all vehicles as either "sad-faced" or "happy" depending on the anthropomorphic design qualities of their headlights and radiator grilles, but now he couldn't decide if these modern, madly overpowered vehicles, clearly designed for other worlds than Argyllshire, had sad, happy, or even angry faces.

Forty minutes later the Nephew came out of sun behind him, down into Boomtown from the megalithic burial grounds up above the Old Folk's home, through that place below Forestry Commission conifers where he once saw a pinecone big as a full-size chocolate Easter egg, one of the ones that he never got.

Bloodstained trousers not too noticeable, he stepped over a picket fence and walked up to Paulette's front door. Doorbell played the Close Encounters coda.

Leaf-pattern glass swung open and an adorable little miniature Paulette looked directly at him cause he was at the bottom of the steps and she says, "Who the fuck're you?"

"Mummy or Daddy in?"

"You're not social services, are ya?"

"No. I'm an old pal of your Mummy's."

"You mean an old boyfriend?"

"Well, goodness me," the Nephew coughed.

"Don't tell anyone," she whispered, "I'm home alone! You can wait out there, I'm babysitting ma silly wee sister; Dad's away offshore, Mum's just down the shop and I've never *ever* to let anyone in."

"Quite correct," the Nephew nodded.

She did her size equivalent of slamming the door, sort of running, heaving at it so's you thought she'd come through that glass. She clicked the Yale, the Nephew thought, with that foul, confident possessiveness of Settled Community kids round their secure little houses.

He sat cross-legged, plucking daisies on that wee lawn; Mary Queen of Scots had her head chopped off. The lawn hadn't been cut for four or five days, so *at least* a week till hubby was home. He took out his Japanese address on that bloodstained piece of paper writ in a very, very shaky hand and put it safe in the shirt pocket. The wee daughters pulled over a chair to the front-room window: stared through dirty double-glazing and giggled toward him. He overheard a cheeky comment about his trousers being far too long.

That doorbell! Yes, the movies were not the Nephew's chosen art form. He recalled, once and once only, the Man Who Walks took him to the cinema, in the Port's fleapit, and paid for his seat in the stalls; there *were* only stalls. It was meant to be a scary film but the Nephew was scared enough by the time he got to his seat. "I can't hear a fucking thing," the Man Who Walks roared, and the woman seated in front of them jumped and her perm shook.

"No characters are talking yet," the Nephew whispered.

The Nephew has never managed in picture houses though he's bought many tickets. The Nephew enters, armed with valid ticket, chocolate-chip tub, or the incredible yellow mustard on his hotdog, but he can see nothing in the gloom. To crash his way to even the nearest seat would be an embarrassment. So he tries waiting for a brightly lit scene that may illuminate his way forward, but no, all the films are so moody these days. The Nephew waits in vain, lurking, sinister-seeming to the back-row dwellers and their furtive ways, so he retreats, pretends he's making for the bogs but instead he leaves the picture house altogether with his valid ticket, escapes the melancholy of some moronic screenwriter's denouement and feels newly invigorated to step out so soon, back into evening airs again, with his copy of Seneca's *Consolation to Helvia* in his jacket pocket; he takes a shivering stance on the street, watching interlinked teenagers brace the thoroughfare in both directions, and lifts the ice cream to his lips, eyes missing nothing. Alive!

When things don't go well for him, the Nephew turns his mind to what is written in wry Suetonius: vain Caesar staring at a bust of Alexander the Great, thinking, By the time he was the age I am now, he'd conquered the world. Or old Art Schopenhauer, his steady gaze being returned for hours by the orange orangutan in Dresden Zoo which the old cynic grew so fond of, toward the end.

The Nephew stood abruptly when Paulette's head on its swan's neck sailed along top of a hedge, like it'd been severed. He groaned at how she still looked and he thought: whatever so mine eyes desired I kept not from them.

Neither smiled nor frowned when she saw the Nephew, but she put down the shopping and lifted a hankie to her nose. Front door came open and two daughters piled out screaming, running round Paulette's denim legs, way that wee dug Trafalgar had bothered me, he thought, till I flung the cunt by its back leg into a wheelie bin.

Paulette looked him up and down, in his conglomerations of clothing, her snozzle was all red and chapped and in nasally voice she says, "Well, least I won't have to worry that I haven't done the vacuuming. Don't! . . . come near me. Less you want a cold."

"Well worth it!" he goes and pecked her on a cheek. Her daughters wolf-whistled. He'd forgot eyes were that color; a few more lines at the side but that was from too much laughing for these lands. He tried to take the shopping bags off of her, but she shrugged negative. He says, "What happened to the hotel?"

"Long gone, stranger, like you."

"Boating accident." He held out his arms, squeezed down on his feet: water fizzed and buzzed still, from top of his boot.

"Chucked off a trawler for too much wanking?" she goes.

"Nah, it's true, bit of canoeing."

She laughed, took a hankie out her sleeve and blew a real grogger.

"I traveled for years, recently I work at Agricultural Supplies, heaving pony nuts for well-to-dos basically."

"No get yur leg over they horsy women types among the alfalfa?"

"Stick to the horses."

"Poor horses. I work at the Sea Life Center these days."

"I know. Saw you in the brochure, they had you everywhere, in the water, behind the till, in the cafeteria."

"That's how it is."

"Our Prince is in the heather once more," he shrugged.

"Your mental Uncle's still doing the runners!" she sniffed. "Why don't you just let him alone?"

The Nephew stopped at the front door, "He's a danger to himself. I'm worried sick about his well-being."

"Ever thought, it's you an yours' mentalness he's tried to get away from; you keep catching him like a stray dug and dragging him back?" She looked at the Nephew out corridors of shadows, one girl-child wrapped round a thigh. "Colin's away, come in if you want, mind your boots on the carpets."

Colin, was it! The Nephew says, "Some cold you've got there."

"Summer colds are aye worser and with these wee ones it's hard taking to your bed any more." She blew that cute snout again.

Front room he goes, "Nae telly!?"

"Against them. Bad influence on these two."

"That a paper there?"

"All you're going to get is the relentless goal machine that is Oban Camanachd," Paulette flicked out yon dreaded local paper (est. 1861) from the shopping bag. "Want a beer?"

Plonked on the armchair of the three-piece suite, a cold Heineken was therefore delivered unto him but with unfortunancy those wee daughters brought an endless series of toys for the Nephew's inspection, Barbies, unfamiliar alien creatures, and a plastic baby that both vomited and pished itself. "I had a cuddly elephant when I was wee called Markus," the Nephew tried.

They were unmoved.

Finally the tallest child dropped a living, all-too-ratlike gerbil from two cupped hands onto his groin area. "Johnstone," she introduced.

"If we want peace, I suggest the washing machine room," Paulette jerked her head, so he shucked off the gerbil and followed her to the washing machine room that was more a cupboard with a Bendix inside, doing a demented cha-cha. With his lower lip pushed out in cursory interest he reread, for fourth . . . fifth time, front page of the newspaper: the customary photo of a minor member of the Royal Family who had strayed within one hundred miles. Also:

STOP PRESS

TULLOCH FERRY SEX ATTACK ON ELDERLY COUPLE
AND DOG MISSING

. . . wish to remain anonymous, managed to reach their phone and summon police . . . embarrassing task of untying them . . . stripped naked, bound with electric wire and exposed to a torrent of verbal abuse by a drug-crazed man IN THEIR OWN HOME . . .

The Nephew looked down the page.

HEAVY GOODS ASSAULT

A lorry driver's nose was broken by an ungrateful hitchhiker . . .

As per usual he flapped the pages and smartly slapped them back to the Personals at the rear, a new editorial innovation.

HE SHOOTS HE SCORES

Dougie, 29 yrs old, into hunting and shooting, looking for a lady who shares those interests. If that's you then reply BOX 436

YOU CAN TALK TO ME

Malky, 28, SINGLE, wants to meet girls. BOX 434

Ah these silver-tongued devils of my homeland! the Nephew thought.

Door pushed in at him and Paulette squeezed through, yelled above washing machine spin, "Awful car crash up the road, they was saying in the shop, must be bad, took the boy away in an ambulance just there."

"Oh!?" he went, quick-slapping yon rag into a folded square and sliding it well in under the washing machine. He noticed these envelopes of silver foil beneath the machine's wheels, to stop it running away or whatever.

Paulette sighed, "Aghhhh!" tiptoe reaching, her slimness perfectly intact, to a shelf for the makings in a Golden Virginia tin, lid clipped into the base and green paint worn silver, then she did a long slide down, sat against the door bottom, legs along the Nephew's, feet *really* close by his thigh, his boot by hers, she got whole-hunkered forward, hair falling into her face with the jerks as those daughters shoved at other side of the door, shouting behind her like some proto-drug squad, but they soon wearied, way kids do these days with all food additives and video games in them, he thought. She went about blowing her nose and asks, "Dinnae have any snot on my top lip, do I?"

He shook his head, mesmerized by her.

Paulette's experienced fingers were sprinkling an rolling up.

He goes, "I know an old gypsy cure for the cold," but she ignored so's he goes, "What age is the biggest?"

"Niamh," she went.

"Neeve," he goes.

"Know how it's spelled?" she says.

"N-E-E-V-E," he goes.

"Nut. N-I-A-M-H. It's Irish," she went.

He didn't flinch, "What age is she?" he says.

"Eight."

He whistled, "Jeez, yonks since I saw you."

She lit up, inhaled, held down, and passed to him. She blew smoke and goes, "I must say, I'm impressed, I was expecting you to be jamp out bushes every night for months, or Colin to show up with his legs broke."

"He's fairly clipped your wild wings, hope this is all paid for," the Nephew sneered and toked deepest of deeps, nodded at the jiving washing machine.

"Want me to straddle it?" she whispered, blew out smoke.

"Bet your daughters do while you're down the shop," he finally says when he couldn't hold smoke in any longer.

She pointed at him, "You will *not* stray within ten meters of my daughters without me being there."

"Don't worry, Paulette, y'know fine they're too old for me. So how d'ye keep the old spark alive in married life then?"

"Who says we're married and at least he can get it up."

"Your memories no frazzled then."

"Hard to forget worst sex of your life."

"I've been researching."

"Aye, on yersel."

"For the day we two would meet again," he bowed, gesticulated.

She laughed, a sort of sneezy sound, and grabbed the toke off him.

He knew he shouldn't smoke dope. Could lead on to major relapse, buying cigarettes and voddy instead of beer, and once back on the spirits you're doomed, man. He'd get the urge for powders and Bob's your uncle! his wee castle would come tumbling down. He thought, Couldn't let myself go that way again. Last time on dope I minded looking at a goldfish bowl trying to decide if the water was behind the glass or surrounding it; I got drawn into a conversation regarding Carpaccio and the evolution of perspective in Venetian art, and I gave away too many juicy ideas of my own, yacuntya.

Paulette was talking, "The older one, Niamh, worries me. One night when she was younger I had a girlfriend over, who was at high school with me. We're both eating tea and my wee Niamh put her chin on the table and says, 'Mummy, there's a battery up my bottom.' Well, panic stations broke out and, sure enough, one of the double AA's you put in a Walkman, a Duracell, was shoved in and stuck up there. She coulda been lectrocuted."

"She's got an illustrious future."

"Shut your gob. So I sit her down."

"She could still sit?"

"And I says to her, 'Now you shouldn't be putting things up your bottom.'"

"Put it in Latin on the family coat of arms! Don't you want her to take after her mother though?"

"'And if you really want to, you must come and ask Mummy first!' 'Oh,' she says, 'does that include food?' So I says, 'Food's meant to be up there, darling,' and she says, 'Even the frozen peas I get out of the fridge and stuff up?' And she'd been getting the froze peas and putting those up too!"

"Ah, the joys of parenting, eh?" The Nephew just started talking, hearing his own voice, not caring that her children were already hopeless psychoanalytic cases, knowing if he looked in a mirror he could never focus on his own eyes. He says, "Paulette; hey, Paulette! Up Bealach an Righ, past Pennyfuir through Tulloch Ferry, choose east or north to you here, I'm no fussed; I went away from old Dalriada, to the army, to a country, to somewhere proper, these lands would play on me at nights, like the shadows on the ceiling. Travel? Travel is for students; don't want to travel, I want to *arrive*, be elsewhere, like old Ovid, concerned with objects that transform themselves."

He took another hit of spliff. "Aye, Paulette; hey, Paulette! Have you ever had a place where things have gone down big time for you, just a place that's going in all directions?"

"You what?"

"Far as your eye can see. Out and lonely among the waters. Ranged somewhere among rock and you've say spent a dod of time there or something happened to you and then you go back to this very place that should mean so much to you and it just, ach, disappoints or something?"

Paulette drawled, with a smile on the sides of her mouth, "I see you still cannie handle a smoke. What're you on about? You're way too deep for me as per usual; all those dictionaries you swallowed burping up again." She was getting fixed to roll another and the fat whopper they worked on was not near done.

"Nah, nah, this isn't book stuff, it's real! I've been to New York, I've been to Rome, seen a million birds circle St. Peter's at dusk, the flocks go invisible until they wheel and flourish like a swarm, opening their wings above the Eternal City, heading west. You come back here and the place seems thinned out, nowhere near as real as it was in your fizzed-up brainbox. Nostalgia. You start to notice tricks time has played. Trees are taller, there's a new something over there that wasn't in your mind's picture, or you'd excluded, foolishly, the way Napoleon warned his generals not to make pictures in their heads but to trust only what their eyes could perceive. Jeez, you get back to home-town you believe you have strong feelings about, to find maybe certain buildings are a whole story higher than you remembered but you kept those cherished memories so sacred! Memory is the mark of love. You find your vision, the product of your love, is grander than the reality. Memory is the mark of love, Paulette. To keep something in your mind and cherish it, what a miracle in this world."

Paulette giggled at him, concentrating, rolleying away, smiling to herself: aroused by some briar she'da been tumbled over in long ago; dumbly superior as if he'd no done that stuff with McCallum sisters, gone and given them some *plein air* memories too; aye aye, a wee nest egg of sweet memories for him also, to take with him when he goes down slow with the cancer or the angina or the pneumonia or the linguistic area of his brain blacked out in a spreading aneurysm's fireworks.

He says, "Aye, like time I had to fight Robert Sinclair when fourteen."

"Here we go," she whispered.

"Hardest guy around. Like some medieval joust, his gang had to meet my gang and it was in this place, way up on the pony-trek to Black Lochs. Fuck alone knows why we'd have chose to meet out there cause we was so knackered by the time we's reached it, on a scorching heatwave day, lucky we could lift our arms, or at least it seemed that way . . . *seemed* it was miles and miles to get there and I minded it as being this lush little plain meadow with all the ben sides seeming to dip down into real rich, long straps of fresh grass. A green basin surrounded by mountains curving away up to the turned-back summits and a full sky above black mounts. Now a few month ago I walked back up there, to find that meadow where I bested Sinclair; a stroll down memory lane sort of."

"Aye, back to your glory days!" Her snigger turned into a mucus release and she darted her beautiful fingers up her cuff for yon hankie. She muttered, "Near as a dosser like you'd get to a battle field, since you gave away yur Action Man."

"Listen, Minnehaha, course it wasn't miles at all; I was there in a jiffy."

Fabric hanging, white and green in front her red lips, there was a giggle. Nodding.

"And it wasn't this grand amphitheater of my mind at all, with embankments all soared away up on every side, it was just this totey wee *cabbage patch*, with some slopes over to wee, *wee* cliffs. See, it seemed so far cause I was all the way there psyching myself up. Hills seemed all round cause when me and Sinclair walked toward each other, the whole world shut out, huge mountains just flew away back with the bang of first punch. It enclosed us, cause there was no way you could escape that conflict, so I felt all mountains round us. Then when I'd triumphed, I recalled it as this, arcadia . . . that's sort of paradise like. What I'm saying is, it's where our head is at that prints our impression of the landscape! I realized early on, growing up in grandeur like this that you and me are surrounded by each day, I sussed that cause I was lonely I preferred landscapes to people, then I was reading Bertie Camus, as you do, and I read in his *Carnets*: 'In our youth we attach ourselves more readily to a landscape than a man. It is because landscapes allow themselves to be interpreted.' And of course they do, but differently depending on the state of your mind."

"You were certainly nae good at attaching yourself to any woman."

"The land is here, all round us, but each of us pulls from it or inserts into it what we want, we all see it different, like we could meet the ghosts of other folks' needs and dreams wandering the places at night."

"Watch you don't meet your own," Paulette curled her lip, a little uglily.

"Exactly. I believe we live in a semi-spirit world. Sometimes the deceased just forget they're dead for a moment or two. Like I knew soldiers, eyewitnesses, who can't agree on where they all were on the field of battle cause you have all these highly excited individual viewpoints jostling with each other. No just Gulf or Falklands or Normandy. Some battles with hundreds of thousands of men, it's been impossible to find the battle site cause no one there could agree; only the burial pits grown over to show for real, like at Culloden. Some battle sites have gone missing, generals arguing it all happened over the next hill. Like the Romans in Scotland, the Ninth Legion marching north to relieve the Tay garrisons, they vanished and it's said at night you can still hear them marching. Aye, when you look at this earth we walk upon with adult eyes."

Some of the conversations folk have in this life, eh? yacuntya.

"Hoi, you've nodded off, ya blethering lightweight."

Right enough, his legs were stunged to billy-o, dope was crashing the Nephew out—knacked; he goes and says, "Aye, look, gotta make a phone call, hardly slept last night."

"Oh aye!?"

"Maybe I could have a quick wee nap of forty winks but you'd wake me later, aye?"

"More like forty wanks with you."

He tried to get to his feet but the pins were wobbling. "It's no the grass," he defended, "I can tak the pace, pal. Suppose I should have something to eat. When did I last eat?"

"It's no grass," went Paulette.

"Eh? What is it?!"

"It's some New Drug. Look, I crush down the seeds under the washing machine, that's why I've aye got it on Spin. There's nothing in the wash."

Right enough, the Nephew leaned down and glared seriously in: the washing machine was empty. The envelopes of tinfoil under the runners were grinding the drug up. His mouth went all dry. He didn't want to tamper with things he didn't understand.

He followed Paulette out the washing machine room, along a corridor of echoes to bottom of the stair. She was carrying his black backpack that he'd forgot existed, he noticed white, semenish stains on it, then salvaged a memory, Dried salt water, he thought. She had another New Drug joint in her other fingers.

"Conducted tour. Girls' rooms, out of bounds."

He nodded, not paying attention, to his later detriment, goes, "Aye aye," he'd realized how hungry he was.

She pointed up the stair so's he led the way, disappointed, sumley supposed she thought she'd grab him if he fell, but he'd been looking forward to watching as her tight behind went up. He ascended.

Top of the stairs she swung a door to a single bed in a wee room and tossed his backpack in on the duvet. Wallpaper was all bright colors; place looked like it was never used. "Luxury," he goes, and she kissed him, aside the cheek.

"Give us a call in a hour or so, I've got to make an urgent phone call. Business."

"Okey-dokey," she sniggered. "It's sort of good to see you, ya lightweight," she pulled the door tight.

He smiled in the true joy that only a woman can give and got the Buddhist snowboarder's breeks off, then sat on the side of the bed, fascinatingly poked at the wasp stings on his thighs that'd come up as hard little lumps. Off with the damp shirt and keks and he wormed under yon bright blue duvet, shivered at coldness, his toes came against something so he reached down. Pulled up a cold, rubbery hot-water bottle from the last guest. He let it slide with a collapsing blurble down on a bedside rug. Then the visions began.

*

Brand-new reg car stopped, raged into reverse. Above the reg the enameled number plate read: WARP SPEED MR ZULU. The Nephew picked up his backpack. The Nephew didn't know if it was polite to let him lean over and open the passenger door or do it yourself, but the driver leaned and shoved it open. "Are fifteen possums going to appear from the trees?"

"Sorry."

"Australian?"

"Nut."

"Are you jogging or do you just have no trousers on?"

The Nephew leaned down to smile and the driver looked disappointed, as if he was about to drive on, so the Nephew clambered in and water poured out his backpack swinging over the gear stick. "I had the old canoe accident this morning," he says.

"Oh, white-watering, I see." Disinterested, he looked in his mirror, accelerated impressively.

"I'm headed for Ballachulish."

"Where's that, is this the right direction?"

"Aye, twenty mile north." He'd got the seatbelt on and looked at the driver's face, realized, just then, immediately and intuitively by that face that they were going to crash in this car. Glued on dashboard top (he could still see a hardened run of Evo-stick down past the clock) was a little cup made of colored glass squares, there was a real candle burning inside. The driver nodded at the candle, "I'm a Buddhist."

"Aye?"

"I'm a snowboarder. A Buddhist snowboarder."

"Right."

Music with a mechanical beat was playing very loudly. The Nephew knew this type of music was called "gangster rap music." It didn't have a patch on Roses or Lizzy. He'd seen it performed on televisions by men moving their arms violently in an effort to back up their articulation. Once, at some girl's house, he'd listened closely to the words; each song was a sort of narrative and, relevantly enough, he'd noticed each song, one after another, was set inside a car. It was the music of a carbound planet. Often cars would draw opposite him when he was thumbing it at Yield junctions and the low sound of that car music was actually rocking the vehicle on its low suspension. With a sinister, subtle motion.

The Buddhist snowboarder took the first corner with the needles on the speedo and revs pointed directly up, gearing in for curves. The Nephew glimpsed a lone sheep in a field with two magpies standing on its back, signifying God only knows what on the luck front. Cars were queued up in the petrol station at the caravan site and he glimpsed an old lady with the petrol nozzle stuck in a jerry can.

"It's summer," announced the Nephew.

"Sure is glorious, eh?"

"There's no snow."

"I thought you had mountains?"

"Aye, but no that high. Few patches lying through summer in the corries but you won't find more."

"Well, shit. I drove all night. I need a cup of tea."

Looking straight ahead the Nephew pondered this relationship between himself and the unknown body part inside him right then that would fail one day, lead to his death. He thought, If only we knew. Way when you look into someone's eyes you don't foresee both will be serrated in a future crash impact, unless you predict futures and bring out those lacerations there yourself. Often the Nephew would dream that all future injuries and fatal ailments on the bodies surrounding him, at a party, or in the street, or with the women he'd lay beside in quiet rooms, that those ailments all immediately manifested themselves simultaneously on the humans around him: tumors fruiting forth, faces tearing open, lungs as heavy as bags of seawater so all destiny was revealed in its sordidness. He believed it would be a mark of mercy to act immediately, invoke those destinies. . . .

Sure as fate, half a mile on, yonder side of the village, they passed a man on a bicycle, the wing knifed so close the Nephew noticed the bicycle had no chain. In the mirror he saw the yellow wellies spreadeagle and the bike's back wheel rear up as the cyclist vanished into the ditch; then another mile on, the Buddhist snowboarder yelled, "Streuth," under-steered a corner, they crossed the road, the Nephew grimaced and, taking forty feet of barbed-wire and rotted fence posts with them, they stopped on the downward lee of a sloped rapeseed field, out of view of the road—two sickeningly colored snowboards almost took the Nephew's head off on their way out through the busted windscreen. The fucking candle was still burning.

"See that, my Buddha looks after me."

The Nephew turned to his driver smiling, says, "A car crash is the least excuse I need. Get your fucking trousers off."

*

Wow! The Nephew jamp into woken-ness, thought himself still in Man Who Walks' dreadful den. It was pitch dark and him no reported in to Foreman, yacuntya! Told Paulette to wake me! He sat up with fiercest of fierce thirsts upon him. Jeezo, what drought! He had to drink. He swung his legs out, stood, thought he was on the New Drug still, cause he floated, then fell

forward on the carpet and bit his tongue so's ornaments chinked out in
that dark there. Jesus Christ, I musta woke the dead, he thought. He held his
breath and listened out for dear life. Not a cheep. His legs weren't there,
they'd got numbed.

"Itchy Magellan?" he says out loud.

His reached-down hand came on the bone hardness of swollen feet,
like as all the wasp poison had sunk down to his toes. He couldn't stand up
his feet were so numbed and invisibled too in such darkness. Where was
the light? That hot-water bottle was beside him, so's he unscrewed the top
and gobbled rubbery-tasted water out it, most gushing down cold onto his
chest and as he gulp-gulped down out of the hot-water bottle he realized,
simultaneous, he was furiously bursting for a pee too! Nothing for it, after he'd
drained the water down his gullet, he got the end of Old Moody, the Marquis
of Lorne, into the hot-water bottle end, trying to spill as little as possible
as he pee'd back into it! Like this cow in a field he saw, drinking from the big
trough his Uncle once had his eye on, a cow drinking and pishing at the
same time, its tail canted out. "In the fields of Abraham," he moved lips to
the words.

He screwed the hot-water bottle top on, realized how chilly it was,
so he pulled himself back into bed and cuddled up, holding warmnesses of
yon hot-water bottle filled with his own urine to his chest. He was famished
hungry.

The Nephew nodded back off into delicious visions but then he was full
awake, needed to pee! Yes, yet again, shamelessly unoriginal and repetitive
but true, and most probably needing to evacuate the same volume of liquid
he had ingested from within the hot-water bottle, now unlikely to receive a
similar volume of urine again back into itself; even taking into account that
absorbed by his dehydrations. For who can calculate the strange ministries
of the body? And should he, say, commence the peeing and find the hot-water
bottle, in simple mathematical terms, pushed to its volumic limits, well,
imagine! How could he hold his head high again after peeing the overflow
onto Paulette's spare-bedroom carpet, especially if she noticed! This would
bring his already low standing, in her and the general eyes of the countryside,
to a new low. In conclusion the Nephew's meditations were led toward one
pulverizing insight, in the manner of that written about by Leibniz or was it
Santayana's essay on Lucretius? Who cares, the conclusion was: Get me to
the pisser, yacuntya!

He got his arms down on carpet, then he lowered his numbed feet. He tried to find those boxer shorts, in case he run into one of Paulette's pesky daughters out there, him in the scud, and he'd be back in the newspaper for child molestings this time! It stung like billy-o getting the keks over the swole feet, they felt utterly ginormous to him, almost frightening, as if they may split, like when Hacker'd whispered to him, if you pulled back hard on your foreskin, the shaft of your knob would come shooting out like a banana, clunking to the floor and you'd never fit it back in again; in the days when it was rumored, also by Hacker, that you could swallow your own Adam's apple!

Too painful to shuffle forward on knees so he'd to hunker self forward on elbows, pulling his dead legs behind him, like a slither of knapdallicks hanging, bloody, from the arse of a ruptured sheep, as his Gran used to intone, for a variety of situations. Even before the Nephew reached the door, the carpet had pulled off the boxer shorts to his ankles and his elbows were tingling. He could reach up easy to the handle of your average door without the use of legs. This was a very average door. He reached up to try sweep the emulsion, find a light switch, but it was so dark, he couldn't make a thing out till his eyes adjusted to the little leaked light from beyond the curtains. His reaching fingertips could just manage a light switch. He thought, Perhaps there's some EEC directive as to exactly what height light switches should be positioned at? Fuck alone knows, cause obviously Glasgow has to be taken into account, and you know what they say, Nay need to replace a light bulb at the Blind Home, yacuntya.

By pattering his fingers, the light burst on. His feet were so swollen with these little toes on the end. Like an orange when you stick it full o' cloves. He sort of panicked at the sight of his feet, maybe he needed a doctor; he didn't like abnormalities at the best of times though fascinated by them in other people, but these were substantially abnormal feet swellings.

Trying to be as quiet as a ghost, he crawled out onto the landing, pulling on the base of the banisters. He listened to the hermetic silence of the slept house and was sure he felt a commensurate arousal in his compressed penis.

There were two other doors. Dragged his poor Old Moody over that acrylic carpet; he too-clearly experienced the insensitive textures of a bargain at Landmark warehouses. The Nephew clicked the door handle and gingerly shoved the first door, perhaps this was the little girls' place and a chorus of wails would arise. Light from his room showed up this other room: he saw gym equipment, one of those torturous-looking weight-lifting mechanisms, and it seemed all other bodies were down the stair. He slithered, bit by bit, over to another door, but by the time he'd pulled it back it was just an airing cupboard with a breath of warm air from a dormant immerser tank, then some bloody towels fell on his head giving him the terrors but he yanked hold of them competitively (as if someone would beat him to it) and continued to crawl, throwing the towels ahead, clawing over them, easing that down the stair passage, planning to use the towels to shroud his nudiness should his crawl be intercepted. He was fair bursting to pee by then.

The stairs were awful steep-seeming in the darkness and blood ran to his head as he began his descent, testicles steadily compressed by each stair edging till he could lay his left cheek on the downstairs corridor carpet. No improvement in the man-made fibers department. Now there were more doors, up and down the infernal corridor. He wasn't even sure what was the washing machine cupboard any more, never mind the locale of the cludgie. Sorta eeny meeny miney mo, he sumley surmised. Made him think of that Traffic song, "House for Everyone," on the first album:

> On the door of one was: "Truth."
> On the other one was: "Lies."
> Which one should I enter through?
> I really must decide.

A Dave Mason composition. I do believe. Yacuntya.

He reached up, gently compressed one door handle, pushed the lightweight, hollow-feeling door in gently, and he was trying to check the walls for kiddies' posters, My Little Pony or Jason Donovan, whatever the fuck floated the boat for these queer nippers of nowadays. Why had he not suffered hisself to get the snowboarder's breeks on? Cause bastardizing things wouldn't get over his blobby feet!

Another unoccupied room almost in darkness; and his people homeless! He noisily elbowed the way in, dragging his legs behind like a snake shucking its own skin. Even a bucket or flowerpot would have to suffice by now.

There was a strange, excited trundling sound in the blackness to his left.

A light went on.

Sitting up on a bed beside him, under a Lion King duvet, so close she could have leaned down and ruffled his hair, was one of Paulette's daughters, the Niamh one. To his left now, in his white cage, Johnstone the Gerbil was frantically galloping on his revolving wheel.

"I can see your hairy bum."

"Hush!"

"Have you come here to have it off with me?"

"No! Shhh."

"Have you come to have it off with Mum?"

"Nooooo, shhhhhhh, your Mummy'll hear," he flicked the towel backward, trying to shield his arse. Some of it got covered by a roping of towel along the crack, so he lay, splayed out, trying to wiggle his boxer shorts back up his shins.

"Why are you crawling? Are you drunk?"

"Look at my feet."

"Yeuch, what's wrong with *them?*" she goggled, fascinated but smiling; she wasn't petrified at all.

"I'm looking for the toilet, darling, and I can't walk."

"Don't call me darling less you want to be my boyfriend and I've two of those already and they'll burst ya if you try an two-time, *three*-time with me," she tiptoed out bed, stepped over him and, to the Nephew's horror, carefully closed the bedroom door, shutting them both in.

"Niamh, now I've GOT to go for a piddle. I'm bursting!"

"Here then," she pattered over to her wardrobe; helpless, his head followed her.

"It's Katia." She was holding up that vomiting and peeing doll she'd waved in his face earlier.

"Eh?"

"You have to fill it up with water, so she pee-pees. A girl can't do it, I try and it goes everywhere!"

"You're joking."

"If you don't, I'll call Mum."

The Nephew looked at the doll's ooo-ing red plastic lips, the pale white of its descending esophagus.

"Come on *then.*"

"You're mad; show me the toilet."

"Fill Katia so she pees real pee."

"What if I . . . spill. It's *dirty.*"

"Careful is what careful does."

"Eh. Well, turn round then."

Something squeaked, it was one of those angle poise lamps she'd next to the bed and she'd twisted it so it glared in his face. "I'd like to watch, please," she says and folded up her legs.

Nothing for it. He coughed and rose to his knees.

Niamh giggled. "It's true what Mum says! You have a tiny one."

He grimaced, took the doll, rolled to the side, away from her so the flaccid, carpet-chaffed tip of Old Moody, the Marquis of Lorne, was placed into Katia's dead, outrageously accommodating lips. The daughter simply stood up on her bed to enjoy a full view, her brown eyes upon him, he sensed the jamming up of pee in his tubes as a massive case of Stage Fright descended, the need . . . the inability! "I can't," he hissed, "with you *staring*."

"Don't be shy."

He looked away from her, tried to pretend the stupid-faced doll's lips were those of others, warm, living faces in the washing sea of lust.

"Go on, pee in her mouth," Paulette's daughter whispered, then suddenly she groaned, all to herself, and it was the privacy of that groan which led to a terrible arousal lifting in the Nephew, not so much at the latest jailable offense but the narrative of this event and how he would be able to slur it in some woman's ear at the perfect moment, as a first few driblets came, then a rich stream, and by angling the plastic doll's head she took it all proudly. He could have written to the manufacturers with admiration, praise, and relief!

The doll grew heavy and warm in his cold hands and, when he was done, wisps of his desperate steam emerged from its lips as if the thing had taken up Marlboros. He was reminded of the drinking days he'd kneel to the chemical toilet in the dark, then light a match to check if there was any blood in there.

He looked at the young girl and licked his lips slowly.

"Men are so disgusting," she said, stepping over him, then very gingerly cradling Katia. She placed the doll in a regimental row of imitation beings. "Night, night, crawl quietly and don't wake Mum."

He began to crawl out again; she made him struggle with the door and she switched off the light; all the way Katia stood in the corner of the girl's room with her dismal gang, watched the Nephew's painful progress with deadened contempt.

Halfway back up the bloody stairs all the lights came crashing on. Least by this time he'd re-hoisted the boxer shorts and perfected a stair-edge hop

to prevent them working down. It was version two on the sprog front.
The Nephew looked down, along the length of his leg at its reprimanding
stare, then he pitifully attempted to accelerate his ascent when the child
walked away, but moments later, pulling a dressing-gown around her and
coughing, Paulette stood, shockingly tall at the bottom of the stairs.

"Why didn't you wake me?" the Nephew whined.

"I bloody tried, you were out the game, mumbling all kinds of stuff, and
what are you doing crawling around nude in the house?"

"Excuse me, but could you direct me to the toilet?" he sighed in normal
volume.

"What in the name of Christ is wrong with your feet?" she says and
honked her nose.

"There was a wasp's nest in the nose of my canoe. I was chastised."

She climbed the stairs and studied his swole feet, then let out a phlegmy
chuckling, "Only one cure for that. Along with a little anesthetic of course."

Paulette rolled him down beneath sodium tangerine street lamps on the
stolen hospital trolley, as all the lights came on in the adjacent houses and the
curtains moved. They stopped where the drive ended in an oval turning place.

"You got a tax disk on this?"

"Does for wheeling Colin in the house when he gets back from the pub
pished mortal. Right. On your feet, son."

With his arm around Paulette's toweling robe they made on into the
Argyllshire Debatable Lands, the familiar tracts where new estates blunder
into reedy fields with a pretense of civilization; where cable TV and sewering
runs out, abrupt, where telephone wires turn back on themselves while
the lazy movements of drifting night beasts rustle against the thistles. Farm
animals wander freely here with the same liberties as the holy cow in India.
A patrol of blue keel marks on sheep flanks show just above the reeds of
the ever-damp ground. A perfect gate stands alone, abandoned on each side
by its fence.

As they labored into so-called fields a particularly virile thistle banged
against his thigh, a fat sappy nettle released its bubbles of poison along a shin
while her terry-toweling threw the plants aside before her. With disappointment he could detect the frazzled end of censorious under-denim round
her trainers.

They halted in unformed fields, deep in dark, the estate just mushrooms of streetlight vapor to their rear, the roofs shining. Paulette blundered him from left to right, almost toppling him a couple of shots till the dimensions were agreeable, his naked legs, gynecologically splayed, both his swollen bare feet were deep sunk in two substantial fresh cowpats, hardened by daylight's sluggish encroach, the crusts digging into blond hairs on his upper feet.

"Best cure for swole feet is the good soak in the fresh cowpats," she announced dubiously, darting out that right hand to his shoulder, steadying him as she lit up two more joints of the New Drug in her mouth and he relaxed but shivered as she popped the now familiar gear in his lips.

"It's great for pain, I took a good toke when I went into labor with Niamh fore they carted me away."

Stood in shit was karmic revenge on him after the Fed, the Nephew thought, and says, "Is there no risk of infection?"

"That what you say to all the girls?"

"When Mockit's old man got sunk on the convoys the men used to pee on their hands to keep the frost out them and they all got infected in their cracked knuckles and that."

"Well, in an open wound, sure, but your own waste can be good, all the supermodels are drinking one another's pee these days. I find that sexy."

"Mmm," he kept quiet, then says, "I feel, Paulette, you run a visceral household."

"I never need Vaseline."

"You're sexy, Paulette, I recall you used to like a man to sing a song in your ear while . . ."

"Is that what you call it? Your singing was no better than your shagging."

The women always have their wee thing, the Nephew thought, like that bint: showers and volcanoes! Yup, if you can find the wee button of their fetish and press it forever, they'll love you okay. Once I get the Man Who Walks' money, a wee trip to Japan might be in the offing, everyone's always on about the dump, and working up a lather with yon caviar whoor in the Jacuzzi, chucking out the soap suds, mmm.

The Nephew, a symbol of his nation, shivered, stood square in the cow shit, musing under cloudy Scotch skies on better days ahead.

*

The Man Who Walks moved down those slopes with a camping pack on his back and his unlit pipe upside down in his mouth to stop it filling with the rain. On the end of each long arm dangled a carrier bag. Both bags were filled full of water, the plastic handles strained against his hands, and he had to hold the bags out to get them clear of his moving legs.

The bag he held with his left arm had a large dead salmon floating inside, curled around against the plastic; you could see its silver flank of scales. The other bag just had water in it that splashed out in response to his erratic walk.

It was still raining when he arrived outside the Hotel. In the Hotel car park, next to two parked buses, he tipped out the water from the bags. He wrapped the salmon in one and laid it by his boot; then, using two fingers, he reached up to his left eye and removed it. It was a glass eye. After he'd taken out the glass eye he poked into the dark recess of the socket and from beneath the little flap of skin he removed a small tinfoil package of cannabis resin. He unwrapped it, used his thumbnail to split away more than half, then swallowed the lump of resin. He wrapped the remaining portion and put it back in the socket behind the eye, which he replaced. He picked up the salmon and crossed to the door of the lounge bar. Inside, the Hotel was busy with tourists from the buses who would have been staying there that night.

When he reached the bar he said, "A score of nips."

"A score? You want twenty whiskies for the bus party?" The barman slid out a tray, then started to count twenty shot glasses.

He shouted, "In one glass, man; in one glass!"

The barman looked at him, sighed, reached for a tankard and started filling it with repeated shots of whisky.

The Man Who Walks slapped the salmon on the bar top. "Cash or fish?" he asked.

The barman said, "Look, sir, barter went out with the Middle Ages, it'll have to be the legal tender."

The Man Who Walks took a very large wad of wet one-pound notes from his greatcoat pocket and, with one eyebrow raised, peeled the paper notes; a few tore in half they were so sodden, but he stuck them down on the wooden bar top.

The barman collected over twenty of the soaked notes and half notes but didn't put them in the till, he laid them out to dry on a radiator by some beer crates. The barman ran up the till and put the change down beside the dead fish. "Can you take that off the bar, please."

The Man Who Walks took the fish off the bar and put it inside the plastic bag. "What a beautiful big fish, is it a salmon?" a nearby tourist asked.

The Man Who Walks removed his glass eye again, grinned at the tourist, then said, "Look into my mind." The tourist moved sharply away.

The Man Who Walks took a small case from inside his overcoat. He opened it and removed his drinking eye. This glass eye was similar to his other but the white of the eye was specially rivered with reddened blood vessels designed to match with his living eye after the consumption of twenty whiskies. He fitted the red eye in.

An hour and three-quarters later it was after closing time and the lounge bar was deserted apart from the Man Who Walks; his tankard still had a good dose of whisky in the bottom.

The barman repeated, "Come on now, sir. I'll have to ask you for your glass."

The Man Who Walks picked up the carrier bag: the upside-down dead eye of the fish and its gaping mouth were inside, pressed against the grayish-looking plastic. He lifted the salmon out by its head, clamping the gills with his grip, he gently tipped the whisky from the tankard into the open mouth of the dead fish, careful not to spill a drop, then banged the emptied tankard down on the bar top. Good night! he yelled. He stepped out of the Hotel into the rainy darkness and held the big salmon's mouth up to his own, then tipped his head back and gulped all that whisky out from the insides of that fish. Then the Man Who Walks took the salmon's tail in both hands, swung back and gave the big bastard a good fling across the road. The fish went spinning through the night, then landed with a bump on the roof of one of the buses— no doubt leading to a lot of shitty speculation among the tourists in the morning concerning the feeding habits of the golden eagle, etc., etc., but meanwhile he was off, striding into the wet black of nightimeness with his thumbs under the straps of his camping pack. He moved along the back roads, across the Concession Lands, between the outlying homes he made his way through the darknesses until he came to a slight gradient in the road where he halted. He stepped into a flat field and strode into the blackness. There was a large crack and a blue explosion as he walked into an electric cattle fence cranked up to the max. He yowled, fell backward into a puddle on his arse. He could not see a thing in front of him, behind him, to his left or to his right, so he did not know where the electric fences were, out there, in the dark, waiting for him.

The Man Who Walks sat still in the raining field and chuckled in the dark, then let out a sound more like a sob. He leaned forward and swung his backpack off. He pulled out a set of poles which clinked together and sounded like tent poles. But they were not. He was unfolding the plastic walls and roof of a child's playhouse that he often used for his camping expeditions. He tried to get up on his feet to pitch the playhouse, but he was mortal as a newt and slumped back on his arse each time. Eventually he unlaced his boots and removed them, then lay back and just pulled the playhouse plastic up to his chin like a sheet.

He started snoring, water made bubbles in his upturned nostrils and there was also the sound, in the darkness, of big raindrops pattering down on the plastic. In the morning his boots were filled with water.

In the afternoon sun, carrying a new bag of water, the Man Who Walks came down off those hills. He entered Old Greyhead's General Store to get provisions. He placed purchases on the counter beside the till, spilling water from his bag all over the floor as he moved. He bought four cans of South Atlantic pilchards and one can of North Atlantic pilchards! He bought Clann tobacco, two copies of the Daily Telegraph, two copies of the Financial Times and two copies of the Times.

"It's brightened up a lot now, hasn't it?" said Old Greyhead.

"Shut your mouth and give us a carrier bag," the Man Who Walks said, and he'd forgotten to change his drinking eye so he had one red eye and one clear one. Although he stinks, shouts, spills water and once shat pilchard skitters on the floor of the shop, then wiped his arsehole with a dead pigeon, Old Greyhead held the Man Who Walks in the highest regard because of the quality newspapers he reads.

"Good afternoon now, sir," Greyhead said, following the Man Who Walks with a swishing mop.

The Man Who Walks moved up the paths to his one-story house on the hill. He emptied the bag of water into a forty-five-gallon drum in the overgrown garden which the rain had already filled, so it poured down the sides. He opened the front door to his house. Afternoon sun still shone over his shoulder but it was dark in there: pitch dark. He shut the door behind him, got down on all fours and dragged the carrier bag of provisions, crawling forward through the network of filthy papier-mâché tunnels and igloos he had constructed inside the rooms and corridors of the house: the papier-mâché made from years and years of unread quality newspapers.

Needle

KYOKO UCHIDA

I dreamed of swallowing a quick-
silver needle, cold as the mirror I stood in,
pinning heavy white folds of a dress to skin
naked as a hooked fish, sewing myself
in. Small double stitches to hold together
these wrists and knees loose as change,
to tailor each line, this breath to the next,
threading myself one eye at a time.
I needed alterations at the hem and waistline,
the untidy mouth. I swallowed the needle then,
wriggling out of my own careful seams, my skin
catching. It pierced my tongue, went down
sharp as someone else's breastbone on its way
to the torn pocket of my heart, where
everything fell through.

JAMES ROSENQUIST

The Meteor Hits Picasso's Bed, 1996–99.

The Meteor Hits Monet's Garden, 1996–99.

The Meteor Hits Brancusi's Pillow, 1997–99.

The Meteor Hits the Swimmer's Pillow, 1997.

James Rosenquist

From 1996 to 1999, James Rosenquist worked on a quartet of meteor paintings: *The Meteor Hits Picasso's Bed*, *The Meteor Hits Monet's Garden*, *The Meteor Hits Brancusi's Pillow*, and *The Meteor Hits the Swimmer's Pillow*. I asked him, "Why hit by a meteor?" And he said, "I don't mean that they were killed. I mean hit by a meteor as in an inexplicable event."

He went on, "In 1938, when I was a kid, I was living in western Minnesota, and, twelve miles north of me, a great big fat lady was lying in bed one night when a meteor as big as a baseball came crashing through her roof, hit her on the hip, and went through the floor. It didn't kill her, but it gave her a giant bruise—and it was the talk of the town! So I thought about that, and I thought about a meteor as a natural disaster that shoots in from space like an exclamation point. What does it mean to be hit by one? That you're lucky or unlucky?"

WALTER HOPPS

Reclined Nude

BRIAN HENRY

How can I blame myself for the vision
I did my best to withstand, a blend
of assertiveness and bland persistence
that, when applied, bled into insignificance?

Well of course I blame myself, for that
and for this, an incursion of little point
or even resistance, and the tears you see
are not the tears I pretend to own. Oh dear.

I left a propeller behind at the fair; some runt
of a boy is fingering it now, its plastic edge.
I'd love to shove that edge right up his

*

Lofty ideals are fine for former corporate
whores, their every missive complete
with self-promoting flyers and brochures.

I prefer the grittier way of conducting
business, refuse to blush or otherwise kneel
to whomever thinks he owns a piece of this.

I suppose it all began when my eyes gave out,
so quickly and with great pain—much much pain—
a scar in a hillside that bungles sight.

Fucking hillside, floating through the ether
as if the sky mattered, as if the trees leaning
against each other did so out of anything but spite.

*

I often feel the need to scratch, so scratch I do.
You wouldn't know the agony this can bring,
the hoopla it pulls a body through.

You try lying here all day, hearing what I've heard.
The worst is knowing others know I'm bored
yet do nothing, pass by undisturbed.

To be ignored when display is the aim:
an insult too great to bear.
How else can I reach out of the frame,
cause an ear to burn, or at least to ring?

*

I saw a woman once—through her
to tell the truth—whose body
must be mine.

Her hair reflected a different light
but her eyes were also green, tongue
blue, nipples pink.

Her legs rose so far above her feet
they soared.

I know those legs, the tight expanse
that moves in bounds, the dimples
beneath the ass.

I watch her so hard she forgot
it is I, not she,

who hangs at another's mercy.

Hiroshima

VLADIMIR SOROKIN

11:48 P.M.

THE YAR RESTAURANT

Lukashevich, the vice president of a modest but stable bank, and Zeldin, the owner of four supermarkets, were sitting at a table set for three. A gypsy choir sang onstage. Next to the table a birch tree grew in a tub. On the table, a carafe of vodka sparkled, and a platter of salmon glowed red.

The two friends were drunk. They had begun at the Pushkin restaurant: 850 milliliters of Russian Standard vodka, cranberry juice, beer, marinated white mushrooms, stuffed pike, veal pâté, Caesar salad, lamb à la Hussar, sterlet in champagne sauce, crème brûlée, crepes with crème caramel, coffee, cognac, Calvados.

They continued at the Biscuit: 380 ml of tequila, green tea, fruit salad.

"No way, Borya," said Lukashevich, carelessly lighting a cigarette. "These gypsies don't rock."

"You don't like them?" asked Zeldin, filling the shot glasses and spilling vodka on the tablecloth. "I love it when they howl."

"Come on . . . it's so depressing," replied Lukashevich, picking up a shot glass. He splashed the contents on the birch tree. "Shit!"

"What, the vodka?" Zeldin asked, puzzled.

"Everything."

"Why everything?"

"I don't like places like this. Let's go to the Bridge. Dance with the girls."

"Right now? Come on, let's have a drink! What gives, Sasha?" exclaimed

Zeldin, embracing Lukashevich. "Everything's great. Hey, wait a minute," he suddenly remembered, "I didn't finish telling you!"

"Telling me what?" said Lukashevich gloomily.

"About the bell."

"What bell?" said Lukashevich in a bored voice.

"The one in Christ the Savior Cathedral! The bass bell! The G note! Thirty-two tons. It's in the southwest wing, I think. Right. Well, that Gazprom broad, you know, the one with lung cancer, she found out that low frequencies destroy cancer cells. She paid them a bundle. So every evening they lifted her up with the bell ringer, and there she was, naked. . . . Sasha, you bastard! I still can't believe you came. Shit! You're really here. You're here, you sweaty old asshole!"

Knocking over the carafe of vodka, Zeldin threw himself on Lukashevich and hugged him with all his might. The table teetered. Zeldin's striped jacket split. Lukashevich snarled, and his large, doughy fingers squeezed Zeldin's swarthy neck. Zeldin clenched Lukashevich's white neck.

"You Moscow scumbag!" Lukashevich growled, and they started choking each other.

11:48 P.M.

CONDEMNED FIVE-STORY BUILDING ON INNOVATOR STREET

Two homeless men, Valera and Rooster, were sitting on a pile of damp rags in the corner of a gutted apartment. A slim crescent moon shone through the broken window. The men were drunk. And they were polishing off a bottle of Rossiya vodka. They'd started drinking early that morning at the Yaroslav train station: a quarter liter of Istochnik, half a loaf of white bread, chicken scraps from the grill bar. Then they rode to Sokolniki Park and collected enough empty bottles to turn in and continue: three bottles of Ochakov beer and two poppy-seed danishes. Then they had a nap on a bench and rode to Novodevichy Convent, where they begged for alms until evening. They got enough for a bottle of Rossiya.

"That's it," said Valera, drinking down the last drop in the dark.

"You finished it?" Rooster croaked. "Fucking shit . . ."

"What?"

"I got the shakes, goddammit. Like I didn't have a drop. I could use another swallow."

"We'll go to Izmailovo tomorrow. We'll load up, man! Tomorrow!

Tomorrow!" Valera began to chuckle and sing something incomprehensible.

"Whaddya mean, tomorrow?" said Rooster, slugging him.

"Shit! I'm pissing in my pants! Again! Holy fuck!" laughed Valera.

"You dick-face . . . asshole . . ." said Rooster, hitting him lamely.

"What're you . . . Oh go fuck yourself!" Valera said, and hit him back.

They were quiet for a moment. A fire engine passed by noisily outside the window.

"A gangstermobile?" asked Rooster with a yawn.

"A cement crusher," Valera objected authoritatively.

They sat quietly.

"Tomorrow! To—moooooorrrrow! Fucking tomooorrrrrroooow!" Valera started singing and laughing again, opening his mouth of rotten teeth wide in the dark.

"Just shut the fuck up, you jerk!" shouted Rooster and grabbed him by the throat.

Valera wheezed and grabbed him back.

They began choking each other.

11:48 P.M.

AN APARTMENT ON SIVTSEV VRAZHEK LANE

Alex, a dancer, and Nikola, a web designer, were lying on the bed naked. Mozart's Fortieth Symphony played quietly in the background. Nikola was smoking while Alex cut cocaine on a compact disc of Alexander Laertsky's *Udder*. They had begun twenty-four hours earlier at the birthday party of a makeup artist friend (0.5 grams + orange juice), then continued at Tabula Rasa (0.3 grams + still mineral water) and Niagara (0.8 grams + still mineral water + two cigars). After that, having drunk a cup of green tea at Shot Glass, they went to a morning show of *Attack of the Clones*. Then they went out to the dacha of a woman designer they didn't know very well (1.3 grams + sparkling mineral water + fruit tea + 150 ml whiskey + apple juice + strawberry tart + grapes + candy + 150 ml of apricot liqueur + strawberries + green tea + strawberries with whipped cream). In the evening they returned to Nikola's place (0.4 grams).

"Just a tiny bit, Kol. We'll finish it off," said Alex, who was making two puny lines with a discount card from a Party store.

"Is that all there is?" asked Nikola, squinting his beautiful glazed eyes.

"That's it, now—all gone."

They silently snorted the cocaine through a plastic straw. Alex wiped up the cocaine dust with his thin finger and gently touched it to the head of Nikola's member. Nikola looked at his member.

"You want to?"

"I always want to."

"Listen, do we have any whiskey left?"

"We never did have any."

"Really?" said Nikola, with tense surprise. "Well, what do we have?"

"Only vodka." Alex gently took Nikola's balls in his palm.

"I'm kinda out of it . . ." said Nikola, stretching.

"I'll get it."

Alex sprang up and went into the kitchen. Nikola stubbed out his cigarette in a steel ashtray. Alex returned silently with vodka and a shot glass. He poured. Nikola drank. Alex kneeled down in front of him and slowly ran his tongue around the lilac-colored head of Nikola's member.

"But first do it like velvet, hedgehog," said Nikola, licking his dry lips.

"Yep, massah," said Alex in English, taking two velvet women's belts— one black and one purple—off the chair.

They lay on the bed, pressed their bodies together, and wrapped their legs around each other. Alex looped the purple belt around Nikola's neck; Nikola wound Alex's neck in the black one. Their lips came together, opened, and their tongues touched. They began choking each other.

11:48 P.M.

A HUT IN THE VILLAGE OF KOLCHINO

Two old women, Niura and Matryona, were kneeling and praying before a dark icon case. The blue flame of the icon lamp barely illuminated the faces of Saint Nikola, the Savior, and the Virgin Mother. It was dim and damp in the hut.

"To you we pray Lord Jesus Christ, Son of God, and to Your Immaculate Mother and our Lord in Heaven and all the Holy Saints, hear our prayers and have mercy upon us."

"Amen," the old women murmured separately. They crossed themselves, bowed, touched their foreheads to the uneven floor, and with a creak began to stand up.

Matryona got up first. She helped Niura up by her bony elbow.

"Oof, God almighty . . ." Niura straightened up with great difficulty, took a step toward the bench, and sat down.

"Maybe you'll write to Vasily after all?" asked Matryona, walking over to the table.

"No. No strength left," said Niura, breathing hard.

"Well, I wrote a note to my folks. Let them come."

"Mine ain't been by for eight months. Oy, everything aches," moaned Niura.

"On with it then, ain't no point. . . ."

Matryona lifted the tablecloth. Underneath, beside the bread and salt cellar, was a plate with one pancake. Matryona took the pancake, sat down next to Niura, and split it in half.

"Here, eat. I made it this morning."

"Just one?" Niura took the half pancake with her thin, shaking hands.

"So what . . . Just one. With cow's butter. Eat."

"I'll eat."

They ate in silence, chewing with their toothless mouths. Matryona finished, wiped her mouth with her brown hand, got up, and took Niura by the elbow.

"Let's go, praise God."

"Let's go . . . Lord almighty . . ." The old woman, chewing her last bite, had trouble standing up.

They went out into the dark mudroom with the rotten floor. Moonlight filtered through the holes in the roof. A hemp rope with two nooses had been thrown over the ceiling beam. Matryona led Niura to the nooses. She helped her put one of them around her neck. Then she put on her own. Niura wore her new white scarf with blue polka dots. Matryona wore her old black one with the white speckles.

Matryona clasped Niura by her bony shoulders and hung on her. Niura let out a sob, and hiccuped. The nooses tightened and the old women's legs gave way.

11:48 P.M.
BOARDING SCHOOL NO. 7, KINDERGARTEN DORMITORY

Five-year-old Rita and Masha lay on their beds, side by side, eyes wide open and staring at the ceiling. The other sixteen children were asleep. On the opposite side of the wall, the nanny and the night guard were making love.

A car passed by outside the window. Strips of light slid across the ceiling.

"A dragon," said Masha.

"Nooo. A giraffe," Rita sniffed.

The nanny's muffled grunts could be heard through the wall.

"What is Nina Petrovna doing in there?" asked Masha.

"She and Uncle Misha are choking each other."

"What does that mean?"

"They lie in bed naked and choke each other. With their hands."

"What for?"

"It's where babies come from. And 'cause it feels good. My mama and papa do it all the time. They undress naked all the way and start doing it. Do yours?"

"I don't have a papa."

They were quiet for awhile. Another car passed by. And another one.

"Oy, oh my, oy, Mish . . . Not that way. . ." muttered the nanny on the other side of the wall.

Masha raised her head:

"Rita. You wanna choke each other?"

"But we'll have babies."

They were quiet for awhile. Rita thought about it:

"No we won't."

"Why not?"

"We aren't a man and a lady."

"Oh . . . then let's do it, okay?"

"Okay. Only we have to take our clothes off."

"Noooo! It's cold. Let's do it like this."

"If we're not naked it won't work."

"Really?"

"Uh-huh."

"All right."

They spent a long time taking off their pajamas. They got into Masha's bed. They grabbed each other by the neck. And began choking each other.

*

The aforementioned Lukashevich, Valera, Alex, Matryona, and Rita didn't see anything in particular during the process of choking.

But Zeldin, Rooster, Nikola, Niura, and Masha observed a series of orange and crimson flashes, which gradually turned into a threatening purple glow. Then the purple light began to dim, changing to dark blue, and it suddenly opened up into a huge, endless expanse. There was an unbelievably spacious, ash gray landscape, lit from the dark purple sky by a huge full moon. Despite the night, it was as bright as day. The moon illuminated the low ruins of a burned city in minute detail. A scattering of stars glittered in the sky. A naked woman walked among the ruins. Her white, moonlit body emanated a mesmerizing sense of calm. She didn't belong to the world on whose ashes she walked. In those ashes and ruins lay people injured by the blast. Some of them moaned, some were already dead. But their moans did not disturb the woman's calm. She moved serenely, stepping over the dead and the moaning. She was looking for something else. Finally she stopped. Among the melted bricks lay a pregnant bitch, mortally wounded. A large part of the dog's body was burned, and her rib bones stuck out through clumps of fur and skin. Breathing heavily and whining, she was trying to give birth. But she no longer had the strength for birthing. The dog was dying; her entire disfigured body shuddered, tensing powerlessly. Bloody spittle drooled from her crimson mouth, and her pink tongue hung out.

The woman lowered herself onto the ashes next to the dog. She placed her white hands on the bitch's singed belly. She pressed down. The dog's dirty, blood-spattered legs spread slightly. She whined and let out a little yelp. Puppies began to squeeze out of her womb: one, another, a third, a fourth, and a fifth. A spasm convulsed the bitch's body. She glanced at the woman with a mad, wet eye, yawned, and died. The wet black puppies stirred, sticking their muzzles into the gray ash. The woman picked them up one at a time and held them to her breasts. And the blind puppies drank her milk.

Translated from the Russian by Jamey Gambrell

AIDAS BAREIKIS

Glad to Hear from You, 2002.
Installation at the Contemporary Art Center,
Vilnius, Lithuania.

Aidas Bareikis

When people are witness to a violent event—a terrorist act, a car accident—
the choreography of the scene takes on an almost schizophrenic quality. The
moment before the event is one of normal, everyday circumstance, and your
actions and gestures are mechanical. But when you're suddenly thrust into a
chaotic situation, your body and expression become disfigured, sometimes even
grotesque. I wanted to incorporate this figurative aspect into an artwork: the
frozen moment of an explosion.

The objects I collected to make this piece had to embody or represent those
qualities of grotesqueness. I picked up tchotchkes from 99-cent stores, masks,
uniforms, cheap things that look weird but betray a certain cruel exploitation
in their purpose or in the way they were manufactured, secondhand things
from flea markets or yard sales that were already invested with a certain history.
I looked for objects that would communicate the idea of potential energy
contained in a gesture, and then the release of that energy. There was humor
involved in my selection, too: I'd pick up a repulsive mask and, because of its
ugliness, come up with a particular treatment for it—inflating it, for example,
so it would take on a quality of exaggerated dumbness. I work with toxic
materials because the greater the toxicity of the medium, the more intense its
color and surface. The explosion or destruction of such objects is subversive.
It denies their significance.

After September 11, friends and family called me from Lithuania, and at
the end of each call they'd say, "Glad to hear from you." The phrase began to
resonate. A few months later I was commissioned to create a work for the
Contemporary Art Center in Vilnius. I decided to incorporate the materials that
I'd gathered in New York and to use Glad to Hear from You as the title of the
piece. I tried to make it geographically and temporally ambiguous to allow for
a wide range of interpretations. Its fragile state—suspended from the ceiling
or mounted on the wall in defiance of gravity, as if it might fall apart at any
second—underscores the idea of leaving things hanging. It makes the viewer
think, This situation is not going to last; it's going to disintegrate. It's a spectacle
without the expectation of entertainment.

A.B.

From conversations with writer and editor Thomas Mediodia

MonoLogical
Poem #1

DURS GRÜNBEIN

Written between 1985 and 1988,
and translated from the German
by Michael Hofmann

If what goes on suddenly
strikes you as atrocious

try to stay calm. Say it
in such a way that the person at the other end

can't help thinking: I probably
wouldn't have put it any differently

myself.

There are hot forms and
cold forms and poems

no matter how you break them and
what you print them on

are always cold (no matter how
hot they were at the manufacturing stage).

And yet hot and cold
sometimes aren't even all that

far apart and it has been known
for the one to turn into the other:

the ripest pathos
becomes the animating gurgle

of air bubbles from a soul
in the depths. Because

what is the whole surreal jokeshop
of terrors compared to the

infinitely chance little
tricks of a poem.

MonoLogical Poem #2

From time to time
I have these days when

I feel like embarking
on a poem again

of a kind that still isn't
all that popular. I mean

one without any meta-
physical refinements or

that thing that lately has stood in
for such . . . that type of

cynical genuflecting
at the stilted progress of history

or standing gasping akimbo
in the tough East-West marathon
as if you were one of

Alighieri's damned
with a stitch. Poems

someone said to me the other day

only attracted him if they
were full of surprises

written at those
odd times when

something still inchoate
a daydream a single

line begins somewhere and
undoes you.

MonoLogical
Poem #4

You pursue your own
eccentric designs you re-

fine the images you order
the moments but you don't

listen to them
as quite differently in their own ways

they pursue their eccentric
designs refine

images show chance movements
move differently

in the same spaces at pains
not to listen to you. That

is the nub.

MonoLogical
Poem #5

Strange what continually a-
mazes me is this suddenness

of some instants,
e.g. the bright flash

of a dolphin's belly
on its upside-down arc

through the hoop the swim-
suited assistant holds aloft. Or

the brittle split second

when a '61 cathode-ray tube
implodes at a stroke and

it is only looking at the shards that it
dawns on you that there never was

any memory (so what was there
to be wiped?). Presumably

all that is generated from
the menacing clearing

in your dream the crooked
tableau all the dead living things

repressed by day into those
diapositive regions where
everything seems so immutable

—yes?—and for all that
lasts barely longer than

a couple of thousand REMS.

MonoLogical
Poem #13

(SONG)

Take a good look, before they
sell you a pup or down the river.
Amigo, the clearest

insight is in the air.
You don't need to
be quicker or cleverer.
(That's part of it.)

There is gainful
employment (which makes it preferable to the pursuit of happiness). In the
hours of enter-

tainment there is still
the discord bridling
between rivals, the

thicket of disappointed glances.

In dead studios, tape-
twitterings to the synced
movements, otherwise
faces like o-

pen newspapers full of
communiqués and de-

sire for a little television
at night and the
deception of a hand

caressing your body-
work.

All About You

A series of impenetrable instants
jammed up together like
rumors by the light of an insistently ancestral politics, a

sequence of rapidly changing grue-
somenesses, the moronic ping-pong
chatter of a few newspaper-
readers on a park bench, and you
you're just enjoying the calm

under a low sky
(in the theater opposite they're rehearsing
Shakespeare . . . "We
humanists . . .").

You wait and then
you choose your moment between
the baby carriages
and the flock of mangy pigeons that

fly up in a sort of *haute volée* gobbling—
You can picture them
with se-
vered
bloody heads in the gutter, a
vivid daydream,

the bespattered extras in an
assassination flick (The
Death of Leo Trotsky) or the usual

BBBBBB films . . . but instead you just
gander on very slowly
to the next crossing, because
today is all about you.

WALLACE BERMAN

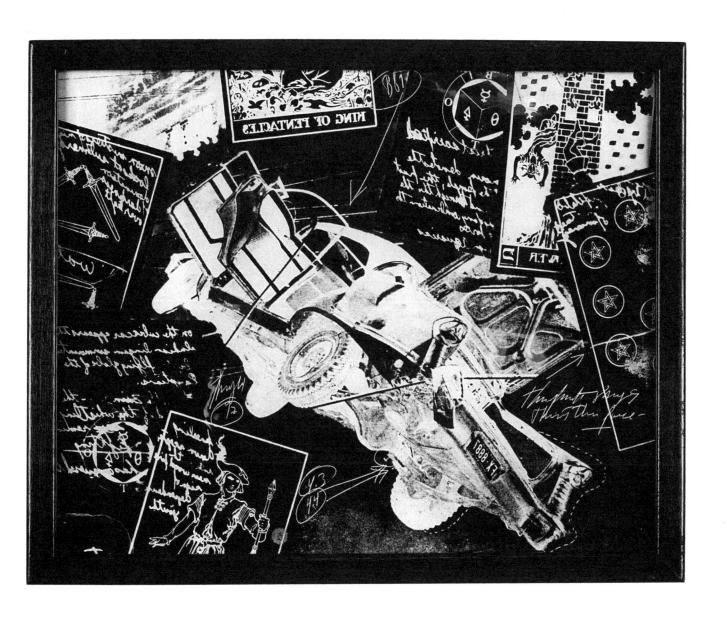

Untitled (Airborne Car with Tarot Cards), 1976.

From Nevada, in Defense of My Marriage

DEBORAH LANDAU

Sunday morning, Laughlin. Heat damns us poolside.
All week we've been trying to shed the marriage bed.

Remember how desire wasn't lilac-petaled?
It was heavy. It swaggered, gave commands,

could make us lie down
in heat in the middle of a workday.

On the empty deck I squint at the Times—
the newspaper's muted violence unfolding in my lap—

while Angie, ex–Vegas waitress in crucifix earrings
and velvet halter-top, speaks to you of Jesus.

When we drove out of L.A., dust warping the windows
of our rented blue Lumina, is this what we were looking for—

this $39 motel room, broken church where we worship
the miracle of too many margaritas and pay-per-view porn?

Later, when I wake to the radio testing the Emergency Broadcast System,
you're sleeping beside me in the sapphire light of the clock's crystal

digits, veins braceleting your wrists, power lines
surging toward the circuit of your wedding ring—

sometimes my restlessness syncopates the day's anatomy
and all I want is to slouch in the darkest bar on the other side

of the continent, numb with wine, dissolving between the borders
of midnight and 4 A.M., a stranger's face leaning toward me . . .

but look, the message light's blinking through the tequila bottle,
tilted amber hourglass, your breath has emptied itself against my breasts,

and we're still here amid the wreckage of flesh—
T-shirt, sandal, minidress, curtains hushing the sun.

We've got hours until checkout. Maybe the door lock's jimmied
but the chain still holds, and for now, I'll take this communion:

your volatile mouth, long scar cracking your chest, anchor
of your face stained with our history, your crucial, exact glance.

Not Light nor Life nor Love nor Nature nor Spirit nor Semblance nor Anything We Can Put into Words

—Meister Eckehart, on God

BRUCE BEASLEY

As the ellipse
of a zero

is to nothing. As
the starfish's

five sucker-tips
are to the mussel's valves

they wrench open, as its
inverted, flung-

out stomach
is to the mussel's meat.

Or as a glacier to the hiss
and crumble of its calving.

As the foghorn
to the offing, no:

as the offing's
visibility, to the fog.

As cadence, to caesura.
Or insomnia

to obsessive dream.
As et cetera

to what's unmentioned,
incognito

to the name. As the *difference*
to the subtracted-

from. As loess
to sirocco,

bioluminescence
to the murk.

As arthritic
fingers to the étude, as

bone-grind
to arthritis. As a saint's

gnawed jawbone
to the reliquary's

purple felt. As *alienation*
of affection

is to *flesh of my flesh,*
bone of my bones.

As breath
to pleura, the clitoral

hood to the tongue:
As *as* is to *as*, I am to You, as

castrati's
scrota, to the song.

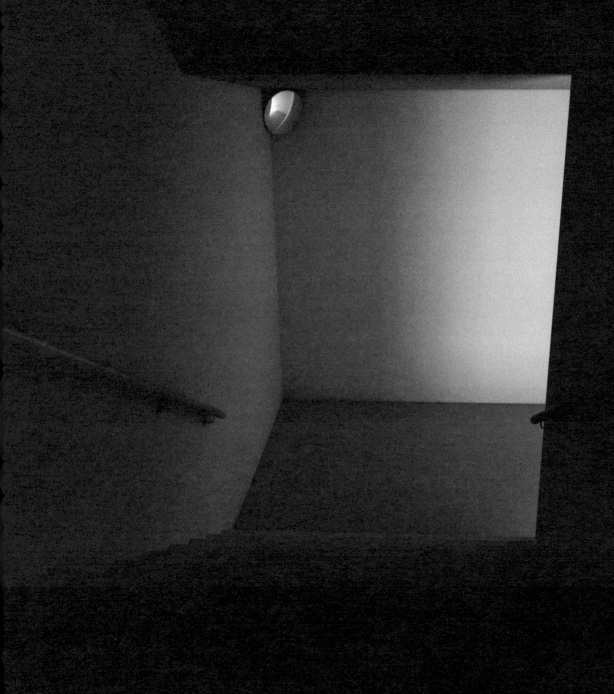

Craig Kalpakjian,
D.S., 2002.

A Little
Like Light

A. L. KENNEDY

You should tell everyone nothing: especially nothing about love.

Otherwise, over and over, there always will be someone who always has to ask about you, about love, about your love, and you'll end up like me— always having to answer.

By now, I know how to, of course, that isn't the problem. I shrug, I wag my hands—sometimes the one hand only—I shake my head, or I offer that little maneuver involving an upward jerk of my chin combined with very mildly rolling eyes. That one gets a laugh, during which I will probably smile, indulgent, and I will not ever say

I'm a sick man—you shouldn't be laughing. I am very seriously ill. I think I have diabetes—I must have diabetes. My current doctor, like all of the others, disagrees with me, but I know—I can assure you that I do have undoubted diabetes, and also leukemia, and this thing which is removing the bone mass from my legs—perhaps elsewhere, too—it is daily reaming out a new fragility in my pelvis, an increasing insecurity when I walk, and a fear that I'll crumble something if I roll over while I'm asleep. I don't care what anyone tells me, I am deeply unwell, I couldn't ever feel this way if I were fit. And you are there and laughing and I am here and scared that I will nocturnally fragment and, set beside all this, my impotence should seem a really, wholly minor matter, but in fact it doesn't. In fact it does not. And every part of this is no one else's business, only my own, just like my love.

I married young: twenty-four: and I have stayed that way ever since. Now I am forty-three. Ten years in, and with the necessary parts still working, I fathered my son. He is called Malcolm John and I am called John Edward and, in this way, the names of our respective fathers have slipped back a notch to settle in subsidiary roles for, most likely, the duration of two other lives.

Actually, I did once think of dropping my John and enjoying the fresh sensation of being Ted. My father was steadfastly an Edward, so there would have been no confusion. I don't know why I didn't do it: a kind of stage fright, I suppose, an unwillingness to fail all over again in another role.

Malcolm, my boy Mal, I would imagine harbors no such fantasies—he thinks that I don't like him. Which is true, I don't. He is, I'm afraid, rather difficult to like. Temperamentally, he's pleasant enough: not that bright, but not so stupid, equipped with acquaintances: there is simply something about him which I find physically disturbing. He isn't exactly clumsy, he just looks as if he will be, he isn't exactly dirty, he just appears unwashed, his clothes aren't exactly rumpled, he just has a disheveled stance. He is a mess, fundamentally. When he was still a baby with the usual murmurs of down on a warm, endearing skin, beguilingly taut with life and little veins, he was also, somehow, cloying to the touch, consistently *tacky*. Some children are born athletes, or predisposed to be good at maths. Malcolm was made to be slightly unfortunate.

Because of this, we spend a great deal of time together. We bicycle round the playing fields at weekends, we visit the cinema, I have taught him to catch, to whistle, and, after a fashion, to swim. But then he will look at me, halt me with a glance from among the trees next to the long jump, or breathlessly red-eyed and glistening in the pool, and I will stop pretending and we will both remember: we aren't having fun. Any treat in each other's company is no treat at all: we are not enough. We are the only real friends that we have and, as a pair, we are a continual, mutual disappointment, frequently prey to these sad, small pauses for thought. After which we hug and hold hands for a while, because we truly are sorry for each other, but sharing sympathy is not the same as love. Then we begin again with what we have to: being a father and a son.

I think, aside from anything else, that Mal didn't get enough daylight, early on. Our house, the only one he's ever known, is snibbed between the highest part of the wall around the school and the tallest, easterly edge of what our current Head likes to call its facade. Direct light will sneak a way down through a handful of our windows for maybe three hours on a clear summer's day, which is enough to keep my window boxes going, but must fall short of what's needed for a boy. We have no garden, and most of his early outdoor playing had to be done in the evenings when the classes were over and their children gone. He still looks his best in late slants of shadow, the silently incendiary glow that closes down the day.

And the buildings are set in gravel, that's another drawback—generations of youngsters have left this place with tiny granite fragments irretrievably embedded in their palms and knees. My son is just the same, little patches of him shimmering with iodine painted across fresh scabs. Now that I'm worried the necks of my femurs may snap with no warning and send me tumbling, we spend as much time as we're able out at the sports fields. We feel calmer when we can anticipate soft landings against grass.

My health also troubles me less when I'm working, although work involves a good deal of striding about. But, on duty, I have the uniform: the shiny shoes, the bunches of keys, the peaked cap and piercing expression: the usual, invulnerable ensemble for the security guard, the prison warder— or for the janitor. I can't imagine ever having an accident while I'm dressed like this, it would offend against natural justice.

In fact, there has only been a single mishap in more than two decades of service: the massive one which continues to puzzle me. I watch my wife, peek at her when she's busy, or reading a magazine, or asleep, and I think: *This is the sort of woman who would marry a janitor.*

She has married a janitor. But I am the sort of man who has never felt like a janitor. I am the wrong man for the job. I have simply continued to be a janitor by default while I have waited to discover what I'm really supposed to do. I am an acting janitor—yes, one of many years' standing, but, all the same—this surely must make me an acting husband, too.

She bought us matching anoraks in the last January sales. They are perfectly pleasant and warm and were once expensive, but they are still matching and still anoraks—blue with blocks of purple at the shoulders and unnecessary woven tabs attached to the zips: a 44 chest for me and a 40 for her. She used to be smaller, smaller everywhere. And out we go, of a Saturday, to shop—the janitor and his better half in their matching anoraks. That can't be right.

I mean, I don't exactly mind my having to play out the janitor's part. Around the house, I tend my paintwork and window boxes the way a country stationmaster might. I guessed this was the right thing to do, and it has, indeed, impressed three successive heads. My bulbs and geraniums flourish and I rarely have to dig out cigarette stubs from among them because, out in the school's world, I keep my population terrified. Among four- to twelve-year-olds—that's the limit to what we take—I am an undisputed king. In the boys' toilets, the only graffiti I won't have removed is a narrow line in smudgy biro that warns of the dangers of me. I didn't put it there myself.

So I don't hate the role, not entirely, it's only that acting the janitor has come to be almost all there is of me. I do object to that: my unwelcome self, the finish to my shift when I swing quickly home—it's not exactly far away—and I prise off the Doc Martens and, soft- and hot-footed, I pad straight into the type of domestic bliss designed to please a janitor, the janitor I am not. Sticky boy, dark house, a wife whose sweat, when fresh, smells large but herbal, something like the after-aroma left by crushed leaves of mint, which is weird, though also cheering and familiar—only not for me. Cheering and familiar, that isn't love.

I used to fuck her while I wore the uniform. That worked for a number of years—once a month, or so. It meant that I could combine the more comfortable side of my duties with the areas that were escalating, developing alarming filaments and structures, like a dry rot spreading up inside my future. She liked it, I think: the costume sex. My buttons were the great thing—the tiny nips of chill from them as she pulled my jacket hard against her skin and the way they'd wink in the gloom of the kitchen, or the gloom of wherever else in the house she'd caught me. Doing it this way suggested types of strange authority. We both enjoyed that.

We differed about my trousers, though. I preferred them at half-mast, this nourishing the longest-running sexual fantasy I've ever had: the one where I'm unmasked suddenly by an admiring, anonymous throng while the pale force of my arse keeps slamming manfully into the space provided between a pair of cocked and shaking legs. I do look at my best from the back—not a bit like an invalid.

My wife wanted me to march up and perform the necessary introduction with just my flies undone, giving her the full experience of the dark blue serge, so to speak. But this felt as if I was trying to screw her from inside a pillar box and, almost immediately, my zip would cramp in and saw at the base of my cock—sometimes in stereo—and then, when I'd managed every-thing anyway, I would tend to be left with stains to sponge off before I could go back out and face the children.

After several discussions, my wife and I, we did the married thing and compromised, took it approximately in turns to be more or less dissatisfied.

And Mal's arrival put an end to our dilemma, in any case. Although I tried to keep my hat on in bed for a time, even after that. I wanted to show willing.

But while I was still performing as the fancy-dress violator, there were some afternoons and evenings, as I marched out patrolling the school, when I would realize that I still smelled of fucking. Nothing obscene, or offensive—more a slight heat in the air when I leaned forward, a vaguely electrical taste under the breath.

This, I am absolutely sure, is what made the cleaners take to me. The two younger guys I was technically in charge of would find themselves teased and harassed, almost daily, but our ladies were purely solicitous with me, as if the slight atmosphere of aftermath I sometimes brought along made them think that I must be tired, or worth spoiling. I was made cups of tea, given baking, loaned a read at their papers and magazines. In return, I'd let a few of them sit in my bothy, have a comfortable cigarette in their break.

Jean wasn't one of the smokers, but she'd wander by, too. Lovely woman, Jean, a truly decent person. When everyone first heard the terms of the private tender: the terrible money, the stupid hours: she cried solidly, right through, until it was time for them to head off home. I had to let her have my armchair and close the door. Terrible.

Now she cleans about as badly as everyone else, but there are evenings when she'll forget herself and suddenly a corridor floor will be perfect—not with a thin, shiny pathway rubbed out between the muck—clean from wall to wall, the old way. Or the taps will end up sparkling, sinks glossed, or a class-room will seem warm and tended, as if somebody cared. I gave her a box of chocolates the Christmas after our change of contracts and she blushed. So now I do it every year. This isn't so much because of the blushes, but because she may well be as out of place in her life as I am in mine. Displaced persons should know one another and be kind. If you can't have love, you can some-times have kindness.

Once I almost told her what happened—why I'm this man and not myself. But people often think the story's funny when I don't want them to, so instead I went back and told everything to Malcolm. It's not what I'd intended, but we were stuck in one of our silences and this filled a gap.

I was hit by a cyclist. Not one on a motorbike—a cyclist: the tinny bell and pump and pedal type of cyclist. Which is ridiculous, I can see. I've been alive, as I've said, for forty-three years, and I've never met anyone else who was hit by a bicycle in broad daylight: they're not tricky to spot, it isn't enormously difficult to step out of their way, they are—as far as everyone else is concerned—quite harmless. Me, I was caught full on by one and hospitalized. I was given a crack in my skull, a dislocated shoulder, and a few other odds and ends that were less important, but the whole thing took up my time when I should have been studying for my first set of proper exams.

In the end I took re-sits. I didn't do well and then I couldn't settle and then, without further reason, I no longer wanted to try. My mother—who cleaned in a hospital, not a school—she'd intended me for great things, and my father and I—not wage-earners—had believed her. We had enjoyed believing. But, after the bicycle hurt me, I couldn't find my pleasant expectations any more. I waited, sullen, at the back of my various classes and passed the time until each reached its end by making an echo come inside my head. Whatever jolt I'd taken to the brain had left me with the knack of modifying everything I heard—I could still do it up until my twenties. If I concentrated, sounds would waver, pause and then tip into a tumbled repetition, as if they were bouncing off my own private cliff, and every time this started up, my solitary—also echoing—thought would be: *My talent, my only one, it had to be this—the magical ability to turn any noise into something you might hear from inside a Hammond organ.* I may not have called it a Hammond organ by name, but that's what I meant.

So I left school with just enough qualifications to be a janitor: first a junior and then a senior janitor. When I told this to Malcolm, I finished with *Wasn't that handy?*—I get to wear a hat not adding in which I used to screw your ma, when I could still manage—your mother, the first girl I met who said that she'd marry me—I was quite sure there would not be another so I didn't look.

And, by the way, my accident is the reason why I am not a physicist, or a diver, or a great, theatrical illusionist: *why I am this way and you are like that. And why did the cycle hit me in the first place? Because I was mooning about at the foot of a hill, imagining*—can you believe it—*the hundreds of things I might do once I was a graduate from a university. An honors degree at Oxford, St. Andrews, or Aberdeen, I had it planned out in detail. Then down came the irony and the bike.*

Malcolm asked me if the cyclist was all right. He has a generous nature, Mal. I told him the man wore a helmet, so he was fine. *That's why we wear our helmets—they keep us safe.* Perhaps I should wear mine in bed.

Not that I cycle as much now as I used to, because of my diseases.

After the story, it was time that Mal turned in. Once he'd got settled, I strolled up and wished him good-night, then sat at the top of the stairs as the evening gradually tilted away toward bedtime for me and my wife. Which is not so good. My marital inabilities have become a source of tension. She has told me to see the doctor, sometimes she shouts, or I do, but for the most part we take care to separate our arrivals beneath the covers with a decent interval and then to plunge rapidly into feigned or genuine sleep.

I pressed my spine against the edge of the highest step and focused on the stairwell, pictured it as the black of a deep pool. It's soothing to think of water, gathered up in a soft column that could be private and hold me, the impression of warm rocks around it and sun and living, undutiful air.

When I first saw Elizabeth, I was doing much the same. My arms were hanging over the banisters, an easy weight, and I was staring, without minding, down from the third floor to the ground and the infants' classrooms. Then she was there.

And it shouldn't be possible to have that much attention simply scooped up out of you by the curve of someone's shoulders, the top of her head, the tone of her footfalls, the March sun through a dirty, south-facing window just slowing across the shape and the sheen of her hair. By the time she'd climbed enough to show me her face, I'd been inhaling for more than a minute. She smiled at me the way pleasant people will if they pass an inoffensive stranger. Packed with breath, I tried to lever my body away from the handrail, but I was locked there, lungs stinging. She walked softly behind me and went on through the fire door and into the top passageway. I couldn't even turn my head.

The light in the stairwell streamed with sheets and flourishes of dust.

I breathed out.

Elizabeth Harrison, permanent replacement teacher for Primary 5B, the most fortunate class in creation. Her predecessor, the manic Mrs. Winters, had slithered from two sick days in the week up to three and then had disappeared entirely. This makes her directly responsible for allowing me to be dumbfounded one spring morning by Elizabeth Harrison who is, in her turn, completely to blame for keeping me that way.

For the rest of the day I couldn't stop it, the dumbfoundedness, the silly, hot pounces of intention—

If I look in her room once she's gone then I'll find . . .

Well, what would I find?

In the end, something. The room, anyway, will smell of her—her room, it stands to reason, it stands perfectly. I could bring her letters from the office in the mornings, check the windows, see how she feels she's fitting in. Tell her she should drink bottled water, the stuff here is terrible: bad pipes, I've reported and reported it.

No. I will not look in her room. Her room is in a building twelve yards away from the home of my wife and son. Which is my home also.

But I don't want it.

But I won't look in her room.

I will show her magic. I will be a magician for her, I will give her that instead.

Prestidigitation: it's another interest I don't share with my family. Useful in school, though. Our present Head doesn't approve, but in the past I have put on shows for the older classes: entertaining and good for the myth of my professional omnipotence. I taught myself; most of the things I know, I've learned about with no help but my own.

Now, in rainy lunch hours, I sometimes let a few kids into the bothy — a second janitor there to chaperon, of course, you can't be too cautious — and I give them tiny, necessary lessons in impossibility. A card can't be in my right hand and, at the same time, in my left: it can't move from somewhere to nowhere and back again: it can't be its own self and also something else. But, then again, it can, if you understand the trick of it.

At the very least, none of my pupils will be taken in by a shell game, or anything like it, and they won't bet on finding the lady: she can't be found. Some of the brighter ones may remember that nice confusion when I've pulled out fifty-pences from inside their ears, or failed to cut off their thumbs with my guillotine. When they realize, much later, that their needs deny physical laws, or that all adults are helplessly, regularly tricked and must frequently be themselves and also total strangers, then I hope they may feel they have been, in some minor way, prepared.

For Elizabeth, I laid on a private show. My hands stumbled and bumped when I opened the door for her, pointed out the best of my chairs, but they settled once I'd started the routine. I drew solid rings in and out of bottles they couldn't fit, poured pints into quarts and vice versa, took her wrist-watch — with her temperature — wrapped it in a handkerchief, destroyed it with a hammer and then gave it back unharmed. She was nervous about the guillotine, so I only used it on myself. The one thing she asked to see again was the old, flip-flop roll of a coin across my knuckles, left to right and right to left, ad infinitum.

"This isn't a trick, though."

"No. I can see that."

"It's a training thing—to keep your fingers supple." This, because of the mood I was in, sounded personal and inappropriate. I kept on talking, so that I wouldn't blush. "The old magicians, they trained to incredible levels. Houdini taught himself to pick up pins using just his eyelashes."

She frowned very gently, shivered the substance of everything, "Why?"

"Because he thought he should be able to."

That, I intended to sound personal and inappropriate.

The following morning, I started to grow a mustache. I wanted to be different for her. Mal said he liked it and my wife said she did not, as if it could interfere with kisses we no longer exchanged. And, Friday afternoon, six weeks after Elizabeth Harrison had arrived, the playground all raw with the scent of spring, no kids, door closed, I leaned along her desk in her classroom and kissed her, Elizabeth.

And this is it now, isn't it? Love.

The mustache didn't interfere.

She'd been telling me about her father. We did this a lot: exchanging information, as if we were forms we'd each have to complete, would enjoy completing. There was no rush, her husband didn't collect her on a Friday, so I'd talked about these two guinea pigs I'd had when I was seven, or eight, and then we moved on to cats, her cat, the way they interrupt you on the telephone, like children—she has no children—and then her father and the way he shouts whenever he rings, as if he had to compensate for the distance set between them, and then she paused and couldn't meet my eyes and then I kissed her. On her mouth.

After that I looked to see if she needed more white chalk and I mentioned something about littering in the playground, and every sound outside was somebody coming to fetch me, to make me stop, but no one arrived and I licked my lips—*she tastes of me, like me*—and she walked, came to stand at my side, and watch the evening start up through the windows.

"Why did they put down gravel, do you think?"

"Because they don't like children." My voice seeming very small, or my self grown larger and hot. "Schools never really do."

"That's a terrible thing to say."

And the room rolled to make me face her, hold her for balance, and again kiss. Elizabeth's hands caught behind me, low, at the small of my back, precisely where a heavy, silvery feeling had started to flower and seep, as soon as we closed ourselves in that first touch.

"I'm glad I have this classroom." Her voice on my neck, sleek under my shirt, inside my ribs: the key to open me. "It gets so much sun."

Trying not to twitch against her, flinch, wanting to be only smooth, secure. "You might not be so glad in the summer."

"I can keep the windows open."

"Yes. You can do that."

When we swayed apart, she brushed the hair above my ear, which made me feel sick: in a good way, sick. I couldn't think of anything to do back. "Well, I'll see you on Monday, then." Which I hadn't meant to sound as if I'd be leaving, but then again, I didn't know how to stay. My pulse had thickened, it was making everything jump, I was sure it would be visible.

And is that what she'd like to see? I mean, are we both being careful, or is it that we're not meant to care when we happen to each other and taste like each other— are we not supposed to say? We do this as if we're not doing this? Does she know that I'm hard now? Does she want that or not? Me or not?

I walked to the door and was, the whole time, dropping into the dark of a pool, something that muffled my breath.

Here I am, though, myself. This is me now, found. This is love.

Schools are watchful places, full of little eyes, but Elizabeth and I, we were invisible, truly. I adored it: to pass across the playground and glance up, find the shape of her, looking down, class out of sight. We would never acknowledge each other, but we would know. Just as we did in the crowd at assembly when I might pass her without a sign, then lean by the doorway, unsteadied as the thought of her rose in me, detonated: so much beauty.

So much beauty. And we do know, don't we? We do both know.

In the end, I told Mal. I didn't want to, but I needed to make my love exist out loud.

At this time, he was five, I think, or just six, and before he slept we'd talk, or I'd read to him, make up stories. *In a desert, in a castle, in a dungeon, there was a prison guard and everyone thought he was nobody special and he agreed.* The guard, he was our favorite—close enough to me to be familiar, far enough away for us to like him. He was called Ted and he fought with the usual monsters, some of them from outer space, but then headed for home to be in love with his lady. *She looked, in each story, not unlike Malcolm's mother, because I'm not a fool. But his love for her was new every time he met her, it made him better than himself, it was like being hungry and on holiday and wanting*

Christmas and feeling that it's close.

Well, how do you describe your love to anyone, let alone a child—and please let us not quite mention that all of this need for Elizabeth removed any erection that I might have still kept for my wife. Nothing doing there for her now, not a thing. Love is like the best surprise you can think of every morning, licking right over your skin. Which probably means that Malcolm thinks love tickles—although that wouldn't really disturb me, as long as he knows it's supposed to be good.

And it is. My face in her hair, yes: being there for the heat, the intention, that lights her face, our hands making every clasp and slip I can imagine, every one, and the first time she opened the seal of her mouth, yes, and easing and setting and pressing my body against hers and trying to think away our clothes, yes—this is mine with Elizabeth, but there is nothing more. We only have love, we don't make it.

So I can't fuck my wife—domestic impotence—and, with Elizabeth, although I'd be very much able and want to and need to and could at a moment's notice, or possibly less, it never does happen, not quite. In accordance with my wishes and against them—either way, I just no longer fuck.

This hurts me, if I think of it. And I think of it a lot.

Once, for two whole free periods we sat together in the boiler room. Elizabeth's class were at the swimming baths without her—drowning in the care of others, for all that it mattered to me. That gave us an hour and a half in powdery, dimmed light, warmth flexing in the pipes around us, and nothing to do but talk about ourselves and what we liked.

There was more to do than that—it was perfectly clear there was more—but we didn't do it. Tugged her in at the side door, I'm not even certain she knew it was there, but she didn't complain—stepped right down and came with me, holding my hand. And then facing each other, whispering, we traded our details, the places, the ways: her first—and once in a park with her boyfriend when she was twenty—the crowd I always dream will catch me—my first—and that, every time, I want to stay inside, even after, to be inside, feel everything.

"So you're demanding."

"No." The air was felty, dry, it kept making me cough. "I'm not. I'm very easily satisfied, but what I like, I like very much."

I'd hoped that she might say the same thing back, or something similar, but she didn't and you would suppose, wouldn't you, that you'd describe these things to each other as a couple, because you intended to both make each other comfortable, happy, fucked. Your conversation would not be entirely purposeless.

That is what you might reasonably suppose.

I ended the afternoon unable to move. She kissed the top of my head—the only time we touched that day—and then she rushed the stairs to be ready for her lift. I stared at the pipes, the storage boxes—full of old sheet music for some reason—and I read the instructions on the fire blanket, over and over again. Something was going wrong in my bones, I realized that, and it seemed I was ill in a number of ways now, or would be soon. My scalp ached where her lips had rested on my hair.

Did you know, the man who invented the in-car cigarette lighter, the one with the little element you plug into the dash, he was a magician. He'd needed to set things burning, unseen, and that was his solution to the problem: very neat. The way I've heard the story, a big car company took the idea and the magician never got a penny for it and no credit either. Stuck in the basement until my legs could bear my weight, I thought about that.

Do all the work and then you get nothing, not a sign of fucking hope. Anticipation with no future, you know what that is—a definition of despair.

And I had long enough there to consider that, if she didn't love her husband and she had started this love with me but wouldn't finish, then perhaps I had opened a door for her and somebody else entirely had used it to slip in.

Do all the work and you get nothing.

I made it across to one of the boxes, crawling, and threw up on multiple copies of "I'd Like to Teach the World to Sing."

Poor Malcolm, he didn't get to sleep at his proper time for quite a few nights after that, although I wasn't keeping him up with stories: I hadn't the heart for Ted, much less for his lady, or his love. I kept to facts. Mal never does seem to be lonely, but I hope that knowing practical information may help him when he's with the other boys. I've let him use a soldering iron—with predictably lumpy results—he can rewire a plug and understands pulleys and gears. I do want to help my son. So, for example, I sat on his bed for those evenings after the boiler-room incident and told him why stars twinkle and why a fire engine's siren changes as it passes and what is inertia. I tried to do the right, the paternal thing, even though I was glad in the deep dark of my heart that Malcolm was so isolated: the frightening janitor's son: and that this meant the shouting matches and screamed comments about my prick were caught firmly inside my house with my family and, equally, any minor mentions of Elizabeth out in the world were kept at bay and I was safe—safe to do very little, but even so.

Malcolm, remember when we drove last summer? On the road there was water you could see, but never reach, because it wasn't really there. It seemed to be magic, but it was only the way the world works.

Sometimes I didn't know if he understood me—he would look puzzled, or else tired, and it was hard to tell between them.

Light—I've told you about light, the way it comes in little pieces and also in long lines, both at the same time and never mind if that's impossible. Well, light always knows the quickest way to go. It's slower through water and cold air, so it avoids them. When we drive, if we're up in cold air and so is the sun, but down on the road there's some warm air in a dip, then the sun's light will pick out the quickest path to our eyes, ducking down through the warm air and then up again. So we see sky light, coming from the ground and it looks like water, reflecting the sun, although there isn't any water there at all. The light always knows what to do, like magic.

This was the point where I started praying: nothing very formal, just requests for help. I am not religious, never have been, my father was a communist, but thinking hadn't helped me and nor had planning, wishing, avoiding her, seeking her out. On a Saturday afternoon, my wife caught me—at prayer. I had to pretend I was looking for something I'd dropped under the bed. Don't ask me why I'd used the bedroom in the first place—Christopher Robin with his elbows on the quilt, or the place I associated most with a need for divine intervention, nothing was clear to me anymore—but that was where I'd ended up. I glanced round and my wife was standing, quiet, behind me, I felt as if she'd trapped me stealing from her, or having a wank, and she gave me a look as if she wished she had. I only spoke to God in the bathroom after that.

And prayers get answered, they do. My sole, repetitive effort certainly got a reply.

"I'm going."

She mentioned a primary school on the north side of our town while my breathing stiffened to a halt and then panicked back in, too fast.

"Bill's already there."

Bill, her husband, was a teacher, too. I'd watched him from a distance—he dressed badly and you'd have sworn that his mother still cut his hair.

"Well, is that good? Do you want to be . . ." I was going to finish with both in the same school, in a voice which suggested it would give rise to tensions and many other kinds of hell. But we already knew about that, so I didn't bother. I sat on the lip of her desk, afraid. "Oh." I couldn't remember being so wholly afraid.

"Once I'm settled, I'll call."

When we kissed I drew her tongue hard into my mouth, hoped it hurt a little, let my hands slide to her arse and hold her as I hadn't often attempted to, for fear of getting nowhere and then going insane.

I am a janitor, I am not a man that women call. No one, ever in my life, has called me, not that way.

I went insane, in any case. Nothing spectacular: I think I was the only one who knew. They were supposed to have a leaving do in school to send Elizabeth off in style, and I was meant to go along and contribute a few tricks. But I wasn't well that week and I think, even before, they'd changed their minds and settled for a pub night out.

On the Monday morning, people talked about their hangovers and said they'd had fun, and walking across the playground was something I avoided for a while, because there was no more Elizabeth Harrison. I tried not to hate the supply who turned up to replace her. Supplies these days, they know nothing, they're what we get instead of teachers.

I kept praying for about a week, but it seemed to bring on no additional effects. Mrs. Campbell, who deals with the dim half of Primary One, is mad enough to consult the I Ching before she makes any decision and is also mad enough to say so. I borrowed her copy, bided my time, and then sneaked with it upstairs, bolted the door, and threw out the little sticks provided to make their pattern on the toilet lid—this not only guaranteed my privacy, I thought, but seemed completely appropriate.

He cannot help whom he follows and is dissatisfied in his mind. The situation is perilous and the heart glows with suppressed excitement.

Those were the only bits that made sense. Except that it did also high-light the bones in my legs that now seemed to feel thinner, raw. It closed with *there will be good fortune* but then I supposed that most predictions would end that way, just to keep you consulting. I wanted to believe it, though: knew that I shouldn't, because good fortune doesn't happen to a man like me.

"John?" She'd phoned my number in the bothy, had to call three or four times, "Hello? Is that you?" until she found me in and, as it happened, alone. "John, it's Elizabeth."

As if I hadn't known.

"Yes, yes, I . . . Hello." That soft pool was yawning for me and I jumped, sprang at it like a happy suicide. "Are you, ahm . . . are you well?"

"Yes. You?"

I couldn't find an answer. Elizabeth didn't wait for one, she only had a minute before she needed to get back, but she wanted to see me, Thursday night, the bar of a hotel I'd never heard of, away on the edge of town.

A hotel.

That week I steered Malcolm and Ted through a barrage of trials and monsters, but I kept them away from the castle. A hotel. If Ted had got near to his lady, I couldn't have been responsible.

A hotel.

My wife got a different story—that I'd run out of good window mastic, but Steve over at St. Saviour's said he'd got some, I'd go over and pick it up, have a drink. Steve enjoys a drink and decent mastic is, occasionally, hard to find. I would have believed me.

And I stepped out on Thursday in nondescript trousers but, underneath that terrible anorak, I wore the good jacket, my nicest shirt—I don't really have many that aren't white—and the best tie. In one of my tiny, stupid, zippered pockets, I had two condoms for no reason.

Not to use, I don't think I'll use them, not one of them. But if I did need them and I hadn't got them, Jesus.

I ought to have known. Primary One's I Ching said: *The situation is perilous. No movement in any direction should be made.* And she is Elizabeth and I am this man and not another and so I should have understood what I could expect.

That she would smell fresh from a bath: those different little perfumes: the quiet, clean evening taste of a woman whenever you breathe in, swallow: and the scent of her skin: her reachable skin that you kiss on her cheek and near her lips, brush with your hand—slowly, seriously, the way it should be done, finding your lady. And you want to see her tonight completely, everything, to break her sweat against you, to howl and race and shiver until you are happy, both of you.

But when we meet, it doesn't make us happy, it just makes us want to be.

I realized, as soon as I saw her face, that she hadn't booked a room, that we would stare at our dinners together in the broad, mainly sand-colored restaurant and that I would drink slightly too much and then would take coffee—I know it seems unlikely, but I think six coffees—to make the meal last.

If anyone had seen us, the way we were, we'd have been in just as much trouble as if we had gone upstairs together, as if we'd fucked across the table while the waiter brought over our eleventh and twelfth complimentary-with-coffee mints.

We stood in the foyer for too long before we left, the porter was edging looks at us, anticipating the final agreement, the turn, the mumbled request for a double room. He didn't know what we're like. Our hands patted and dabbed at shoulders, forearms, and nothing connected properly. Quietly we wished each other the good night we weren't going to have and walked out to separate cars in the dark. I shouldn't have been driving, but then there are lots of things I shouldn't do and I wouldn't be myself without them.

This is love. This terrible feeling. This knowing I would rather see her than be content. Even the way that we are is so near to being enough. This is love.

This is love as I understand it. I could be wrong. I would rather not talk about it, I do imagine that would be best. Malcolm, though, whenever I think he's moved on, he'll sit up in bed and want to hear about it. In the end, he always has to ask. Perhaps he realizes that I probably need him to, that without him I would come back from February's restaurant, April's cinema, May's hotel: from each of my unconcluded meetings with Elizabeth: and I wouldn't know what to do.

Although it won't ever be anything other than inappropriate, I would like to tell him, to really say:

The best love is a little like light. It is unremitting, cannot fail to find you, to take the shortest, surest way, as if that were marked out as part of your nature, the line where you and love are made to meet. It is your law, the physics of your life. It will move from somewhere to nowhere and back again and it will make you lost. It is beautiful and terrible and blinding and you will never understand the trick of it.

ISABELLA KIRKLAND

Isabella Kirkland

Drawing inspiration from sixteenth- and seventeenth-century Dutch still lifes, California painter Isabella Kirkland has created a series of seductive ruminations on wealth, biological diversity, and our voracious, often fetishistic relationship with the natural world. "Taxa" (from the Greek taxis, meaning order) comprises four sumptuous arrangements of meticulously rendered, anatomically accurate life-size plants and animals set aglow by rich dark backgrounds. With their luscious colors and high-gloss finishes, these elaborate oil paintings celebrate decorative beauty while at the same time delivering a disturbing narrative of environmental degradation and homogenization.

Descendant (1999) is a memento mori to some of the many species that have been endangered by human activity. In the painting's counterpart, Ascendant (2000), a perfectly ordinary orange house cat stares confidently out from beneath a large array of flora and fauna, all of which are species that have overtaken the habitats into which they've been introduced. On the left, a delicate feather drops from a mongoose's mouth, alluding to that animal's disastrous introduction to Hawaii, where it was meant to kill off rats brought ashore by foreign ships. The diurnal mongoose rarely crossed paths with the nocturnal rat; instead, it feasted on the indigenous Ne-Ne bird until that species neared the point of extinction.

Trade (2001) and Collection (2002) address the effects of commerce and scientific study on the natural world. In Trade, a large tusk carved with a parade of elephants arcs across the canvas; perched nearby are birds whose frothy plumes were a turn-of-the-century fashion obsession. Collection features plants and animals that excite our desire to possess—the horn of a black rhino used to make dagger handles; the jaws of a great white shark, which can bring up to $10,000 on the black market. These works are true natures mortes, showing lives endangered or cut short in pursuit of precisely the kind of drawing-room luxury this style of genre painting originally typified. In resurrecting this style, Kirkland also draws a sly parallel between our own intoxicatingly prosperous era, with its bursting speculative bubbles, and a time—some three and a half centuries before the term "biodiversity" was coined—when a frenzy for rare varieties of tulip turned the Dutch economy upside down.

SUSAN EMERLING

Trade, 2001.

Descendant, 1999.

Ascendant, 2000.

Collection, 2002.

from Dart

ALICE OSWALD

I met a man sevenish by the river
where it widens under the main road
and adds a strand strong enough
to break branches and bend back necks.

Rain. Not much of a morning.
Routine work, getting the buckets out
and walking up the cows—I know you,
Jan Coo. A wind on a deep pool.

Jan Coo: his name
means So-and-So
of the Woods,
he haunts the Dart

Cows know him, looking for the fork in the dark.
They know the truth of him—a strange man—
I'm soaked, fuck these numb hands.
A tremor in the woods. A salmon under a stone.

I know who I am, I
come from the little heap of stones up by Postbridge,
you'll have seen me feeding the stock, you can tell it's
    me
because of the wearing action of water on bone.

Postbridge is where
the first road crosses
the Dart

Oh I'm slow and sick, I'm
trying to talk myself round to leaving this place,
but there's roots growing round my mouth, my foot's
in a rusted tin. One night I will.

And so one night he sneaks away downriver,
told us he could hear voices woooo
we know what voices means, Jan Coo Jan Coo.
A white feather on the water keeping dry.

Next morning it came home to us he was drowned.
He should never have swum on his own.
Now he's so thin you can see the light
through his skin, you can see the filth in his midriff.

Now he's the groom of the Dart—I've seen him
taking the shape of the sky, a bird, a blade,
a fallen leaf, a stone—may he lie long
in the inexplicable knot of the river's body

       *

Exhausted almost to a sitstill,
letting the watergnats gather, for I am no longer
able to walk except on a slope,

the river meets
the Sea at the foot
of Totnes Weir

I inch into the weir's workplace,
pace volume light dayshift nightshift
water being spooled over, now

my head is about to slide—furl up my eyes,
give in to the crash of
surrendering riverflesh falling, I

come to in the sea I dream
at the foot of the weir, out here asleep
when the level fills and fills and covers the footpath,

the stones go down, the little mounds of sand
and sticks go down, the slatted walkway
sways in flood, canoes glide among trees,

trees wade, bangles of brash on branches,
it fills, it rains, the moon
spreads out floating above its sediment,

and a child secretly sleepwalks
under the frisky sound of the current
out all night, closed in an egg of water

(Sleep was at work and from the mind the mist
spread up like litmus to the moon, the rain

    a dreamer

hung glittering in midair when I came down
and found a little patch of broken schist
under the water's trembling haste.
It was so bright, I picked myself a slate
as flat as a round pool and threw my whole
thrust into it, as if to skim my soul.
and nothing lies as straight as that stone's route
over the water's wobbling light;
it sank like a feather falls, not quite
in full possession of its weight.

I saw a sheet of seagulls suddenly
flap and lift with a loud clap and up
into the pain of flying, cry and croup
and crowd the light as if in rivalry
to peck the moon-bone empty
then fall all anyhow with arms spread out
and feet stretched forward to the earth again.
They stood there like a flock of sleeping men
with heads tucked in, surrendering to the night.
whose forms from shoulder height
sank like a feather falls, not quite
in full possession of their weight.

There one dreamed bare clothed only in his wings
and one slept floating on his own reflection
whose outline was a point without extension.
At his wits' end to find the flickerings
of his few names and bones and things,
someone stood shouting inarticulate
descriptions of a shape that came and went
all night under the soft malevolent
rotating rain. and woke twice in a state
of ecstasy to hear his shout
sink like a feather falls, not quite
in full possession of its weight.

Tillworkers, thieves, and housewives, all enshrined
in sleep, unable to look round; night vagrants,
prisoners on dream-bail, children without parents,
free-trading, changing, disembodied, blind
dreamers of every kind;
even corpses, creeping disconsolate
with tiny mouths, not knowing, still in tears,
still in their own small separate atmospheres,
rubbing the mold from their wet hands and feet
and lovers in mid-flight
all sank like a feather falls, not quite
in full possession of their weight.

And then I saw the river's dream-self walk
down to the ringmesh netting by the bridge
to feel the edge of shingle brush the edge
of sleep and float a world up like a cork
out of its body's liquid dark.
Like in a waterfall one small twig caught
catches a stick, a straw, a sack, a mesh
of leaves, a fragile wickerwork of floodbrash,
I saw all things catch and reticulate
into this dreaming of the Dart
that sinks like a feather falls, not quite
in full possession of its weight)

I wake wide in a swim of
seagulls, scavengers, monomaniac, mad
rubbish pickers, mating blatantly, screaming

and slouch off scumming and flashing and hatching flies
to the milk factory, staring at routine things . . .

LOS ANGELES FINE ARTS SQUAD

Isle of California, 1971–72.
Hormel Building, Los Angeles.

Isle of California

MIKE DAVIS

Ever since their arrival in the land of the earthquakes, Anglo-Americans have had night terrors of Southern California being flushed away into the Pacific. The Reverend William Money, who claimed that Jesus accosted him on a Manhattan street corner and ordered him to Los Angeles in 1840, published bizarre maps ("Wm. Money's Discovery of the Ocean") that depicted San Francisco and L.A. underwater. Half a century later, a number of the Pentecostal revivalists who witnessed the Holy Ghost's rain-of-fire visit to Azusa Street in downtown L.A. had lurid visions of a final earthquake and flood. By the time Montana writer Myron Brinig penned his darkly funny L.A. novel *The Flutter of an Eyelid* in 1933, there was only one conceivable demise for the Land of Sunshine:

> Los Angeles tobogganed with almost one continuous movement into
> the water, the shore cities going first, followed by the inland communi-
> ties; the business streets, the buildings, the motion picture studios in
> Hollywood where actors became stark and pallid under their mustard-
> colored makeup.

In 1972, when the Los Angeles Fine Arts Squad—Jim Frazin, Victor Henderson, and Terry Schoonhoven—completed their apocalyptic trompe-l'oeil mural on the outside wall of a recording studio near Santa Monica Boulevard, most Angelenos were still trembling from the aftershocks of the previous year's big quake in the Valley. The area was also reeling from an aerospace recession, the Manson murders, mass arrests at local colleges, fires in Malibu, violent wildcat strikes, Eastside riots, and police shootouts with the Black Panthers. Reactionary mayor Sam Yorty was still bunkered inside City Hall, and nervous liberals were packing their bags for the East. *Isle of California*—however much it horrified the boosters—defused the panic with wonderful magical-realist irony. Even the angels laughed.

Vija Celmins,
Alliance, 1982.

Two Stories

JORGE LUIS ARZOLA

The Night They Gave Orders for Us to Be Killed

Perhaps it was foggy that night when they took us and put us in the cell.
Or perhaps not. Anything is possible.

But I think it was foggy. And I remember that there were many of us, and
the cell was as dark as a cave, or a swamp, and they took us at night, and we
were drenched in blood. I remember it dimly, as if it happened three millen-
nia ago or as if it had not yet happened at all.

If I can state anything categorically, I would say that most of us were
dying, our open wounds like bloody stars, and that our enemies were very
like us.

I can remember neither why we had become enemies, nor what weapons
we used in our war against them or they in theirs against us to wound us
in that way. All I can tell you is that they caused a lot of blood to be shed.

Sometimes, too, I ask myself what it was made of, that cell they locked
us up in, but the only conclusion I can reach is that it wasn't made of wood,
because if it had been, we would have been able to escape.

For of one thing I am sure: we knew about working with wood. How do
I know that? I'm not sure, but from somewhere or other I can still hear the
piping of a quail chick that I found one day caught in a trap made by me or
by one of my family.

More than that, I can't really say. All I know is that our enemies hated us,
and all night, until break of day, they hurled insults at us, and stones. At times,
when none of the bosses were around, some felt able to treat us like people
and spoke sadly about their homeland and asked about ours, and regretted

the fact that dawn was approaching. I can't quite remember now.

At night, the bonfires burned tirelessly. At daybreak, they took us out and gave orders for us to be killed.

Essential Things

Many things are now just a black space in my memory. But there was the sea, the fragrant journey and the galley—from Carthage?—and that boy so very like me (my friend, I believe), with his lover, that girl whose eyes spoke of desires and things of which I knew nothing then. . . . Or was I the lover, and was the boy the one who trembled to receive in his mouth the woman's small, salt breast?

But I could just as easily have been the girl. The three of us probably came from the West—from Rome, from Gaul, from some far place in the future: from the kingdom of Castile, from the Socialist Republic of Cuba? Or did we come, my two dark-skinned boys, from the past, their silken rosebuds between my lips; and the girl who, one moonlit night, behind a crate of salt, showed me, gave me the first taste of a breast perfect for my adolescent lips, the lips of a girl almost?

I was running away: the girl and her lover, and the other boy too, we were all escaping—from what, from whom, from where and to where? I was coming, going, running back home, and there was the smell of the sea and, of course, the sea itself and a port from which to weigh anchor, and a galley, a sailing ship, a vast steamship ready to weigh anchor.

No one now can clarify the precise circumstances of this story. The three of us were running away, this is all that can be known. But the point of departure was doubtless a suffocating village, and we had decided to try our luck on the vastness of the sea.

I was the friend of the lover, and while I did not desire his girl, I had never desired anyone as much as I desired that girl. And there, in that loathsome village, I used to spy on them when he rocked like a boat on the sea between her legs.

Or was I perhaps the girl? And who was spying on whom? Sometimes I felt sorry for him watching us, but it was pleasurable too, the sight of his almost frightened face watching from afar. . . . I would lay my lover down on the grass and I would sit on top of him until I had had my fill, and I would offer up to him (to the boy) the sight of my breasts erect as tremulous promises.

(Ah, gods, did they not tremble like that too, those bunches of grapes loaded onto the back of a mule being driven to market by a peasant from a vineyard near the village?)

I was the girl, I was the lover, I was the friend who dreamed of the girl sitting on top of him, not on his pubis, but on his chest, on his mouth. Then I was the lover who sensed both the veiled offers being made by my girl and my friend's covetous blushes.

And which of us planned the escape? Who convinced whom that there was a reason to escape?

I accept that it was me, the friend of the lovers. I had more than enough reasons. The girl wanted me, and I wanted her. In fact, once, as if by accident, she showed me one charming breast, while she was explaining to her lover that they had a surplus of oranges that year, enough to be able to sell some.

The important thing, though, was that the three of us decided to run away from the village together. And early one morning, we left. I remember that it was a long, hard walk until we found the sea and could feel that we were rendering null and void that now distant, unimaginable village, which may never have been anything but my way, our way, of giving a name to our fear, although now I don't even know why I mentioned it, since I've never said anything about neighbors or judges, with which all villages everywhere are crammed.

The fact is that, one day, we found the sea and set sail joyfully, and that on another day, at last, my beloved and the boy met behind a crate of salt on the deck. At the time, I was (perhaps) in my first-class cabin drinking whiskey, or talking to the man in charge of the galley while he whipped the Scythian oarsmen, who complained ceaselessly.

But I could have been the girl. I was the girl, and sometimes I think I can remember my beloved standing there in the port—of Samos? of New York?—while our ship sailed swiftly away. I can still feel the unexpected sadness of seeing him left behind there, gesturing and shouting. . . . But before us, immense, lay the sea, and on my waist I suddenly felt the boy's hand. It was a delicate, almost girlish hand.

The sun was setting in the distance and there was a breeze and we were free. And then I no longer felt quite so sad.

Translated from the Spanish by Margaret Jull Costa

ATI MAIER

Tales to Tell, 2000.

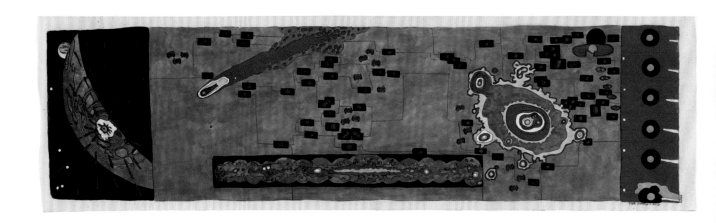

ABOVE: The Sword, 2001.

RIGHT: What Goes Around Comes Around, 2002.

Life Force Radio, 2002.

Ati Maier

For the last ten years Ati Maier has been making exquisite science-fiction-tinged drawings with ink and wood stain on paper. Depicting happenings on earth and in outer space, they often evoke a sense of mystery and occasionally peril. Familiar hazards include tornadoes and forest fires, but there are also hints of otherworldly forces: ominous explosions, radiating magnetic fields, and strange vapor formations emanating from earth and the heavens. The scenes of our world (if it is indeed our world) are presented from an ambiguous aerial perspective. Maier's subtly anomalous vistas—a flock of blood red birds dipping into a low horizon, a pair of horses on a vast yellow mountain plain (illuminated by four suns), a volcano puffing perfect white clouds—seem too far away to be pictures from an airplane. They suggest the view from a UFO instead.

Maier's latest drawings occur mostly in space and are packed with celestial bodies that travel in vivid orbits amid a crossfire of cosmic rays. Spacecraft traffic is frantic and all matter appears to be relentlessly smoldering, sizzling, and speeding. Galaxies that should be light-years apart are fused in a playful and hallucinatory vision of the space-time continuum. Some of the works contain painted monitor-like insets and zones of high and low image resolution, indicated by pixelated squares, as if the viewer were facing a screen. These references to computers and digitization emphasize the scenes' scientific edge but equally their fictional qualities.

There are never any humans in Maier's drawings. Instead, animals take on the aspect of mythological creatures, and emancipated space vehicles move with the canny awareness of living things. It's both eerie and invigorating to enter these territories entirely free of man, ruled by forces as transparent as they are arcane. Maier's works are a kind of visual flight simulator that propels us beyond our routine perspectives and earthbound imaginations into fanciful spheres where logic meets magic and future meets past while still offering a sense of intimacy and inclusion—just like good science fiction.

SABINE RUSS

Indian Summer

MICHAEL KRÜGER

Translated from the German
by Richard Dove

Before we close up the house,
the wine must be poured down the sink
and the light must be made to vacate the rooms.
Every word spoken from this point onward
requires approval.
And don't you go and forget the trash-liner.
The friendly mirrors
in the hallway are bowing,
each with a mournful face.
Leave the key in the lock.

The ark is waiting by the shore;
the dog, in the bow, is lunging for flies,
his tongue busy diving in all directions.
From now on the swallows will mow
the grass. Don't forget Love
either.

Already on the water,
we see the hills in flames.

Cello Suite

From the window
I see the train coming—
a rusty insect
with pupils dilated.
It's pulling those coffins so sprightly
through the sunny valley!
Twenty-one, twenty-two . . .
Are they occupied or empty?
Now, with a hiss, it's letting off steam,
which gently floats across to me
like some unclear message.
I turn the radio up:
a cello suite. In the background
is the musician's panting
breathing, quite audible.

NEO RAUCH

Sturmnacht (Stormy night), 2000.

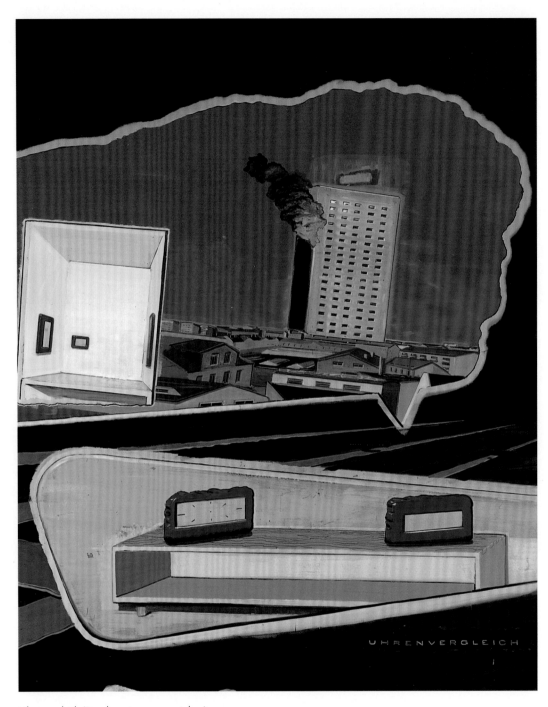

Uhrenvergleich (Synchronize your watches), 2001.

Harmlos (Harmless), 2002.

Schöpfer (Creator), 2002.

Neo Rauch

Sir Thomas More coined the term "utopia" in 1516, as the title for his satire of England in which the island-state is imagined as a paradise. Since then, a utopian has been defined as someone who believes in the perfectibility of society, yet to describe an idea as utopian is basically to admit that it's impossible to achieve. This slippage in meaning—a kind of linguistic bait and switch—underscores the gap between faith and fallibility.

Neo Rauch, who grew up in the East German town of Leipzig, experienced firsthand the consequences that can occur when utopian-as-noun collides with utopian-as-adjective, and those collisions are central to his art. In Rauch's paintings, sleekly propulsive elements of pop figuration and minimalist abstraction lock horns with obdurate echoes of Socialist Realism. While references to other artists—Balthus, Max Ernst, Max Beckmann, Andy Warhol, Gerhard Richter—are many, Rauch's style is uniquely his own, as is his subject matter; it suggests that more than any other polity in twentieth-century history, the German Democratic Republic embodied the failures of modernism with a poignancy that borders on the sublime.

While scarcely democratic, the GDR did apply the tenets of central planning with ruthless efficiency; the result was a Marxist consumer culture of which the country's Soviet overlords could only dream. Still, however proficient the GDR was in plying its citizens with televisions, radios, cars, and other basic amenities, its economy eventually wound down in the late 1950s. The ensuing time warp proved especially problematic when the two Germanys united. Unlike West Germany, the East was never officially de-Nazified (as a Marxist state, it could hardly be held accountable for the rise of Hitlerism), and so ghosts of fascism remain. It's no wonder that in a painting like Hatz (Chase, 2002), Rauch imagines the German landscape as a frozen lake presided over by floating, hockey-playing burghers, who seem undisturbed by the ominous larval forms emerging from its icy depths.

No less than Richter, Rauch is a painter of memory who collapses the distinction between imagery and abstraction—much as memory itself does. Richter's chilly disdain for ideology led him to help invent the postmodern idiom; Rauch, who is almost thirty years younger, makes work that is just as bound up in skepticism as the older artist's, but is nonetheless warmer in one way: it recognizes that where there is fallibility, there is inevitably faith, too.

HOWARD HALLE

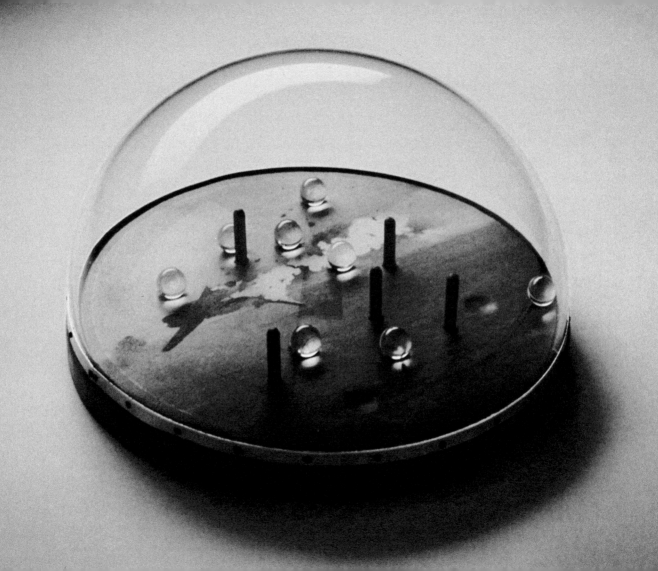

Breakout

WILLIAM T. VOLLMANN

With few, but courageous allies . . . we must take upon ourselves the defense of a
continent which largely does not deserve it.

—Joseph Goebbels, 1944

I

Until July 1942, Lieutenant-General A. A. Vlasov, Commander of the Second
Shock Army of the Volkhov Front, remained one of those heroically immaculate men of Soviet marble, each of whom bears a glittering star centered in
his forehead like an Indian woman's caste mark (why didn't German snipers
shoot at it?), each holding his gleaming black gun in white hands, aiming with
confidence. So the old photographs portray them, all highlights bleached into
blank purity. Vlasov cannot be descried among them now. Nor has he been
found deserving of a citation in the *Great Soviet Encyclopedia.* There is, indeed,
an angry entry about "Vlasov Men." That befits, for the crime that Vlasov
committed was of a collective nature: he organized an army of traitors to fight
against their own motherland.

He is said to have been both brave and coolheaded in the foredoomed
defense of Lvov. In a series of energetic attacks, he led a breakout right
through the German pincers, saving his troops for future fighting. Repeating
this dangerous and thankless accomplishment when the enemy took Kiev,
he preserved the remnants of Thirty-seventh Army. (No doubt he was aided
both times by the rumors, each day less deniable, that the Fascists were

machine-gunning prisoners by the thousands.) He reached Moscow shortly before that city came under siege. The people around him were as faint and intermittent as his reflection in the broken, blacked-out windows. Most of them had never even thrown a hand grenade. Vlasov visited his wife and tried to prepare her for the worst. On 10 November 1941, he was summoned beneath the five-pointed Kremlin stars of ruby glass (each of which weighed one ton, and each of which was illuminated from within by incandescent lamps), and so he came into the presence of Comrade Stalin himself. It was literally the stroke of midnight. Rigidly polite, he awaited honor or death.

Stalin demanded his opinions on the protection of Moscow. Vlasov gave them without mitigation but without defeatism either, recommending a deeply echeloned defense to delay the Fascist Army Group Center until winter. In particular, the Mozhaisk defensive line should be strengthened. Ground might be given, in Kalinin for instance, but it must be contested. Meanwhile, it was essential that we use the time purchased with the lives of a few more hundred thousand peasant boys to form up the Siberian reserves.

Stalin raised his haggard head. He asked: Where will the enemy break through?

Vlasov rose, approached the situation map, and said: I've already mentioned Mozhaisk. Generally speaking, the Iartsevo axis will soon be endangered.

Speak the truth, like a Communist. Will we lose Moscow?

I think not. By the end of this month they'll start freezing to death, and then we can counterattack. . . .

With what?

Well, Comrade Stalin, as I said, with the Siberian reserves.

Anybody can defend Moscow with reserves.

Vlasov nodded obediently.

Nevertheless, your analysis is correct, Comrade Vlasov. I'm going to give you fifteen tanks. As for this echeloned defense, you'll present your diagrams to Comrade Zhukov in one hour's time. . . .

And that very day, the 450,000 shivering, famished Muscovites who'd been mobilized (three-quarters of them women, for all conditionally fit men had been sent to the front long ago) began reifying the Mozhaisk defensive line with their shovels. Mozhaisk fell. The survivors regrouped to dig more trenches according to Vlasov's specifications: deep and narrow, like the corridors of the Lubyanka. Within hours there were blanket-wrapped corpses in one ditch—magnified representations of the worms that would eat them come summer. Firepoints of concrete blocks sank down into place like tombstones. As for the still immaculate man, he went to take command of Twentieth Army with his fifteen shopworn tanks. The night sky was already turning pink under Fascist artillery fire. This time he had no chance to say farewell to his wife, who, white-faced in her dark winter coat and shawl, too sick to dig trenches, sat against her cold samovar, hugging herself for warmth with her hands inside her coat-sleeves, the apartment lightless but for a candle. Soon she'd be sleeping underground with the others, beneath the arched roofs of the metro station. Somebody in raspberry-colored boots was asking a railroad man which train for Kuibyshev would be the last. As for Vlasov, he expected to be dead within a week at most.

In December, Twentieth Army and First Shock Army launched successful counterblows against the German Fascist command. Solnechnogorsk was liberated; the enemy had already set fire to Volokolamansk in preparation for retreat. The commissar called on the soldiers of Twentieth Army to increase their efforts. He pointed out that thanks to Comrade Stalin we now had fifty-four tanks. He invoked the neck-high pyramids of antitank traps made entirely by girls in Leningrad. Vlasov, who'd been studying the strategic maxims of Napoleon, emerged from his dugout, at which the commissar's speech got routed by many cheers. Vlasov smiled shyly. That night he led them back into battle, showing admirable contempt for his own safety. Abnormally tall, he stood out above the other shapes of men bulked and blocked by winter clothes, heads swollen and flat-topped like immense bolt heads, shoulders swollen and squared. They conquered Volokolamansk. General Rokossovsky sent a radio message of thanks and congratulations; the commissar for his part warned the security "organs" that A. A. Vlasov might be an unreliable element.

By New Year's Eve, when his photograph appeared in the portrait gallery of prominent generals in *Izvestiya*, they'd recovered ground all the way to the Lama-Riza line. More than half a million Germans died in the snow. Their corpses were often found clad in clumsy straw overshoes, for the Fascist high command had not issued them any winter supplies. The liberation of Mozhaisk was imminent. On 24 January 1942, Vlasov received the Order of the Red Banner.

He was now a lieutenant-general. Throughout those years of pale men staring down at maps there were many careers of a meteoric character—

instant promotions and executions, loyal initiatives, heroes' funerals—but none more dramatic than his. He was a modest, bookish sort who knew well enough when to leave politics alone—namely, always.* Until now, to be sure, that abstinence had been a virtue. In meetings with his staff officers he was less inclined to cite the inevitability of a Soviet victory than to bring to their attention some brilliant field maneuver of Peter the Great's. From somewhere he'd obtained a treatise by the executed Tukhachevsky. Later it was also remembered against him that he'd dared to praise the operational genius of the Fascist Panzergruppe commander Guderian. Vlasov felt that knowing the enemy well enough to steal away his science was sufficient; he need not squander time in detesting him. Priding himself on his rationalism, which was truly a species of courage (indeed, it bears comparison with the noble atheism of the true Bolshevik, who fights and dies without hope of any unearthly reward), he failed to foresee how weak a perimeter it might prove against the spearheads of an alien will.

At the end of February he embraced his wife for the last time. The hollows beneath her eyes were yellow and black like snow-stains where a German *Nebelwerfer* shell has exploded. She whispered good-bye almost with indifference; he couldn't tell whether she'd decided to endure.

In March, shortly before the premiere of Shostakovich's Seventh Symphony, Comrade Stalin appointed him deputy commander of the Volkhov Front. The strategic aim: to break the siege of Leningrad. Of course the assignment was impossible, but at this stage of the war, what wasn't? Vlasov said: Comrade Stalin, I accept the responsibility.

That night they airlifted him into a sinister taiga zone beset by snow. Two divisions of nearly prewar strength awaited his command. No retreat would be tolerated. Nor could anyone allow himself to be captured by the Fascists, for that meant collaboration. Vlasov therefore had every motivation for success.

He is said to have infused his sector with an almost monastic resolution. His untrained, half-starved Siberians adored him. (In our memory, why not depict them with the scarlet cloaks and halos of Russian icons, the forest darkness between their faces traced with capillaries of gold?) Mild whenever possible, yet plain-speaking always, getting his point across with common proverbs (he was, like any Communist hero, the son of poor peasants), he reminded them that in victory lay their only hope of delaying death. Some of them were equipped with antitank rifles. Every other nation had long since

* In our Soviet Union, of course, one may only be apolitical in the most enthusiastic and even militant fashion. It's said that on one occasion Vlasov, having just denounced the brutal, hypocritical murderousness of a certain article in *Pravda*, was interrupted by the visit of a Party apparatchik. Quickly he began to praise the selfsame article. When the guest had gone away at last, Vlasov's wife, standing numbly in the kitchen doorway, said to him, "Andrei, can you really live like that?"

given these up, for the man who fights a tank can hardly hope to win the contest, but in those days the Soviet army had no other recourse.* The Siberian riflemen smiled at Vlasov, smoking their *mahorka* cigarettes. Then they went and died for him. The arc welder's glare whenever a tank was hit became their own eternal flame. Nonetheless, our attack faltered and froze.

They dwelled in a pocket shaped like a hammerhead, its neck crossing the front line between Novgorod and Spaskaya Polist, then widening to a rounded flatness on the west side of the Luga River. German tanks pointed guns at them, although the tanks were frozen and the gun barrels filled with snow. As long as the cold endured, Second Shock Army was safe. (Ranged against him: Eighteenth German Army's two hundred tanks and twelve hundred self-propelled guns.) Sleeplessly poring over that static game board, Vlasov reread the essays of Guderian. A certain reference to the errors of military traditionalists haunted him: *These men remain essentially unable to break free of recollections of positional warfare, which they persist in viewing as the combat form of the future, and they cannot muster the required act of will to stake all on a rapid decision.* Guderian's criticism rang true. The only question was in what wastes of operational philosophy he, Vlasov, remained frozen. Positional warfare had superseded cavalry charges because a single machine-gun nest could decimate the bravest, most inspired brotherhood of horsemen. What could warriors do but dig themselves into trenches? Then came tank and plane, the Panzer group, the Blitzkrieg. Positional warfare was obsolete forever. And yet the very success of Blitzkrieg had already afflicted it with its own traditionalists. Panzer warriors charged ahead with the same recklessness as their cavalrymen fathers. Supply lines lengthened; the Fascist machine had run out of fuel before Moscow. How could this phenomenon be exploited across the map?

Disobeying the commissar's recommendation, he reread Tukhachevsky, who insisted that Blitzkrieg could be defeated through planning, determination, and operational reserves. Of these he could call upon neither the first nor the last. He said to the commissar: If we only had a hundred tanks . . .

He reread Culaincourt's account of Napoleon's defeat at Moscow. Time, space, and weather had worn Napoleon down.

Once in a great while, his sentries at the rear might see a truck convoy's many furry eyes of light in the night on the ice-road. The Fascists rarely shot at it. Sometimes an airplane landed, bearing emissaries of Comrade Stalin whose task it was to brief and debrief him. Ensconced in a ring of minefields,

---

* Here we might as well insert another allegory. The metal of the day was steel. Hitler and Mussolini had their Pact of Steel, "Stalin" is a quite literally steely pseudonym; all hearts were supposed to be hardened and armored. But it remains a sad fact that in our Soviet smelting plants we most often find steel being alloyed against corrosion by means of neither that utopian substance, platinum, nor even the perfectly adequate nickel; rather, manganese gets pressed into this role, because it's abundant and cheap in the U.S.S.R. So it is also with our weapons and even our fighters . . .

he was now full commander. They'd promised to send him the Sixth Guard Rifle Corps, but it didn't happen. They assured him that First Shock Army would rejoin him before the thaw, and then he could outflank the Fascists at Lyuban, save Novgorod, liberate starving Leningrad. They demanded to know why he hadn't already broken through. His appearance deteriorated rapidly. He knew very well that Second Army could expect nothing other than what the enemy called *Kesselschlacht*, cauldron-slaughter. Meanwhile he ate no better than his infantrymen and never hesitated to expose himself to enemy fire. Call it emblematic that beside the dugout which served as his command post that spring, a corpse's frozen hand was seen upraised from a heap of ice and steel.

2

By 24 April, General K. A. Meretskov, Vlasov's erstwhile superior, was more than anxious about the situation of Second Shock Army. —If nothing is done then a catastrophe is inevitable, he said to Comrade Stalin. Stalin shrugged his shoulders.

This Meretskov had already been arrested once on suspicion of anti-Soviet activity. The fact that no evidence of guilt was ever found only made the case more serious. At the very least, he could be convicted of defeatism. Like far too many commanders, he kept demanding reinforcements and begging permission to withdraw. (There were no reinforcements; and any further withdrawals would mean the fall of Moscow.) That was why Stalin had dismissed him from the Volkhov Front just yesterday. He was lucky. Several of his colleagues had been shot for losing battles. On 8 June, this round-faced, curving-eyebrowed Hero of the Soviet Union would be restored to all his dignities, with Stalin's apologies. Indeed, he'd outlast Stalin himself. Assistant minister of defense, deputy to the Supreme Soviet, seven-time recipient of the Order of Lenin (Vlasov received it only once), he lived to be buried honorably in the Kremlin wall.

Meanwhile, Vlasov's infantrymen kept sighing to one another: If Comrade Stalin only knew to what extent his policies are being sabotaged!

A black cloud hovered above a tank for a photographic millisecond, soft, almost like an embryonic sac, but then it fell, comprised of earth, rubble, and steel beams.

Vlasov was summoned to speak with Comrade Stalin on the V-phone.

What's your objection to continuing this offensive, Comrade Vlasov?

We can hold the sector for a few days longer, but deep enemy penetration has compressed our bridgeheads.

Explain this failure.

Well, their tanks aren't frozen anymore. The Fascists have regained their mobility. . . .

For a moment Vlasov could hear nothing but heavy, weary breathing, and then the metallic voice said: We can spare you no reinforcements.

Perhaps if First Shock Army—

Impossible. The Northwest Front would be endangered.

Then Sixth Guard Rifle Corps—

No.

In that case, I request permission to break out immediately.

Your analysis is incorrect, Stalin replied. You will hold the line at all costs.

The connection ended. Vlasov sat mournfully in his candlelit dugout. Holding the receiver against his ear for a moment, he nodded. He even smiled. He remembered a sentence: *These men remain essentially unable to break free of recollections of positional warfare.*

Well, Comrade General? said the commissar.

Withdrawal is premature, he says.

I understand how you must feel. Still, once Comrade Stalin has laid down the line, there's nothing for us to do but follow it.

Then we're doomed. Within a week, they'll enfilade us with artillery fire—

In an exasperated voice, the commissar replied: Everything you say may be correct from the military viewpoint, but politically speaking it's quite incorrect. You'd better be more careful. I've heard that your eldest brother was shot for anti-Bolshevik activity during the Civil War. . . .

There came the "general alarm" signal.

Telephone communications are broken, sir!

Send me the liaison officer.

He's dead.

On 24 June, the German pincers having long since squeezed shut, Vlasov informed his soldiers that no further hope remained unless they could break out in small groups. This having been said, he wished them good luck, and Second Shock Army disbanded into fugitives.

That twenty-day interval when Vlasov dwelled between the Soviet and the Nazi systems was, as biographers love to say, "crucial to his development." In the first stage, he continued in all good faith to discover a gap in the Fascist lines, so that he could repeat the near-miracles of Lvov and Kiev. This period came to an end on the day after he, the lieutenant-colonel, and the scout had eaten a family of drowned field mice somewhere near Mostki. The scout was already through the barbed wire and the lieutenant-colonel was holding two corroded strands apart for Vlasov to crawl between when the upraised needle of a distant tank-gun began to move. When he'd returned to his body, he found himself covered with blood, but it wasn't his. Sun-flashes on German helmets and German guns sought him out. Rolling down into the shell crater where his companions lay, he closed his eyes but could no longer remember his wife's face. In good time, when the artillery explosions seemed to be growing louder to the east, he dodged south, into the swamps. He continued to seek a way back to immaculateness, but he'd lost confidence, and the sounds of motors harassed him almost as much as the flies on his bloodstained uniform. Silver streams and silver skies, sandy ooze, immense trees, and every now and then a uniform containing something halfway between flesh and muck—this taiga bogscape, shrinking limbo of Soviet sovereignty, remained as blank on both enemies' maps as a hero's forehead. —Should Vlasov have entombed himself there? Ask Comrade Stalin.— In any event, hunger flushed him out.

He was well into the second stage when just off the Luga road, not far from where Pushkin had fought his fatal duel, he came across the bodies of fifty peasant women in the open air by their ruined hearths. They'd perished variously, as people will, some ending face-down in the dirt, others on, say, their left side, legs twisted in a final spasm, and one even lay inexplicably on her back, with her hands folded across her heart, as if somebody who loved her had laid her out for a funeral. What welded these manifestations of individualism into an enigmatic parable of universal fatality was the fact that each victim had been shot in the base of the skull—a method of execution that the German language, so capable of inventing words for all eventualities, names a *Nackenschuss*. Cartridges glittered in the bloodstained grass. I suspect that not even Vlasov himself could have described his feelings at the moment, although he'd seen as many horrors as any other military man, especially

130   WILLIAM T. VOLLMANN

during the fall of Kiev. On the battlefield, corpses tend to clump randomly together, their nested kneescapes and elbowscapes resembling mountain ranges photographed from high altitudes. Vlasov had taught himself to look on such deaths as accidents. But these women lay in an evenly spaced line, like deserters after the commissar imposes sentence. It may not be out of place to mention that in the course of Thirty-second Army's retreat to Moscow, certain secret dispatches inadvertently left behind (orders to hold the long since overrun Stalin Line) had given Vlasov occasion to return to a village they'd evacuated an hour before. I am sorry to say that he found the peasants, with utter contempt for Soviet power, already preparing the bread and salt of traditional welcome, which they clearly meant to offer to the oncoming Fascists. Not without difficulty, Vlasov prevented his machine-gunner from feasting those traitors on lead. Perhaps this inaction is something to reproach him for. Indeed, his aversion to murder was the very reason he'd requested permission to withdraw from the Volkhov pocket. What was the use of allowing Second Shock Army to be slaughtered without hope of any operational or tactical breakthrough? But Comrade Stalin had replied: You will hold the line at all costs.

These fifty corpses (fifty exactly) proved the correctness of Comrade Stalin's order. Had the collapse of Second Shock Army been prevented, these women would still be alive. Exhausted by heartache, anxiety, and guilt, Vlasov came near to regressing to the first stage. But then he heard engines. Scavenging through the ashes of the nearest hearth, he found a few charred potatoes, tumbled them into his coat pockets and ran across wet, sandy ground, circling the village until he reached a place where he could hide. He thought of Zoya the Partisan's last words (as reported by the *Pravda* journalist Lidin): *You can't hang all hundred and ninety million of us.* Closing his eyes, he seemed to see that photograph of her frozen, mutilated breasts. It was not strange that that image could still cause him to feel wounded in his own heart, for he still retained his immaculateness. Like Zoya, who perhaps had wept quietly before the Fascists executed her, he could be enveloped and annihilated, but no one could break through the impregnable marble of his convictions. Not long after he'd crawled into the tall grass to eat his potatoes, a line of mobile assault guns came grinding up the Luga road, their barrels and tank treads shining, and helmeted German boys were sitting on top, half-smiling into the lens of history. What had Second Army ever possessed to oppose them? A few Sokolov Maxim 7.62 millimeter machine guns, which resembled farm machinery with their two wheels and towing yoke, their fat barrels pointing backward as if to drop leaden seeds into the fields (five hundred per minute of them)—how ludicrous!—And with this reflection, he entered the third stage.

All this time he'd kept one of the cartridges from the massacre clenched in his left hand so tightly that the fingers bore greenish stains. When the Fascists had gone, he brought it close to his spectacles, to read the marking: Geco, 7.65 millimeter, of German manufacture.

4

The fourth stage in General Vlasov's development followed inescapably from the third, given his logical bent. The intellect that read Napoleon, Culaincourt, Guderian, Tukhachevsky, and Peter the Great with fairness to all prided itself on its willingness to admit the sway of physical laws, even and especially if those laws operated to its own disadvantage. *He who says I have failed is more likely to be sincere than he who declares victory.* Datum: The Fascist invaders outnumbered the Soviet military forces by a factor of 1.8 in personnel, 1.5 in medium and heavy tanks, 3.2 in combat planes, and 1.2 in guns and infantry mortars. Leningrad must fall this summer, and likewise Moscow. The enemy would soon control the oil fields of the Caucasus. They could not be defeated. This was the fact. Therefore, any attempt to defeat them was absurd.

(He remembered the lieutenant-colonel's last words: *I don't understand how the Fascists were able to cross the Stalin Line. . . .*)

Here, in the roofless ruin of the dacha he hid in (on the wall behind the bed's skeleton, someone had drawn a heart with the initials E.K. and D.D.S.), other facts and memories seemed to linger like his wife's miserable face peering around a half-lifted blackout curtain whenever he left her. So many sad chances faced him now! General Meretskov had whispered in confidence that *ten thousand lives* were lost in the evacuation of Tallinn alone. How many of these could be ascribed simply to numerical inferiority, how many to incompetent leadership, and how many to madness beyond cruelty? (*Andrei,* said his wife, *how can you live with yourself?*)

Consider the case of the *Kazakhstan*'s Captain Kalitayev. (Meretskov had told Vlasov that tale, too.) Knocked unconscious by a German shell, he fell into the water. The *Kazakhstan* sailed on without him. After his rescuers carried him to Kronstadt, he was shot for desertion.

For that matter, everybody knew that Stalin and Beria had shot Army Group General Pavlov, then generals Klimovskikh and Klich, for the crime of defeat. Their under-strength, untrained battalions had rushed into action with a few bullets apiece, commanded to hold the line while the Fascists got vanquished by half a dozen tanks "donated" by some collective farm. No enemy breakthrough could be permitted. The last thing those dying soldiers heard was a metallically amplified speech of Comrade Stalin, played over and over again, reminding them of the virtues of the new Soviet constitution.

Vlasov had known all these things, but in the interests of that certain kind of "realism" that allows us to live life, he'd never *confessed* them until now. Now he shuddered. He saw into himself. He grew more rational than ever before.

(Two days before he dissolved Second Shock Army, with the pocket already nearly as narrow as a corridor of the Lubyanka, the Supreme Command had sent a Lavochkin SFN fighter to fly him out. Vlasov refused, preferring to remain with his men. Was he brave? Everybody said so. But Comrade Stalin had told him that no retreat would be tolerated. He preferred not to share the doom of generals Pavlov, Klimovskikh, and Klich.)

Munching on a handful of bog bilberries, he heard artillery bursts from the direction of Leningrad. How many ditch-digging schoolgirls were dying there today? Supposing that their bravery equaled, since nothing could excel, that of the pair of Russian soldiers at Smolensk who'd hidden for ten days in a tank's hulk beside the decomposing corpse of their comrade, radioing the positions of the German victors who passed all around them, what then?

(What must have happened to those two soldiers in the end? Discovered, shot.)

5

Directed by German fires shining between roof-ribs, he found an old peasant who fed him. The peasant said: When there is no more Red Army, the Germans will give us our land back.

Mutely, Vlasov held up the Geco 7.65 millimeter shell.

The peasant said: Excuse me, Comrade General, but in the last war the Germans behaved very correctly.

Vlasov had his own memories of war. They resembled the hardened blood on his uniform, mementos of the lieutenant-colonel and the scout.

6

On 12 July 1942, about the time that Stalin issued Order Number 227 ("Not a Step Backward"), Lieutenant-General Vlasov was captured by the Fascists. He'd been betrayed yet again, this time by a village elder of whom he'd begged a little bread. How did he feel when the lock-bolt clicked behind him? Let's call his night in the fire-brigade shed the fifth stage of his political development. Nobody brought him even a cup of water. Late the next morning, when he'd begun to swelter, he heard the growl of a vehicle, probably a staff car, coming up the bad road. He heard the hobnailed footsteps of German soldiers. The bolt slammed back. Through the opening door he saw two silhouettes with leveled machine guns, and then a voice in German-accented Russian shouted: Out!

Don't shoot, he murmured, exhausted. I'm General Vlasov. . . .

For the moment they allowed him to keep everything except his pistol. (In the pocket of his greatcoat was a shell: Geco, 7.65 millimeter.) Perusing his identification papers, which were bound in the finest morocco leather, they lighted upon the signature of none other than Comrade Stalin himself, and stroked it in a kind of awe. Just to be sure, they made him show them his gold tooth, which had been mentioned in the "wanted" messages.

Strangely enough, they did not place him in one of those open boxcars already crammed with Russians packed and stacked vertically—still alive, most of them (soon they'd commence eating each other). Nor did they give him unto those German murderers straight and clean whom archivists and war-crimes prosecutors would later spy in photographs, lightheartedly posing halfway down the slope of the newest mass grave. Instead, they took him to the front-line stalag to be classified.

Their field police recognized him immediately. They said to him: Don't worry, General. You're a politically acceptable element.

Vlasov kept expecting to be shot. But instead they conveyed him respectfully to the headquarters of a German general in a field-gray greatcoat. The name of the German general was H. Lindemann. He commanded Eighteenth Army. And General Lindemann said to Vlasov, with exactly the same gentleness as he would have bestowed on one of his own wounded soldiers: Well, your war's ended. But I must say you fought with honor. Upon my word, dear fellow, you gave us a devil of a time—

Vlasov bowed a little, sipping the tea that General Lindemann's orderly had poured out for him.

If you'd ever gotten the reinforcements you deserved, you just might have outflanked us! Ha, ha, look at this map! Do you see that break in my line down here just behind Lyuban? Every day, oh, until almost April, I should say, I used to tell my staff officers: Gentlemen, we'd better pray that Vlasov doesn't get reinforced. . . .

General Lindemann, would a German officer in my place have shot himself?

Heavens, no! Capture's no disgrace for someone like you, who's fought with his unit up to the very last instant. . . . Why do you look at me that way?

I beg your pardon, General Lindemann. I'm a little tired. . . .

We are not the monsters your Premier Stalin makes us out to be. We are human beings.

Vlasov smiled dryly, waiting to be shot.

I suppose you've wondered why we came, said Lindemann. Personally, I was against it, but personal opinions are of no importance nowadays. Fate has sent Germany a great genius: Adolf Hitler. We must obey his will.

Vlasov was silent.

Now let me tell you something, continued General Lindemann with the utmost kindness. To my mind, Bolshevism is a crime inflicted against the world in general, and Russia in particular. You Slavs are perfectly capable of ethical conceptions, as I know from Dostoyevsky and—hmm, Tolstoy's not really manly—and yet you've allowed yourselves to be tricked into following these, well, excuse me, these *murderers*.

On that subject I can hardly begin to answer you, General Lindemann.

Both of them heard the scream of the incoming shell, but that meant nothing. Then the adjutant rushed in with a dispatch, stood a little foolishly, then slowly backed out, still holding that piece of paper which after all must not have been so important. The Russian shell continued overhead and finally exploded dully somewhere to the west.

Very well, General Vlasov. What if it's not true? What if we are in fact monsters? Tell me why that should invalidate our critique of *your* monsters. Think about that. And now I'm afraid our lads in Military Intelligence must impose on you a little. . . .

And so he was swallowed up by Germany. Germany was a monster of rubber, oil, gold, steel, and chromium ore.

The man behind the steel desk offered him a cigarette. A blackout curtain covered something on a wall, perhaps a military map. The man said: Don't think I approve of all these measures.

Which measures?

And now he talks back to me, the man said. Imagine that. It's 1942, and I have to tolerate a Slav talking back to me. I don't give a shit what the General says. This must be happening in another country. This must not be Russia. What do you think, Slav? You think that explains what's going on here?

Vlasov waited to be tortured or shot.

Where were you?

I was captured in Tukhovetchi Village.

We know that. Now tell me why it took so long for us to catch you.

I never stayed in one place.

Who hid you?

I've heard about your Barbarossa Decree, said Vlasov, expecting to be shot.

So you don't want your partisan friends executed. Your little Zoya took care of you, eh? Well, we can understand that. We'll get their names and locations out of you later. But maybe you have incorrect ideas about us. We don't mind working with people who admit their mistakes in full.

I've made mistakes, said Vlasov palely. Otherwise I wouldn't be here.

Well, think about it, said the man behind the desk. You have all the time in the world.

How much time?

The rest of your life.

They all kept telling him to think about it. General Lindemann, who was an extremely handsome man and was rendered still more resplendent by the black cross at his throat, the glittering metal eagle, the row of six buttons each as glowing and glaring as the sun, had advised him to consider the issue of moral equivalency. Vlasov was compelled to remind himself that such arguments were not in the least objectively motivated; nevertheless, they might be true. He thought about it. Even when they asked him how many tanks and artillery pieces he'd commanded in the Volkhov pocket and he told them, they asked him to reconsider, just in case he might be forgetting something. When they asked him about Meretskov's new divisions, he told them (his head awkwardly bowed just as it would usually be in the official photographs of the propagandists, his dark strange new uniform—plain and brown, not German—too big for him, enwrapping him like bends of sheet metal) that his soldier's honor prohibited him from any comment, and they said that they understood. Then they suggested that he contemplate the matter further. Pale and anxious, he traced invisible arcs on a map with his forefinger while General Lindemann looked on. Their typist recorded everything. They thanked him for his information, which they said was very helpful and important. Half-guilty now, he wondered what he'd given away, or whether that was just one of their tricks. . . .

But he said to himself: I need to be realistic. I need to save what can be saved.

A military intelligence officer poured out two glasses of cognac from Paris. Vlasov was shocked by his own gratitude. The officer remarked: I admire your fanatical determination. The Polish campaign won't get more than a paragraph in the history books. But we're going to have to write an entire chapter about you Slavs! Do you know what I told my wife last summer? I told her what my commanding officer promised me. Don't worry, I said. The Russian question will be solved in six weeks.

Vlasov laughed a little, not disliking the man. Outside, an amplified voice sang almost pleasantly: *Jews and commissars, step forward!*

Nonetheless, with our new eighty-eight-millimeter guns, your tanks won't have a chance.

Anyway, said Vlasov with a sad smile, we've already lost twenty thousand tanks.

9

After a thorough but correct interrogation at Lotzen, they sent him to Vinnitsa in Ukraine, where a comfortable prison camp awaited him—a really nice one, in fact, where each of the reprieved lay licking up sleep as a cat does drops of milk. It was a hot journey, but the Fascists kept him in a special train car where he could stretch his legs, in company with some perfectly correct SD policemen. —Don't be alarmed, said the captain, but before crossing into the Reich every Russian must be deloused at Eydtkuhnen Station. . . . Composing his face into an aloof smile, Vlasov awaited developments. His former life's freedom of action now seemed wondrous, but he reminded himself that it had hardly been his choice to get inserted into the Volkhov pocket to fight there uselessly. What if something good could come of all this? Certainly when Comrade Stalin had dispatched him to China he hadn't known what to expect, and yet he'd been able to do his duty there without disappointing anyone; he'd even been awarded the Order of the Golden Dragon by Chiang Kai-shek, although as soon as he reentered the Soviet Union, the secret police confiscated it for reasons of state. His wife had been disappointed; she'd wanted to see his golden dragon. . . . Hoping and believing that he could break out of his new difficulties, he replied courteously but not obsequiously to the small talk of the SD men, who wanted to know which features of the Crimean landscape he considered most beautiful. (He'd fought there with distinction in 1920, against the monarchists.) After that, the SD captain told him about a certain sailing excursion he'd once taken on the Bodensee, seven years ago it was, when his lucky number came up, thanks to the Führer's "Strength Through Joy" program. Had General Vlasov heard of the Bodensee? Vlasov nodded, clearing his throat.

Seeing that he made no attempt to escape, they finally told him where he was going. —Yes, Vinnitsa, he replied with one of his meaningless smiles. I remember when that was General Tyulenev's headquarters. . . .

(Over one-third of the peoples' armed forces were already out of commission—if we didn't count all those schoolgirls now dying for the sake of useless antitank obstacles. That figure kept exploding within his forehead, malignantly trying to break through.)

Although their conveyance passed several of the newborn concentration camps in which Russians huddled in bare fields sealed off by barbed wire, thirsting and sickening, digging up mice and earthworms with their bare hands so as to extend the term of starvation, Vlasov is said to have seen nothing. After all, window-gazing is not one of the pastimes permitted to prisoners-of-war. Nor would it have been fair to impute any evil to the German administration on the basis of those camps, for it takes time to put conquered dominions in order. Soon, when these zones were better Germanized, the survivors, the one-in-ten, would be inducted into striped uniforms. They'd wear a red triangle superimposed with the letter R.

Vinnitsa, where in the words of a German policeman-poet, *we saw two worlds, and will permit only one to rule*, had only recently been cleansed of Jews. Nowadays we'd probably label it a "strategic location," for it was rapidly becoming a junction for military traffic of all kinds. From behind barbed wire, the prisoners could often see processions of armored troop carriers cobblestoned with German faces and helmets. (Yes, it's all true, a grief-crazed major muttered into Vlasov's ear. At Smolensk alone, they caught a hundred thousand of us. . . .) Long hospital trains clanked rearward; truckloads of ammunition and jaunty dispatch riders went the other way. Just a couple of weeks ago the Führer had established his latest military headquarters on the edge of town, in a discreet little forest compound called "Werewolf." Precisely because Werewolf was such a secret, even the inmates of the prison camp knew all about it. It was said that the Führer wanted to give the drive against the Caucasus oil fields his personal direction. Stalingrad wouldn't halt him for long! Nobody knew when Moscow was slated to fall at last, but the drama of approaching victory excited everyone into a rage of impatience at considerable variance from the resignation one might have expected; for the "Prominente" could not help but feel that six months from now, when the war was over, it would be too late to prove themselves to their new masters. As for Vlasov, his unexpected proximity to the head of the German government gave him hope. (Every wall regaled him with posters that said HITLER—THE LIBERATOR.) He sufficiently understood his own worth to be aware that rationality itself required the Führer to redeem him into usefulness. At this point, he still didn't know what he wanted. He remained determined to ensconce his own integrity within the deepest, most concentrated defenses. But on his face he felt the seductive breath of opportunity.

A photogenic old peasant, magnificently muscled and bearded, kept saying to everyone: As soon as the Communists are finished, we can all go back home.

You see my face, General? said a Polish colonel. With all due respect, when your Red Army captured me back in '39, they knocked half my teeth out. I wouldn't sign anything, so they propped my eyelids open on little sticks. . . .

Frankly, I'm surprised to see you here, Vlasov replied. I was under the impression that the Fascists were liquidating the Polish officer class.

It's not so simple. In fact . . . But there's a compatriot of yours in our

barracks; his name is Colonel Vladimir Boyarsky. He can explain it all
to you. . . .

Although it was this Boyarsky whose assurances finally persuaded Vlasov
to sit down for discussions, first with the diplomat Gustav Hilger, then with
Second Lieutenant Dürken direct from the OKW Department of Propaganda,
and ultimately with Captain Wilfried Strik-Strikfeldt, without whom there
might well have been no Vlasov Army, Boyarsky remained no more than the
doorkeeper of fate.* Much the same can be said of Hilger. But less than
a week after that interview, Vlasov was summoned into Second Lieutenant
Dürken's presence. A guard led him toward the commandant's office. And
now from across the parade ground he already spied a man, a man pale and
slender, sunken-eyed, narrow-lipped, with the white death's-head on his black
collar tab and an Iron Cross just below the throat; a man with a swastika on
the breast pocket, a man whose dreamily quizzical expression proclaimed him
master of the world. Vlasov thought him one of the most sinister individuals
he'd ever seen. During his various battles, breakouts, and evacuations, he'd
spied the corpses of Waffen-SS men, and only those; they never permitted
themselves to be taken alive. There was a certain deep ravine near Kiev, called
Babi Yar. Vlasov remembered it very well. He'd read in *Izvestiya* that a week
or two after the zone fell into Fascist hands, Waffen-SS men had machine-
gunned thirty thousand Jews there; but the tale seemed implausible. He'd said
to his wife: That sort of conduct would only interfere with the German war
effort by turning people against them. Besides, what threat would unarmed
Jewish families pose to the Wehrmacht? You know, when I was in Poland I
found out that most of what *Izvestiya* said about class exploitation there was
lies. The peasants eat better than we do. . . .

I believe you, Andrei, she'd wearily replied. You don't have to argue the
matter with me. But please lower your voice; somebody might be listening. . . .

No, General, they have their honor, Boyarsky had insisted in turn. There's
a positive mist of propaganda in this war; it obscures everything! I won't deny
that reprisals were taken against a few Yids right here in Vinnitsa, but their
cases got thoroughly investigated beforehand. I've been told that they were
all Stalin's hangmen.

But women and children—

It wasn't like you think. They're all partisans! And it was humanely done.
When the Jews saw how easy it was to be executed, they ran to the pits of their
own free will. After all, have you been tortured here? If not, then how can you

* Accounts of his fate vary.
The reader is invited to
select one element from
each of the following pairs:
a bullet or a noose; the
Germans or the Russians.

GRAND STREET

Subscribe now and save 16% off the cover price

Name

Address

City   State   Zip

Gift subscriptions to:

Recipient's Name

Address

City   State   Zip

Name

Address

City   State   Zip

Signature (a gift card will be sent in your name)

$25 One Year
2 issues at $5.00 off the cover price

$48 Two Years
4 issues at $12.00 off the cover price

All foreign (including Canadian) orders $35 per year, payable in U.S. funds. Institutional orders $30 per year.

○ Payment enclosed   ○ Bill me

PLEASE CHARGE MY:
○ American Express   ○ Visa
○ Mastercard

Account Number

Expiration Date

For more information, call **877-533-2944**
or visit **www.grandstreet.com**

2371A

GRAND STREET

Subscribe now and save 16% off the cover price

Name

Address

City   State   Zip

Gift subscriptions to:

Recipient's Name

Address

City   State   Zip

Name

Address

City   State   Zip

Signature (a gift card will be sent in your name)

$25 One Year
2 issues at $5.00 off the cover price

$48 Two Years
4 issues at $12.00 off the cover price

All foreign (including Canadian) orders $35 per year, payable in U.S. funds. Institutional orders $30 per year.

○ Payment enclosed   ○ Bill me

PLEASE CHARGE MY:
○ American Express   ○ Visa
○ Mastercard

Account Number

Expiration Date

For more information, call **877-533-2944**
or visit **www.grandstreet.com**

2371B

BUSINESS REPLY MAIL
FIRST-CLASS MAIL   PERMIT NO. 147   DENVILLE NJ

POSTAGE WILL BE PAID BY ADDRESSEE

GRAND STREET

PO BOX 3000
DENVILLE NJ 07834-9919

NO POSTAGE
NECESSARY
IF MAILED
IN THE
UNITED STATES

BUSINESS REPLY MAIL
FIRST-CLASS MAIL   PERMIT NO. 147   DENVILLE NJ

POSTAGE WILL BE PAID BY ADDRESSEE

GRAND STREET

PO BOX 3000
DENVILLE NJ 07834-9919

assume that they were coerced in any way? Just think about that. And these SS whom everybody keeps complaining about, they're actually quite noble in their way. You know how an SS man takes out one of our K.V. II tanks? I've seen it myself. First he shoots off a tread. Then he charges right up and plants a grenade inside the muzzle of the cannon! You have to admit—

Let's be rational, Vlasov interrupted him. Nobody runs to get shot unless—

I know it's hard to explain. So let me ask you something else: Do you *want to live without hope*?

I beg your pardon?

General Vlasov, until the war's over we won't be able to calculate the number of victims on both sides. But think back on the purges of '37—

But—

Excuse me, General! Think back on the mass arrests, the horrors of collectivization, the disastrous and utterly unnecessary casualties of the Finnish war. How would you sum all that up?

In a quiet, earnest voice Vlasov replied: *Lack of realism.*

(And indeed, it had always struck him as not only unrealistic but unreal. He seemed to see his wife, brown-eyed queen of his integrity, feebly rising up from her bed of illness to say: Can you be sure? Andrei, did you *see* Stalin's men murder all those millions? Can you live with yourself if you're wrong?)

All right, Boyarsky was insisting. And wouldn't it be *realistic* to hope that the other side might be better? Because the side we come from is so impossibly evil—

As it turned out, the man with the white death's-head wasn't Second Lieutenant Dürken at all, only a sort of doorkeeper. He inspected the pass that the guard presented, signed a receipt for Vlasov, and led him into a waiting room, where he indicated a bench. Both of them sat down. Feeling intimidated, Vlasov would not have launched any conversation, but his keeper kept looking him up and down with bemusement and finally said: General Vlasov, we have something in common. You survived and defended yourself in the Volkhov pocket. I myself was surrounded by your armies at Demyansk!

That would have been our Eleventh, our Thirty-fourth, and then our First Shock Army. . . .

That's correct. You commanded Second Shock Army, I believe?

I—yes.

Fanatical fighters! laughed the SS man. You put a lot of pressure on us even after we forced you to the defensive!

Thank you. . . .

Don't be despondent, General. You may be a Slav, but I respect you as a man. Care for a smoke?

Yes, please.

I'm curious. A shock army is what exactly?

An instrument of breakthrough, Vlasov replied a little stiffly.

Ah. The Lieutenant is almost ready to see you. He didn't have time to finish reading your file until now. He feels that preparation is especially important in a case like this.

What exactly do you mean?

The Lieutenant will see you now.

And he led Vlasov into a room that was painted white.

Second Lieutenant Dürken did not rise. Smiling, he said that he was quite ready to grant Vlasov's men the status of *semi-allies*.

I must request that you clarify, said Vlasov, feeling all his apprehensions return.

In due course. I see here that you joined the Communist Party in 1930, General. Did you take that step out of political conviction?

At that time, yes.

In other words, your present attitude may or may not be different. All right. We'll get to that. I'm very interested in Communism as a phenomenon. How about you, General?

I don't know what you mean.

Your form of rule was discredited long ago by Plato. In the *Republic* he points out that true democracy is mob rule. And that's what you Slavs have. Why do you think we were able to conquer you so quickly? Because mob rule purged the best thinkers in your officer corps!

I beg to disagree, Vlasov replied. Those purges were organized by the Soviet leadership—

That's not important. The point is that unlike our system, Communism leaves no place for individual merit. I've heard that you admire General Guderian. Well, we Germans also give credit where credit is due. Some of us don't mind calling your Tukhachevsky a genius, even though—well, it was out of fear of his genius that you shot him. We would have made him a field marshal!

I myself have often wished we'd followed his line with respect to tank development—

Ah, you use his name, General Vlasov, but can you quote him? No doubt the tyrannical Jewish-Bolshevik regime—

With an ironic smile, the Russian recited: *It is necessary to observe the promise of privileged treatment to those who surrender voluntarily with their arms.*

Oh, he said that? Hmm. Perhaps he wasn't ruthless enough for today. Anyway, you shot him.

Lieutenant, it wasn't I who pulled the trigger!

Of course it's *never* anyone in particular! But does Stalin really exist, or is he just the convenient projection for a hive of Jews?

He exists, all right. I've met him. These are very peculiar things you're saying, said Vlasov in a tone of exasperated pride. And, if you don't mind my saying so, you haven't conquered Russia yet.

Oh, come. Leningrad and Moscow may hold out another six months, but what then? You've been known to say that yourself! Most of your high-quality elements were destroyed long before we came. Consider yourself fortunate, General, that you were captured in time to be saved. . . .

What do you truly want?

We want a democracy of the best, a society in which all aristocrats are free and equal, so that they'll give their best to the State. Imagine an officer corps with free rein! No more purges . . .

And everyone else?

Serfs, of course. For now, we need them for their productive value. Later on, when robots can take their places, we won't require them for anything.

You'll exterminate them?

Of course not. We'll let them share in our accomplishments, as long as they obey us unconditionally. The measures that we're obliged to take in wartime are simple self-defensive necessity.

Is it true that you're shooting all the Jews?

Propaganda! They're all being resettled in labor camps to help the war effort. But let's not waste time talking about those vermin—

Vlasov hesitated. Then a bitter smile traversed his face. Between thumb and forefinger he began turning and turning a certain memory-token: Geco, 7.65 millimeter.

In the end, he could not bring himself to cooperate with Second Lieutenant Dürken, whose attack on his moral defenses had lacked depth and evinced a vulgarly linear character. But at the urging of Colonel Boyarsky, he wrote a letter directly to the Reich, requesting permission to establish an autonomous Russian National Army. It's said that when the authorities received it, they adorned its margins with exclamation points.

11

At last the enigmatic organization Fremde Heere Ost dispatched one of its own, a certain Captain Wilfried Strik-Strikfeldt, who was to play a crucial role in the Vlasov game—indeed, he might have been more important than Vlasov himself. As it happened, Strik-Strikfeldt was a Baltic German who'd been to university in Saint Petersburg. Our Führer teaches that blood calls to blood; and in this case racial kinship did facilitate the project. With his wry, half-ruthless smile, his merrily narrowed eyes and clean high forehead, his military crew cut and naked ears, Strik-Strikfeldt achieved a dashing appearance. Vlasov liked him at once.

Sitting alertly in chairs made of crooked birch limbs, enjoying the July days on the dusty plain of Vinnitsa, they faced one another across the long table. Beside each of them sat German officers with their military caps on, and then at the next table, which was well within earshot, a German in dark glasses pretended to be reading a newspaper while a female stenographer typed everything. Behind her, the log cabin barracks lay sleepily silent, and trees rose all around.

Strik-Strikfeldt had already begun to feel like a new-made American millionaire. This Russian general was decent, intelligent, capable, and ready to be guided by somebody who didn't make Dürken's mistakes. *Vlasov spoke openly,* he remarks in his memoirs, *and I did also, insofar as my oath of service permitted me.*

How peculiar life is! he remarked. I fought in the Imperial Russian Army and now I'm serving on the German General Staff. Sometimes I can hardly catch my breath—

Vlasov smiled sadly, eyeing the lyre-like decorations on his dark collar, and the German eagle below.

Not really disconcerted, Strik-Strikfeldt continued: My dear fellow, do you think Stalin would have allowed me to enlist as the lowest private in the Soviet Army? *Nine grams* was what he would have fed me. Nine grams of lead—

I suppose you've seen my memorandum, said Vlasov, a little impatiently.

To be sure. A number of us have studied it. Have I mentioned that before the war I used to run a business in Riga? Don't think I'm indifferent to Mother Russia! And let me tell you something. *Now is the time*, when the territorial situation is so fluid, to push through certain measures. I swear to you, we can make good all Russia's losses. . . .

Clasping his hands, Vlasov replied in a harsh voice: Only if I put human values before nationalist values would I be justified in accepting your aid against the Kremlin.

My, my, but he goes straight to the point! I admire your earnestness, General. Well, we have several issues to discuss, but it's not impossible that I can help you.

Vlasov waited, perceptibly anxious.

First of all, we need to know your attitude on the subject of the Stalin government. I suppose you've suffered—

The Soviet regime has brought me no personal disadvantages, said Vlasov flatly.

Ah.

The tall Russian sat glowering at him, so Strik-Strikfeldt, who was very cunning in such situations, said: And doubtless you were given every assistance and reasonable orders in carrying out your command—

Wilfried Karlovich, at Przemysl and at Lvov my corps was attacked, held its ground, and was ready to counterattack, but my proposals were rejected. At Kiev we were commanded to hold almost to the last man, to no purpose except to hide the vanity and incompetence of our leadership; you know as well as I how many thousands died as a result. When they refused to allow Second Shock Army to pull out of the Volkhov pocket while there was still time, that decision murdered more and more and *more*—

It was as if Vlasov could not stop talking now. Strik-Strikfeldt gazed unwaveringly into his anguished eyes as he spoke of collectivization, purges, murders, arrests. The man was truly pitiful.

Well, my dear fellow, don't worry, for we'll be able to put everything to rights within a few months—or do you think that Stalin has any chance of escaping defeat?

Vlasov fitted his fingertips together and said: Two factors must entail our loss of the war: first, the unwillingness of Russians to defend our Bolshevik masters, and second, the inadequacy of a military leadership debilitated by interference from the commissars. That was what I wrote in my memorandum.

Yes, of course. I merely wanted to make sure you hadn't changed your mind. You told Dürken that we haven't conquered Russia as of yet—

Well, this Dürken—

Say no more. He just doesn't realize . . .

12

Once, not too long ago, I was lying in the arms of a woman who'd explained that she still loved me but could no longer endure to go on in the dishonest, enervating, frightening, exhilarating, and unspeakably sad way that we'd gone on. She, the one who for years had always clung to me, wheedling just a moment more and then a moment more in my embrace, now grew restless there on the bed. She'd already refused to make love with me one last time, because it would be too pitiful and she didn't know how one ought to go about lovemaking for the last time. Should she put her all into it, or . . . ? Then I too agreed that doing that really would have been too sad. I kissed her once, desperately, then lay back with her still in my arms, her body, having determined that mine was now inimical, trying politely not to squirm away from mine. —But putting it this way is so unfair to her! She really did still love me, you see; it wasn't that I bored her; it was simply that everything was over. —I wondered whether I should stop calling her darling now or next time we met. I knew that as soon as I stood up, everything really would be over forever. But she was still mine for another five minutes, and then another five minutes while she yawned and asked whether we ought to get up and take a drive or play a board game. And it had come to this point between Vlasov and his immaculateness. (She was always far more admirable, sincere, honest, and decent than I.) Strik-Strikfeldt was explaining that under the secret direction of the Experimental Formation Center, *a Russian National People's Army had already been formed!*

13

Wilfried Karlovich, said the prisoner in a tone of almost childish eagerness, what did you really think of my memorandum? Was it clear? And has the German leadership made any comment?

Ah, said Strik-Strikfeldt. Well, it's an admirable document, but, as drafted, too Russian. Shock tactics!

Do you know, laughed Vlasov irrelevantly, once I gave my parents-in-law a cow, and in consequence they got punished for being kulaks!

14

My friend, if you don't mind my asking you, what are you doing with that spent cartridge?

It's a souvenir, Vlasov replied in a suddenly lifeless voice.

May I have a look at it? Why, it's a Geco, 7.65 millimeter. I'm told that the Führer himself carries a Walther pistol of that caliber. Good for close work, they say. Does it have some sort of sentimental value, or am I getting too personal?

Awkwardly stiff, round-faced, his hair receding, Vlasov watched everyone through round heavy spectacles that gave him an impression of half-comical surprise. Even his mouth was round. Round buttons descended from the sharp triangular points of his collar. He said: It reminds me not to make any commitments I might later regret.

Hmm. Well, that's a worthy goal, to be sure, remarked Strik-Strikfeldt in a tone of brooding alertness. I wonder if there's something you're trying to tell me? But no, you didn't call attention to . . . Well, let me rephrase the question. Is there something that you disapprove of, or that perhaps worries you a trifle?

Vlasov was silent.

Strik-Strikfeldt sighed. —I beg your pardon if I've inadvertently offended you. Well, well, here it is, and may it bring you good luck.

Wilfried Karlovich, if I told you that I found this in a burned village, about ten days before my capture, would you understand me?

Of course. Now it's quite clear. I'm sure you saw something regrettable. But *there was a reason*. . . .

What reason? No, I—

When Stalin purged the officer corps, did you see what happened to the men who disappeared?

No.

And, you know, we never want to admit the invincibility of death. I myself, well, once I was at the front with some colleagues who'd become dear friends, not too far from here actually, in this same forest terrain, and partisans ambushed us—the spawn of Zoya herself! I was the only survivor. Well, well, Vlasov, I'm sure you've seen worse; the point is that even though they were both quite obviously, you know, *dead*, and I was even drenched with their—

Vlasov was staring at him.

As I was saying, the point is that I couldn't have forgiven myself if I hadn't rushed them to the field hospital, just in case. But they were *dead*, *dead*, *dead*. But what if they weren't? So I understand your position perfectly, my dear fellow, because it's so difficult to believe in death. So you can't be *sure* that Stalin's actually committed atrocities, whereas what you saw when you picked up this bullet—well, what exactly did you see?

Nothing important, said Vlasov in a strangled voice. A few corpses—

Listen to me. You've assured me that you believe in rationalism. There's always a reasonable explanation. You don't know who killed those people or why. Now I'm going to tell you something. This is top secret, so if it ever gets out that you heard it here, it's the concentration camp for me. But I'm trusting you. When our forces entered Poland, the *causus belli* was an attack by Poles on a German radio station at the border. Well, that attack was faked. The propaganda organs supplied the bullets, the uniforms, and the bodies. They were *dead*. But how and why they died, and who they were, well, death doesn't always play a straight hand—

I know that, Wilfried Karlovich.

Good. Just give everyone the benefit of the doubt. That's all I ask. Don't be hindered by unverifiable assumptions. I grant that thousands of Russian prisoners may have died from hunger and cold. But let me assure you, my dear General Vlasov, that our own soldiers froze to death on hospital trains last winter! Just consider the conditions under which both of our armies must fight! If anything, the suffering we share should bring us together. . . .

Vlasov longed for Strik-Strikfeldt to think well of him. They had to trust one another. Here was Vlasov's chance to fight for something he believed in. (Where he came from, one was free to choose: Death at the hands of Fascists, or death in our execution cellars.) He couldn't demand too many conditions. When he expressed uneasiness about the way that so many Russians were being treated, his new friend replied: Some of that might well be true. But I swear to you, the Führer's a flexible man. We can persuade him to change his mind.

Vlasov was easily led to assume that Strik-Strikfeldt would never have said such words had they not been authorized at the highest level. In fact, the latter belonged to the category of what Khrushchev privately called "temporary people"—rich and powerful serfs whose master could cast them into the pit at any moment. (Khrushchev, of course, was talking about the minions of Stalin. In our Greater Germany, no such perils exist.)

In fact, many of us disagree with Berlin on a number of important points! And I want you to think about that, General Vlasov. If I were a Russian and I announced that I disagreed with Moscow, what do you think would happen to me?

And so his scruples were crushed by concentric attack.

That evening, the musically talented inmates organized a serenade for Vlasov, on balalaikas provided by the Germans.

15

He dreamed that once again he was standing over the massacred peasant women in the burnt weeds where the Geco cartridges glittered, but this time he understood enough to bend down and gently cleanse the blood from their faces with a black scarf dipped in the river; and as soon as he had done this he realized that the blood wasn't even theirs; unwounded, immaculate, they opened their eyes, sat up, and kissed his lips in turn.

16

Summoning him back to the commandant's office, Second Lieutenant Dürken invited him to sign a propaganda leaflet calling on Soviet troops to surrender.

Vlasov replied: As a soldier, I cannot ask other soldiers to stop doing their duty.

Then we'll take out the part asking them to desert, Dürken replied eagerly.

Vlasov signed.

On 10 September 1942, just as General Paulus's Sixth Army began to run into trouble at Stalingrad, the Germans dropped leaflets on the Red Army, inviting them to desert. These leaflets bore Vlasov's name.

17

On 17 September 1942, thanks to a word from Second Lieutenant Dürken, the Fascists installed Vlasov in the Department of Propaganda on Viktoriastrasse, Berlin. (Reader, think of them as the mechanized corps of the third echelon, meant to exploit breakthroughs.) — You may feel a bit fettered here in the Old Reich, Strik-Strikfeldt had warned him. There's more legalism here than in the occupied territories — more obstructionism, I should say. As for the men in the office, I don't really know them that well. If you have any problems, just ring me up, old fellow. I won't desert you. . . .

When will I meet Hitler?

Oh, right now he's busy trying to decide how quickly our Tiger tanks ought to be fitted with the new eighty-eight-millimeter cannons —

Vlasov's new offices were brightly lit, if windowless, and the administration gave him plenty of liquor. On the wall glared the face of HITLER — THE LIBERATOR. Sometimes there were hilarious drinking parties with the secretaries, who almost seemed to have been selected for their voluptuousness (if I may be permitted to employ that word to describe creatures of the Slavic race). Sitting back on a faded green sofa, Vlasov smiled a little awkwardly while a drunken Cossack poet whose parents had been shot by the Bolsheviks back in '21 declaimed strophes pertaining to *this antipodal realm / where summer burns eternal.* (You're quite the relativist, but I don't blame you! laughed a lieutenant-general who hailed from the coldest part of Siberia.) A German girl was desperately kissing a Russian girl in the corner. — Well, let them all take their pleasure where they can, thought Vlasov with an impersonally pitying affection. Soon enough they'll be fighting for their lives. — Perhaps because he himself had become a little drunk, they reminded him of the *mahorka*-smoking troops he'd commanded during the battle of Moscow. Bivouacking under the snow (for the Fascists had burned down all the peasant huts), they too got tipsy, sang songs (*I'm warm in this freezing bunker / thanks to your love's eternal flame!*), played chess, crushed lice, cleaned their weapons, and prepared to die. At those times Vlasov found his war stories much in demand. Pouting, a typist named Olenka demanded to know why he hadn't saved his Chinese Order of the Golden Dragon for her. — I would have worn it around my neck, Andrei Andreyevich, I really really would. And do you know what else? Every night I would have kissed it. . . . — Vlasov chuckled and pinched her, his face relaxing into good-natured ugliness.

It was on this very same green sofa that in company with a certain M. A. Zykov (soon to be liquidated on account of his Jewish antecedents) Vlasov wrote the famous Smolensk Declaration, which begins: *Friends and brothers,* BOLSHEVISM IS THE ENEMY OF THE RUSSIAN PEOPLE! Their colleagues toasted them with vodka and then again with schnapps. It was signed on 27 December 1942 and published on 13 January 1943, one day after having been approved by the Führer. Although it was meant for the Red Army, Reich Minister Rosenberg arranged for it to fall on the occupied territories, where, in Strik-Strikfeldt's words, *one could come across gray wraiths who subsisted on corpses and tree-bark.*

By then the Germans had already lost the strategic initiative. Rommel was in trouble at El Alamein; then came the landing in French North Africa; Stalingrad was encircled. Even the Führer kept saying now: The Russians will break through somehow. They always do. —As the Barons of the East began to perceive an alarmingly fluid operational situation, they cast about for a way to redirect policy. Maybe their fiefdoms could still be saved, if somebody like Vlasov . . .

And so Vlasov felt that he had somewhat reestablished himself in the world (or, if you prefer, that he'd stabilized his defensive front). This new life offered no "security," it's true, but nobody had been secure under Comrade Stalin, either. Nor had he stained his conscience in any way. To be sure, all of our decisions, even self-destructive ones, contain opportunistic elements; but really the safest, most comfortable thing would have been to ensconce himself in that office on Viktoriastrasse and sign leaflets dictated by his German masters. He refused to do that. He wanted to fight for the liberation of Russia. And so the propaganda officers, promising him an imminent escape from this pleasant limbo, photographed Vlasov in his new regalia, raising his right hand in a sort of Indian salute, with smiling German officers at his side as he paced down the wall of imaginary volunteers.

Listening to Liszt on the gramophone in his new quarters at the Russian Court Hotel, he continued to believe in a German victory, if only because any other kind would have such evil consequences for his dreams. (What *were* his dreams? He lay down, his feet hanging off the edge of the bed, and dreamed that his wife was embracing him, but she was a six-armed monster with a face of brass and she was choking him and he could not break free. He woke up gasping, and for the remainder of the night lay staring up at the ceiling in infinite bewilderment and distress.) Europe was becoming (to appropriate Guderian's words) *a fortress of unlimited breadth and depth,* and there was no reason why that fortress could not thwart any breakthrough. The disaster at Stalingrad gave him pause, but in the end he merely thought it all the more urgent to return to the front line and apply his talents, instead of signing his name to other people's propaganda. His colleagues kept invoking the Führer with such reassuring conviction that the forthcoming meeting would obviously settle everything. And Strik-Strikfeldt rang him up again with the news that he'd now obtained the support of a powerful faction in the Supreme Command. . . .

Indeed, our merry Balt, whose motives gamboled within an inviolable perimeter of goodness, continued to do whatever he could to set up his friend on what he called "solid foundations." If his influence was not quite as powerful as Vlasov imagined, it remained nonetheless considerable. He wrote poems and plays about the misery that Germany had brought to the East. He sent them to a winnowed list of Wehrmacht officers, many of whom were quite moved. To his more immediate colleagues he insisted: We cannot alter policy. But in the name of improved security for our combat troops, we can introduce a new factor that may persuade Berlin to reconsider policy. —And to a third constituency he proved capable of speaking still a third language. Thanks to the war, staples, goods, and even luxuries kept flowing from the occupied territories into the Old Reich, where (as seemed only right) they sold for more than they had cost, which was nothing. Strik-Strikfeldt happened to be in touch with certain sources of supply. All he needed to do was bring them into contact with some factory owner, general's nephew, or bored actress in order to retain his financial freedom. So when he became Vlasov's partisan, he got in touch with a few well-chosen individuals and said, putting the case in their language for the sake of courtesy: Gentlemen, it's like this. Since the Slavic-Asiatic character only understands the absolute, disobedience is nonexistent among them. They'll follow our orders blindly, don't you see? We'll require Vlasov to do the impossible, and there'll be no complaint—

Allow us to ask just how you think we're supposed to accommodate our-selves to such a shameful alliance. *They're Slavs!*

That's just a trifle! Think of all the blood they'll cost Stalin! Don't worry about that. And afterward we can . . .

He did his best, he really did. Slipping on his glasses, he wrote many a memorandum. The Russian National People's Army now comprised more than seven thousand paper volunteers. But General Keitel, who reported directly to Hitler, had already ruled out any Wlassow-Aktion.

As for Vlasov, he played patience alongside Zykov, who was excellent at all card games. He rolled another cigarette from last week's German newspaper. He reread Guderian: *These men remain essentially unable to break free of recollections of positional warfare.* What could better sum up the mistakes of the German leadership at Stalingrad? He wondered why Guderian had not been consulted there. (He didn't know that Guderian had been relieved of his command in disgrace long ago for seeking to contract the defensive line during the battle of Moscow.) He asked for Napoleon's memoirs, but they told him that that sort of thing wasn't considered very uplifting. Olenka made him dance with her. Through his dreams the following words writhed in vain attempts at alignment: *operating, fortified, undefended.*

By now the Soviet propaganda machine, which had first kept silence, then insisted that he was either dead or an immobilized object of Fascist propaganda, had begun to take note of his charismatic appeal. Denouncing him as a Trotskyite, it now connected his stale life with the counterrevolutionary conspiracy launched by that exterminated snake Tukhachevsky. It revealed him to the peace-loving toilers of the Soviet Union as a Hitlerite, an imperialist henchman, a traitor to the motherland.

These compliments were timely, for on 1 March 1943 the Department of Propaganda opened Dabendorf Camp, where under the rubric of paper fantasias real Russian soldiers began their training at last. (The German inspection report concluded: *Discipline: Slack. Men do not rise to their feet on the entrance of a German officer.*) A captive Russian artist prepared no fewer than nine sketches of a proposed insignia, each one of which got returned by the authorities, each one defaced by the prohibitory "X." Vlasov is said to have remarked: *I'd really like to leave it that way—our Russian flag crossed out by the Germans because they fear it.*

Finally they were allowed to utilize the Cross of St. Andrew, blue on a white field.

The next step was to actually start fighting. That was bound to happen any time now.

18

Strik-Strikfeldt said: Unfortunately, he didn't agree. But I have a friend who often goes hunting with none other than Obergruppenführer Friedrich Jeckeln—

Very slowly Vlasov raised his head from the row of cards that he was turning over as industriously as the woman who rolls muddy corpses face-upward until she can verify the particular death that will permit her to grieve. Then his crude, almost simian face sank back between the nicotine-stained thumb and forefinger of his left hand. He crossed his long, long legs. He yawned. He said: You can't even give a suit that fits, and you want to conquer the world!

Don't get bitter, my dear fellow. After all, this is wartime, and you have a peculiar build.

Listen to me, Wilfried Karlovich. I want to go back to the prison camp. This feels like being half awake all the time. It's . . .

The Führer is always convinced by results. Your Smolensk Declaration had more impact on the occupied territories than a hundred anti-partisan detachments! Once he understands that the only possible way for us to keep our territorial gains is to give your Russian National People's Army something to do—

But—

Isn't that the reality of the situation?

And so once again the bolt clicked shut, and Vlasov found himself back inside his sweltering conceptual prison, the notion that logic, limitation, and realism informed the doings of influential men.

The second half of "Breakout" will appear in Grand Street 72, Fall 2003.

ROMAN SIGNER

Kajak (Kayak), 2000.

Ballon mit Rakete (Balloon with rocket), 1981.

Beobachtungskiste (Observation box), 2000.

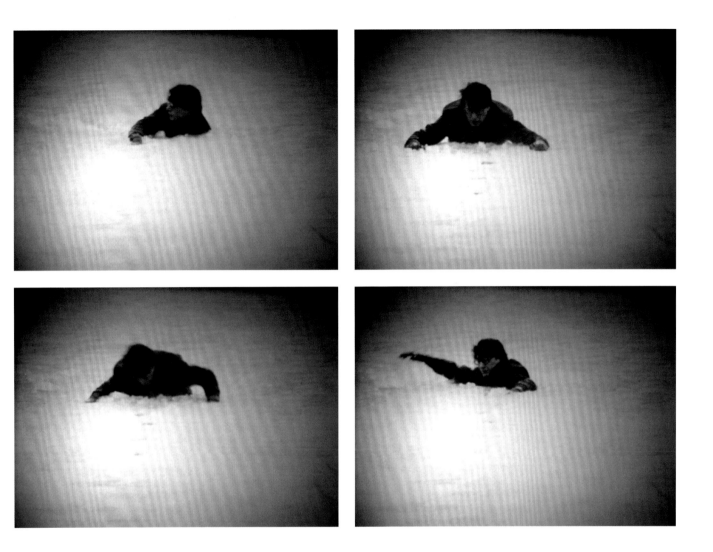

Einsinken im Eis (Sinking into the ice), 1985.

Rakete mit rotem Band (Rocket with red ribbon), 1990.

Roman Signer

For the last thirty years Roman Signer has been staging "sculptural events" with unpredictable outcomes, involving simple props that interact according to the basic laws of Newtonian physics and act on the artist in turn. He perceives his role in these actions as that of a machine: he sits stoically in a kayak that is dragged down a country road, connected by a towline to a van going twenty miles an hour; he walks toward the center of a frozen lake, and its unstable surface collapses beneath him. Yet Signer does not pursue situations that hinge conceptually on risk. His behavior is more gelidly empirical, as if to ask: What happens to a 175-pound mass on thin ice? But of course the mass has consciousness, and we have conscience, and thus the experience of watching Signer sink into freezing water up to the waist, then armpits, is compellingly torturous.

In Signer's world, objects set in motion are observed, and cameras have perspectives that we as voyeurs can occupy. He is interested in the "suffering camera" and in the "lives" of his objects. In his reverence for nature and in the understated but crucial element of beauty in his work, Signer seems less twenty-first-century Swiss Conceptualist than nineteenth-century German Romantic; he grasps at the ephemeral and shows by implication that objective truths are unknowable. Perhaps it's the alchemy between Conceptual and Romantic elements that gives Signer's work its strangely irreducible quality. In an action that seems symbolic of the nexus of meanings his events produce, rockets trailing red ribbons shoot in opposite directions across the expanse of a rushing white waterfall. The ribbons intersect and create a momentary, wafting X—an ethereal crossroads before a wall of water, one locus on an infinite set of points.

Chris Burden famously constructed a less diaphanous pair of Xs: gasoline-soaked beams that he laid across both lanes of a Los Angeles freeway and then ignited. As Burden later commented, the piece was "made for just one person"— whichever motorist first happened on the two Xs in the roadway, burning against the night sky. Signer's work seems less about substantiation by a viewer than about the viewer's own transience in the natural world. His fluttering X is entrancingly beautiful, and made even more so by the discomfiting notion that we matter to this fleeting moment of aesthetic harmony not at all.

RACHEL KUSHNER

BRUCE CONNER

MUSHROOM CLOUD, 1963.

Alfalfa Farm

NATHANIEL
BELLOWS

From the highway I see the open, unmown fields, two silos the same
battered blue, the sign with its white letters still singing the name

Alfalfa Farm. And next door, the house of an old friend, long gone,
now redone and different from how I knew it: raw, dug-up lawn,

cracked storm door, a van in the driveway balanced on blocks where
his sisters would play under a pile of ratty afghans. We watched them

from an appliance box with a slot cut out for spying. Now there is
a birdbath, a potting shed where their mildewed dollhouse sagged.

The farm is unchanged. Barns upon barns, the same cows wearing
the same canvas hoods alongside the highway where the cars fly by.

We used to count them, cows and cars, out in the field for no other reason
than to stay out of his house where Christmas lights, cheap cordials,

Easter grass lay around for no discernible holiday, the same warped box
of a chocolate sampler spoiling on the counter. For the flies, I thought.

The flies that clung to the eyes of beasts in the barns, ate their fill from
around the lids, flew up in a frenzy when we ran through the kitchen.

The same flies, calves, and shabby stallions in the fields. I see them all
as I pass by on the highway. The falling sign, crooked like a sleeping head,

the rusted tractor punctured by reeds in the swamp. This new house
has a gazebo in the yard where we stood on the stone wall, watched

men slaughter the black bulls they'd linked to a concrete slab by the rings
in their snouts. The air was sharp with blood and howls and struggle,

the men took running starts, gouged the bulls with pikes, dragged them
down the hill where they bled a dark blot of blood on the pond.

This is not the same house—now it's painted sky blue with white trim, crisp
as an unsliced cake beneath a plastic dome—not the same house I

barely remember leaving. My friend's sisters wore their bathing suits
all day, his mother was locked in the bathroom with a stranger whose car

was parked on the lawn. The manure cooked, piled in its rank monument.
I was a child then. I believe that was part of my childhood.

Hide-and-Seek

ELIF SHAFAK

In the afternoons, time lay down to nap in the garden behind the house. Every day without fail its eyelids grew heavy at the same hour, closed for the same interval, and reopened at the same moment.

While time slept, the child sat idly under the sour-cherry tree and ate the fruit that had fallen to the ground. If she wanted more, she might dare to reach for the branches, but she seldom needed to do that. Every day without fail dozens of sour cherries abandoned the tree. That was the way of the world, she knew—but why, she wondered, couldn't she do the same? Why couldn't she abandon this house?

The house she couldn't abandon was the color of salted green almonds.

The salted-green-almond house was her grandmother's house.

When time lay down to nap, the child almost believed that she could walk away without even leaving a trace behind, that right then, that very minute, she could go somewhere entirely different. Ah, to walk away, to follow a trail of cherry pits tossed by who knows whom, who knows when, to walk away quickly, steadily, without cherry trees sprouting in her tracks. To walk away. Not to arrive anywhere in particular, just to walk away.

As long as time slept, she could eat sour cherries to her heart's content—first the ones on the ground, then, if she felt like risking it, those on the

branches. Who would have seen her? When time slept, almost everyone
and everything else slept as well. The salted-green-almond house reverberated
with the sounds of snoring—Grandmother downstairs, upstairs Auntie
Madam Kiymet, the owner of the house. The entire neighborhood turned
into a giant cradle, and the breeze murmured lullabies. *Shush shush* slept
the children and the cats and even the street vendors, the kites, paper dolls,
and candied wafers. As long as they slept, she could eat sour cherries to
her heart's content.

She liked to throw the pits as far as possible—all the way to the zinc roof
of the coal cellar in the neighbor's backyard. As they fell pitter-patter on
the zinc roof, the child imagined she was rousing a hailstorm. Sooner or later,
every pit she threw would puncture the roof and disappear inside its own
hole. Perhaps, if she ate enough sour cherries—if she finished not only those
on the ground but also the fruit on the branches—she could turn the zinc
roof into a big colander. Pit after pit after pit, the holes would multiply
until there was no space left to puncture—no wound left to maim—and the
coal cellar would make one last attempt to hold up its battered roof. The
plaster would swell and crumble, the void below would rise up and overwhelm the lacerated skin, and then the coal cellar with the zinc roof would
vanish forever. The coal cellar couldn't hold its tongue. *Rat-a-tat*, it kept
chanting while the pits rained on its roof. The cellar didn't know that if you
talk too much, your tongue will bleed.

If you talk too much, your tongue will bleed, Grandmother always said.
She said so and kept her lips sealed, tough and ruby red like pomegranate
rind. If the rind cracked open, word-seeds would scatter everywhere, but
Grandmother was not like other women. They talked too much.

*

It was the women's *aghda* day. Early in the morning, they assembled on the
ground floor of the salted-green-almond house and placed their small, blackened pans on the stove; they inhaled the languid smell of the homemade
depilatory mixture of sugar and water as it heated, and gossiped until it
achieved the right consistency. At noon, while the women sat side by side on
the floor and, grimacing, peeled off the thin strips congealing on their legs,
the child wandered around, licking a wad of the sweet concoction wrapped
around a pencil. She was restless. Her fingers were so sticky that until the

aghda day was over she couldn't touch anything in the house. Even the walls would stick to her fingers. She had no choice but to perch by the window and watch the rain, which hadn't stopped since that morning. She watched the garden being threshed and pounded, caressed and renewed by the rain. Soon the women would wash their legs and hands with soapy water and, their beauty ritual over, share a lunch of steamed dumplings. The child tried to avoid looking at them. She sensed that *aghda* was something shameful; she didn't want to be an accomplice to the unsightly secret she'd witnessed.

When the rain turned into a downpour, she got up and walked lazily to the kitchen. That was when she noticed the glass teaspoons on the counter. They were removed from their ribboned velvet box only when Grandmother was receiving guests. On days when no visitors came, the child stirred her tea with a tin spoon that twisted and bent easily. She gripped the counter and pulled herself up to take a closer look at the glass teaspoons. She hadn't seen this set before. Their handles were adorned with tiny, brightly colored glass butterflies, poised as though ready to fly away at any moment, yet they didn't seem to want to fly. Next to them were two large round trays lined with newspapers. The women would soon be preparing dumplings. There were small squares of dough, and in the center of each was a bright pink ball of meat. The squares hadn't been folded yet. They looked like tongues, yet they didn't seem to want to speak.

The child snapped the wings off the butterflies one by one and put them aside. Then she placed the glass teaspoons in a mortar and pounded them thoroughly. Trying not to cut her fingers, she carefully picked up the pieces of glass and placed them in the center of each pink meatball. The dumplings swallowed the glass as eagerly as thirsty soil absorbs raindrops; in the blink of an eye, all the pieces disappeared. Unless you looked intently, you wouldn't notice anything odd. The child left the squares of dough unfolded. Whoever had prepared them could now come and fold them, and the minced-meat-and-glass dumplings would be ready to cook.

She didn't know why she did any of this. But she was aware of what she had done, as well as what might happen. She could prevent it, if she wanted to. She could go back to the living room right away and tell the women — who were by now quite hungry — that they shouldn't eat the dumplings, that if they did, their tongues would bleed. There and then she could have squelched the mad voice inside her; she could have turned herself in.

She had just taken a step toward the living room when she saw

Grandmother's long shadow on the floor. Grandmother was probably coming to fold the dumplings. She hadn't noticed the child yet. The kitchen had another door that opened to the garden behind the house. Quietly, the child slipped through it.

It was still raining, pouring into the countless cracks that opened in the gloomy gray sky. The child began to run, stumbling in the mud, squishing the worms that the earth flushed out each time it rained. She ran and ran until she crashed into the coal cellar and fell flat on her face.

vilevilecoalcellarvilevilecoal

Her knee was bleeding, and she looked at it anxiously, fearing germs. She imagined that she was holding a bottle of iodine and pretended to douse her wound, grimacing wildly while blowing at the painful spot. But the wound was only caked with coal dust, which she decided was harmless. It could be swept off by the wind, washed away by the rain until not a trace remained. Coal dust wasn't like a cherry pit; it didn't send roots down wherever it fell.

When she was younger, the child used to swallow sour-cherry pits, hoping that trees would sprout and blossom inside her. Now she was old enough to know that such a thing wasn't possible. Now she knew that, no matter how many pits she swallowed, sour-cherry trees would never grow in her stomach. The pit on its own, once stripped of its tasty flesh, was just refuse. Even if it managed to enter the body, swallowed by accident, it had to keep its visit brief. It had to return to where it came from.

The last raindrops fell on the garden, and the sun smiled lazily on the earth, glistening like mother-of-pearl.

*

After the rain, the air became perfectly calm. The gurgle of dumplings in the steamer joined the chorus of snoring women exhausted after their *aghda* session. The ground became a wooden cradle, rocking lazily; the neighbors sprawled drowsily on their beds, strolling through the resplendent forests of their dreams. While they slept, the child leaned against the sour-cherry tree and ate the fruit on the ground. The more she ate, the more she wondered how the sour cherries managed to abandon their branches.

All of a sudden, time's sleep was interrupted by a sound like the sighing that a spicy sausage makes when its casing is peeled. Then a shriek arose, then another and another. The screams were coming from the second floor of the salted-green-almond house. Auntie Madam Kiymet, the landlady, was leaning over the iron railing of her kitchen balcony, and she was shrieking as loudly as her lungs could muster.

The child panicked. Each spring, Auntie Madam Kiymet allowed her downstairs tenant to pick sour cherries from just three branches. Grandmother made jam and never neglected to send a few jars upstairs as a token of gratitude. It was forbidden to touch the rest of the sour cherries. They were reserved for Auntie Madam Kiymet and her sons. In fairness, the child couldn't be found guilty today since she had only eaten the cherries on the ground. But come to think of it, she couldn't prove her innocence either. Hadn't she committed the crime just yesterday? Hadn't she secretly plundered the branches all day? Could it be that, since Auntie Madam Kiymet seldom left her house and always inspected the tree from above, she was just now noticing the missing sour cherries?

Auntie Madam Kiymet was the fattest woman in the world, though no one ever saw her eat a thing. Her feet were so large and fleshy that she never wore shoes, and instead shuffled around, winter and summer, in her slippers. Her legs, each as wide as the waist of a child, were covered with veins in every shade of purple. Some of the veins were as stiff as clothes left to dry in the cold; others drooped slackly like the elastic of a slingshot at rest. But most of them were like telephone cables, thick and ropy. Whenever Auntie Madam Kiymet climbed the stairs of the salted-green-almond house, the child stood quietly below, imagining the old woman stumbling on the top step and rolling all the way back down. As that huge body came tumbling toward her, the child imagined herself stepping aside at the last second to escape being crushed like a bug. The thought always sent shivers down her spine. But Auntie Madam Kiymet never fell. She wheezed, gasped, and sweated and still managed to climb all the way up. Besides, she rarely left the second floor—only on the first of each month, when she had to collect rent from the houses she owned up the street. And when she went out to get liver for Elsa.

Auntie Madam Kiymet adored Elsa. She didn't care for animals in general, or even other cats; she just loved Elsa. She picked out liver for her with her own hands and prepared it herself. The second floor of the salted-green-almond house reeked of it. When her varicose veins kept her from walking two streets up to the Faraway Butcher, she sent the neighborhood children to fetch the liver, but she always suspected that, despite her warnings, they bought less than the amount she ordered and pocketed the difference.

Sometimes she suspected the butcher, too—of sending the most inferior cut of liver, even though he knew perfectly well for whom the liver was intended. On days when she could bear her varicose veins better than her suspicions, she would confront the butcher herself. The burly, mustachioed man would offer a thousand and one apologies and wrap a new package of liver, all the while patting his forehead to calm the vein pulsing across his temple. Frowning, Auntie Madam Kiymet would take her package, thank the man dismissively, and, on her way out the door, issue a final threat for good measure. As soon as she turned the corner, the butcher would hurl the rejected package of liver at the wall; afterward, he'd complain bitterly to every customer who entered his shop. The customers were well trained in this routine. Each time, they comforted the butcher with a few kind words and reminded him that he had to humor the woman. After all, like every other house in the neighborhood, this dreary butcher shop also belonged to Auntie Madam Kiymet.

That afternoon when time was napping, Auntie Madam Kiymet couldn't sleep. She tossed and turned and finally decided to get up and cook. She wanted to cook stuffed eggplants. Her middle son, Nureddin, had loved them since he was a child. The dried eggplants were hanging on the kitchen balcony that overlooked the garden. She put a string of them in her apron, and then it struck her that sour-cherry syrup would go well with the meal, so she glanced down at the sour-cherry tree. All of a sudden, she made a sound like the sighing that spicy sausage makes when its casing is peeled. She let out a shriek, then another and another.

Auntie Madam Kiymet's shrieks startled the neighbors out of their afternoon sleep, and they swarmed into the garden. So did the street vendors, who always seemed to materialize wherever crowds gathered. The garden had never seen so many people. Everyone looked up at the shrieking woman on the kitchen balcony, until it occurred to some of them that they should go upstairs, and so they did. But they couldn't glean anything from the stricken woman, nor could they understand why her eyes were as wide as divination stones, until finally someone thought to look not at Auntie Madam Kiymet but down at the sour-cherry tree.

A dead body was hanging from a branch of the tree. The dead body of a cat. Once everyone else took in what she had been seeing all along, Auntie Madam Kiymet regained her power of speech.

"Ah, my baby! How could they do this to you! Strike their hands, Almighty God!"

The neighbors who had gone upstairs to comfort Auntie Madam Kiymet now rushed down in a tumbling mass, while her youngest son, Zekeriya, began climbing the tree to cut the dead cat down. At first he climbed eagerly, but the cat hung near the top of the tree, where the branches were very thin, and he soon realized he wouldn't be able to climb much higher. So he balanced himself against a sturdy branch and, reaching up with a rolling pin, began swatting at the dead animal. He hit whatever part of the body he could—first its tail, then its nose. The sour-cherry tree shook and trembled, cherries pattered to the ground, a languid cloud of dust descended through the leaves and rained softly on the crowd, but the dead cat wouldn't budge.

Then the neighbors, who couldn't bear to witness such misery inflicted on the dead—cat or human—took matters into their own hands. Rolling up their sleeves, they began to shake the sour-cherry tree, in which Zekeriya was still perched. Within seconds, dozens of cherries, then the rolling pin, then Zekeriya, and finally the dead cat came down in a cloud of dust and smoke. There was no doubt about it. The corpse was Elsa. She had been blindfolded with a cherry-colored scarf that had tiny seashells embroidered along its edges. Flies were swarming over her exposed mouth. She had no visible wounds, but there were blood clots caught in her whiskers.

When the scarf was removed, the neighbors leaned over to inspect Elsa's eyes. She gazed back as if she were unaware of her own death. She even had sleep in the corners of her eyes. There was nothing eerie about her appearance; rather, she gave the impression that she might come to life at any moment, stretch lazily, and, yawning once or twice, curl up on an inviting lap.

The neighbors wiped the sleep out of their own eyes, erasing the remains of their disrupted naps. Nobody wanted to resemble the dead, whether cat or human. Just then came a stirring in the crowd and Auntie Madam Kiymet appeared. With surprising agility, she swept through the crowd and threw her body over the dead Elsa, weeping and wailing on the ground. Now the neighbors were wiping away tears. Eventually Auntie Madam Kiymet raised her head. She looked at the faces around her carefully, painfully, hatefully. Suddenly her eyes, which looked like bowls of blood from crying, focused on the child.

"She did it! That child did it! From day one she has been cruel to my Elsa. She's the devil's accomplice! Say it, child—'This scarf is mine'! Admit it, bastard child! Speak!"

The crowd's tears were gone, replaced by questions. Could it be true? Could a small child have committed such a horrible crime?

Grandmother pleaded with Auntie Madam Kiymet and finally convinced her to come inside. The neighborhood women scrambled to set the table. A young girl swiftly put down plates, while an older girl lined up forks and knives. Two big-bellied women followed, carrying big pots, and divided the dumplings among the plates. Behind them came a tall neighbor, who poured yogurt sauce with plenty of garlic over the dumplings, while another neighbor, carefully balancing a small frying pan, drew curlicues of sizzling oil across them. Everyone sat down at the table, and a few polite guests picked at the edges of their dumplings, but no one could eat after what they'd witnessed in the garden. At the head of the table, Auntie Madam Kiymet continued to weep, and the women near her took turns rubbing her wrists with cologne. But then, quite unexpectedly, she stopped weeping. She began spooning up the dumplings in front of her. She ate so fast that all the women in the room watched her with their mouths agape. *Crackle crackle*, she kept chewing. Each time she cleaned her plate, she was offered another serving.

That afternoon, under the astonished gaze of everyone in the room, Auntie Madam Kiymet finished fifteen plates of dumplings. When not a single one was left, she leaned back and said, "Elsa used to love dumplings too!" She had barely finished her sentence when everyone in the room began to scream. Auntie Madam Kiymet's mouth was overflowing with blood.

*

"You and I will be friends. You know, friends can tell each other everything."

The doctor was young, with thick glasses and blue eyes like beads, and he had no mustache. The child was his first patient.

*

As the moving truck left the neighborhood, the grandmother, who was sitting next to the driver, turned and gazed with tears in her eyes at the salted-green-almond house where she had lived for twenty-two years. Just this morning, she had knocked on the upstairs door to plead one last time.

"Madam Kiymet! I beg you, please don't throw me out of my home. I've been your tenant for so many years, have I ever troubled you? Haven't we been good neighbors? Haven't we always seen eye to eye? Trust me, she will leave. I sent word to her mother and father. They'll come and take her away. 'You know times are bad,' my son said. 'Keep her a little longer. We'll come and get her soon.' So I didn't argue. She is my grandchild, I said to myself. I didn't see it until now. How could I have known that the devil was inside her? If I'd known, would I have allowed her to stay with me? Take pity on an old woman, Madam Kiymet. I beg you, don't throw me out of my home. I swear on the Qur'an, she will leave soon!"

As the saying goes, Auntie Madam Kiymet saw Noah yet refused to call him prophet.

The moving truck stopped in front of a five-story building at the opposite end of town, where the grandmother's daughter lived with her husband and their three children. The grandmother climbed the stairs, spewing maledictions against everyone who had a hand in forcing an old woman to live like a derelict in her son-in-law's home. The child followed behind her.

This house had no garden. It only had a balcony, filled with empty flowerpots. The child went out and placed a few sour-cherry pits inside each of them. She knew there was no soil in the pots. It didn't matter. She would leave this place soon.

*

"You know, you can tell me if something bad happened."

The longer the silence lasted, the more anxious the doctor became; every few minutes, he removed his thick glasses and wiped them with a soft cloth. Without the glasses, his beady blue eyes that couldn't see past the tip of his nose assumed a bashful glow. The child was amused by his uneasiness. She enjoyed watching him.

"All right, all right, fine," said the doctor, stretching his arms out, admitting defeat. "At least explain this to me. Before moving out of your grandmother's house, you climbed onto the roof. You got everyone very worried. Would you like to tell me why you climbed onto the roof?"

*

When the child first moved into the salted-green-almond house, summer had just begun. Grandmother had opened her little suitcase and laid out its contents one by one on the sofa. Shorts, socks, underpants, hats, and brightly colored marbles.

"Don't you have anything else to wear?"

By evening, the child was wearing a brown long-sleeved dress Grandmother had bought for her.

"Now you look a little more like a girl."

Grandmother closed the suitcase and set it on top of the armoire. The clothes in the suitcase were not to be worn, either outdoors or in the house. The child knew she shouldn't wear shorts outside, but she couldn't understand why she had to observe modesty inside. Who would see her in the salted-green-almond house? Grandmother left the question unanswered.

*

"What do you see in this picture?"

A stove with chestnuts roasting on it. A big fluffy floor cushion. And a red ball of yarn.

"You didn't look carefully enough," the doctor said, handing the picture back to her. "Please look again, this time more closely."

Next to the stove with chestnuts roasting on it, on top of the big fluffy floor cushion, there was a cat playing with the red ball of yarn.

"Did you know that I have a cat? Perhaps one day I'll bring him here. You can pet him. Do you like cats?"

*

Grandmother chewed her food so slowly that by the time she swallowed it had become tasteless pulp and she'd forgotten what she was eating. It didn't matter anyway. Being choosy about food was a sign of ingratitude. That's what Grandmother said, and from time to time, she spoiled the meals she cooked on purpose. Sometimes she didn't put in any salt, other times she added too much spice or left out the oil. The child had to learn to eat anything. Or to eat nothing at all.

Grandmother often fasted. The debt of past and future Ramadans could never be paid in full. Though she didn't demand that the child join her, she expected her to fast too, and the child never refused. She put nothing in her mouth while she was with her grandmother, but as soon as she could go outside, she ran to the sour-cherry tree. One day her grandmother grabbed her fingers speckled with cherry stains and looked straight into her eyes. When she finally spoke, her lips—tough and ruby red like pomegranate rind—curled inward with a mocking smile.

"Suppose you were able to fool me. Do you think God doesn't see you eating those sour cherries?"

*

"You don't have to talk if you don't want to. But if you're silent, that means you're not my friend. And if you're not my friend, then you can't visit me anymore."

He removed his thick glasses and began to clean them. The threat worked. Her lips sealed until then, the child began to speak anxiously. She told the doctor all the fairy tales she knew. Then she invented new ones. She didn't worry that her voice was waning or her mouth was parched, or that her tongue might start to bleed; she talked and talked and talked.

As she spoke, the doctor's beady blue eyes grew cloudy and a look of dismay spread over his face.

*

The child opened the package her grandmother gave her. She was expecting a new dress, but out came a scarf instead. A sour-cherry-colored scarf with tiny seashells embroidered around the edges.

That day she learned how to pray. Mimicking her grandmother's motions on the prayer rug, she listened to the sounds of the seashells. They were all speaking at once. She couldn't understand what they said. When her grandmother folded the prayer rug and put it away, the child followed her.

"So when does He watch?"

"Do you think He lives by my clock or yours?"

God was beyond time. Even in the hours when time curled up and napped, He did not sleep but kept watching the human beings. The child folded her prayer rug and put it on top of her grandmother's.

"And why does He watch?"

"Blame your mother and father," her grandmother said wearily. "They have taught you nothing. They want you to be like them, poor miserable souls."

The child looked as if her thoughts were elsewhere, but just as her grand-mother was leaving the room, she shouted, "And at night? When it gets dark? Can He see even in the dark?"

Her grandmother turned around and examined the child from head to toe, as if she were seeing her for the first time.

"You must hold your tongue. If you talk too much, your tongue will bleed."

The child's mind flooded with thousands of answers her grandmother might have given her. She was certain about daytime: whether inside or out-side, she had to be careful to remember that she was always being watched. But perhaps nighttime was different. Perhaps God wasn't watching the earth at night. That's why it was so dark. The night was as black as coal. As black as the coal cellar.

*

"I hear that you're eating a lot nowadays. Is that true?"

The child nodded enthusiastically. She didn't want to lose her friend, so she leaned back and began to speak. She described a little house: the windows made of candy, the door of almond paste, the chimney of macaroons, the lawn of strawberry pudding, the fence of twice-roasted Turkish delight, the walls of nougat, the roof of chocolate, and Hansel and Gretel caught red-handed by the most evil witch in the world.

The young doctor held his head in his hands and stared while the child told this story. On the coffee table in front of him was the sesame ring that she had left half-eaten.

*

"Stay still," said the stranger. "Stay still."

He didn't need to say that. The child wasn't moving. Not that she had suddenly stopped or stood frozen—rather, she was utterly still and incapable of moving, as if she had never moved before, not even once, in her entire life. Her stillness resembled that of an ant trapped under a glass turned upside-down. There was an outside beyond the glass. But the child wasn't outside. She was inside. Inside the coal cellar.

"Good for you," said the stranger. "Now we will play a game together. The counting game."

In the neighbor's backyard, there was a coal cellar with a zinc roof and two doors. One door was always closed, and the other always open. A big padlock hung on the closed door, behind which coal was stored for winter. The open door needed no lock. Thieves wouldn't steal emptiness.

Behind the open door, it was always dark. There was a tiny window with broken glass, but the sun's rays faded just inches beyond it. Inside, glass shards, pieces of wood, long-lost marbles, faded newspapers, a woman's shoe missing its heel, a tattered tea strainer, rusty nail-clippers with a clipped nail still stuck inside, broken razor blades, a prayer charm to keep ants away, scattered chickpeas from a crushed amulet, all huddled in the dark and whispered. There were also children, sometimes. Children playing hide-and-seek.

(The coal cellar confused the seeker more than any other hiding place. Since it was the most obvious choice, no one planned to hide there, so the seeker would seldom bother to check it. But since the seeker seldom bothered to check it, the coal cellar ended up serving as a frequent hideout after all.)

"You know how to count, don't you?"

Of course she did. She had come to the cellar in an attempt to hide from numbers. As soon as the seeker pressed his face against the wall, she and the other children had dashed off like arrows released from a bowstring. After hesitating briefly, she had decided to jump over the garden wall and hide behind the blazing crimson car that belonged to Abdullah, Auntie Madam Kiymet's oldest son. That's when the seeker had shouted "One!" in his most piercing voice. The seeker had shouted "Twoooo!" as the child was passing by the coal cellar. The crimson car suddenly seemed too far away. She changed her mind, dashed into the cellar, and shut the door.

There was someone else inside who wasn't part of the game.

There was a man inside. A stranger. He sat beneath the window, where the sun's rays faded just inches beyond the broken glass. His face was partially illuminated. Leaning against the wall, he rested his head in his hands. He looked anxious.

Perhaps he was crying. His clothes appeared to be clean. His shoes shone brightly despite the coal dust. Obviously the man was not a gypsy. The child knew that she had to stay away from gypsies. Gypsies did not wear shoes like his.

The man was a stranger. (Who was he?) Beware of strangers. (Yet how unhappy he looked!) Best to tell someone. (What was he doing here?) Best to leave the cellar. (But the seeker would find her right away!) A stranger inside. (The seeker outside!)

The child avoided making the slightest sound as she sat near the door. She couldn't take her eyes off the stranger. Outside the children shouted in protest when the seeker found them, and the seeker cursed and swore at them in turn. He had such a foul mouth that one of the mothers marched into the street and threatened to report him to his father that night. In the midst of this chaos, the child could also hear a faint patter in the cellar. Like little feet stepping carefully on the zinc roof.

The stranger rose to his feet. He moved so slowly that he looked almost inhuman. Perhaps he was a marionette stitched together from a pattern in a fashion magazine. The fabric must have run short—his jacket was too tight. There was a marionette like this in the imaginary drawer where the child kept all the things that caught her eye. A puppet she'd once seen at a fair. Among the blond dolls with painted lips, toy cars, multicolored tops, phosphorescent yo-yos, long-tailed kites—among all these things was a marionette with loose strings, waiting patiently. He held three balls in his arms. If she could strike the balls, the marionette would be hers. She couldn't.

The stranger's eyes were more beautiful than those of the marionette— olive green. He had no hair on his face. The child sat quietly, her eyes fixed on the man, her ears on the children brawling in the street. Outside, the seeker was still cursing and swearing at his quarrelsome prey. The irate mother must have gone back inside, for her voice could no longer be heard. The game was coming to an end. Soon the seeker would concede. Soon she would have to come out of hiding.

"Would you like to play a game with me? A counting game. Would you like to?"

Like his eyes, his voice was beautiful.

"Together we will count to three," he whispered. "You know how to count, don't you? What do you say, shall we count?"

The child knew how to count, of course; after briefly hesitating, she nodded. Then the man caressed the child's cheek. His hands were beautiful, like his eyes and voice.

"Good for you! When I say 'One,' you close your eyes. When I say 'Two,' you open them. The game isn't over until I say 'Three.' You don't leave the cellar until you hear 'Three.' Agreed?"

Outside, the children were calling her name. They were starting a new round; someone else would be the seeker. Her name called to her. She had to come out.

"One!" said the man. "Close your eyes!"

As soon as she closed her eyes, the child was surrounded by darkness. She looked straight into the darkness and there she saw the figure One. It was otherworldly. One resembled a pregnant woman, whose solitude would last only a little while longer. Soon it would produce another living being. Staring at the figure One, the child felt scared. She had to escape right away, without waiting another second, before she could see what this new life would look like. To escape, she first had to open her eyes, but her eyes were caught in the figure One.

She checked her dress with her hand. She was relieved to be wearing the dress Grandmother had bought for her, not to be standing nearly naked in front of this strange man.

"Twoooo!" the man said. "Open your eyes."

As soon as she opened her eyes, the child was surrounded by light. She looked straight into the light and there she saw the figure Two. It was otherworldly. Two resembled a side street that had broken free, strayed from the course of the main avenue. You could easily see where it started and where it curved, but its destination remained hidden. Staring at the figure Two, the child was terrified. She had to escape right away, without waiting another second, before she could see where it would take her. Her eyes were no longer closed, but they were caught in the figure Two.

Where Two stood, there was another. The other was a pink piece of meat. Encircled with twisted black strands of hair and hanging down like the tongue of a thirsty animal. It must have enjoyed being watched, since, as the child stared, it solemnly raised its head. Little by little it changed, grew longer, wider, darker. Bolder, vein upon vein. These veins bore no resemblance to the purple cables crisscrossing in Auntie Madam Kiymet's legs.

Just when the child began to think that if it continued to grow at this rate it would soon overwhelm the cellar, it stopped. Stopped and began to wait. The children playing hide-and-seek outside must have stopped, too, since not a sound could be heard, not a leaf rustled. Somewhere in the depths of this stillness, the child sensed a pair of eyes watching. Eyes that belonged neither to her nor to the strange man. Eyes that were neither far away nor near. She was being observed by a living being; who or what, she didn't know.

She wanted to find the origin of the gaze, but she couldn't spoil the game; she couldn't take her eyes off the other.

The man began to approach her. The child told herself that there was nothing to be afraid of. Three was the next number. Three always followed Two; it was never late. In fact, it arrived so quickly that if you didn't hide by the time the seeker shouted "Two," you would most likely be caught in the open. When Three was called, this game would end, and she'd finally be able to leave. She would leave the coal cellar and never set foot in it again. She would never again play games with strangers in the cellar. She was sorry to have begun this game at all, but now she had to wait until Three was released. A little longer, and she would be saved.

But the other arrived before Three did. Arrived and pushed its way into her mouth. The child stood frozen. The man was wheezing softly. It reminded the child of Elsa. When Elsa's neck was caressed, she made a similar sound. But the wheezing became louder, quicker. And now the child thought of the retired history teacher across the street who suffered from asthma. Whenever he climbed stairs, he made exactly the same sound. But the wheezing grew even quicker. Soon it was so intense that the child couldn't compare it to any sound she knew. The pink piece of meat moved back and forth in her mouth, but the child could no longer see it. She could no longer see anything. She didn't even know if her eyes were open or closed. She felt nauseous.

Then, just when her stomach raised a flag of protest and she neared the end of hope, just when the universe began spinning so fast that it overwhelmed all traces of the previous stillness, just when the man's wheezing turned to moaning, the number at hand expired, and like all numbers that expire, it gave way to the next number. Two was done.

The other withdrew. The emptiness it left in her mouth was filled with a strange liquid. Sticky. Repulsive. Unable to bear it, the child unlocked her stomach's door. She began to vomit. Whatever it was that had been vomited into her mouth, she vomited out.

When there was nothing left to vomit other than bile, she raised her head. On the verge of tears, she peered into the emptiness and saw that the absence of Three was worse than One, worse than Two, even worse than Three itself. The man had left.

Left.

Without saying "Three."

In the neighbor's backyard, there was a coal cellar with a zinc roof and two doors. Inside, a child was trapped.

It made no difference whether she opened her eyes or closed them. Open or closed, her eyes could see nothing but the blackness of the coal cellar. Everything, everyone was painted the color of blindness. The whiteness she vomited, the sour cherries she ate, the veins on Auntie Madam Kiymet's legs, even Abdullah's crimson car, all were black, as black as the coal cellar.

*

"Aren't you tired of telling fairy tales? Because I am tired of hearing them. Do you understand?"

The young doctor paced nervously. Exasperated, he collapsed into his armchair and sighed, "That's enough." Suddenly there was a cracking sound in the room, like the sound of a heart breaking. The doctor jumped to his feet and, looking behind him, discovered that he had sat on his glasses.

*

She was swimming in a lake as black as the coal cellar. The water was warm. She didn't feel cold at all. Earlier there hadn't even been a puddle here, much less a lake. She had created the lake herself. She had created it with her tears. And she felt great relief at the thought of having cried so abundantly. Perhaps if she cried a little more, the emptiness around her would be inundated with her tears, and the cellar door would open all by itself. Then she could swim to safety, and no one would blame her for not having waited till "Three."

Just as she was about to fall into the current, her nose detected something that made her grimace. The lake she'd imagined was a puddle of urine. She had wet herself. Anxiously, she ran her hand over her eyes. They were dry. She hadn't cried, she hadn't even shed a single tear. A stabbing pain lodged itself in her stomach. Bent double with agony, she sensed again that she was being watched. But this time she was determined to find the eyes. And this time she did find them.

Sitting on the windowsill, beside the broken glass, Elsa stared at the child. Her raw green eyes were insolent. As though they had been there since the beginning of time, as though they had left no secret unrevealed, no sin unrecorded. They were witness to everything that had happened in the coal cellar. The child rose to her feet, shaking uncontrollably. She grabbed a piece of coal from the ground and hurled it at the cat, but she missed.

Enraged, she watched Elsa disappear through the window. There was no sense in staying in the cellar. She had been a willing accomplice to evil, and despite that, she had not shed a tear. Elsa had seen everything, everything that should not have been seen.

A sinner and her witness cannot inhabit the same world. They cannot face each other. Even if they both want to forget, their faces reawaken the memory.

The best thing would be to leave, like the sour cherries that abandon their branches. The world was big. East or West, there had to be a place where Elsa couldn't see, a place where Elsa couldn't be seen.

The house she longed to abandon was the salted-green-almond house.

The salted-green-almond house was her grandmother's house.

*

"I'd like you to color this picture. You can use any colors you want. But you have to color the entire picture. Leave no spot uncolored. Let's start."

There was a box of crayons on the coffee table. The child glanced at the crayons. Each color reminded her of a different kind of food. The more she looked at the colors, the hungrier she became. But she didn't say anything about this to the doctor who was carefully observing her.

The picture showed a family. The father was in an armchair, his legs crossed. He was reading the newspaper. The mother was ironing. The grandmother was on the sofa, knitting. Two small children, a boy and a girl, were playing on the carpet, surrounded by toys.

The child colored every item one by one, from the father's slippers to the mother's iron, from the grandmother's ball of yarn to the children's toys. The slippers she colored spinach green, the iron milk-pudding white, the ball of yarn candy-apple red, the toys egg-yolk yellow.

"What about the balloon?" the young doctor asked. "Why didn't you color it?"

The child was puzzled. There was no balloon in the picture. It was only the interior of a house. But looking closely, she realized that the doctor was right. She could see a tiny piece of sky through the window in the room where the family sat. There, floating among the clouds, was a balloon. The child tried to pick a color while she pressed her finger to the balloon to keep it from flying away. The doctor leaned forward and looked at her finger. Its skin chewed, its hangnail bitten, the finger noticed being watched, and it panicked. It quickly retreated among the crayons.

*

The child's face turned pale. How could she not have realized before! Angrily, she looked up at the broken lightbulb hanging from the ceiling of the coal cellar. Neither this cobweb-covered ceiling nor the zinc roof above could hide from God all that Elsa had seen.

There was a steep hill in hell, lined with cauldrons of hellfire. Sinners, shouldering baskets filled with their sins, climbed up to escape the flames. But the path was slippery, their burden heavy, the slope steep. Drenched in sweat and blood, the sinners lost their footing and tumbled back down the hill. Their sins scattered everywhere, but each one returned to its owner, who began the climb again. That was what Grandmother said, and every time she climbed a hill, she stopped and prayed that she wouldn't slip. That was what Grandmother said, and she warned the child to stay away from hills. They were the paths to hell.

The child looked fearfully at the ceiling of the coal cellar. Night was her only hope. Because if it was already nighttime, if it was sufficiently dark, if the coal cellar was as black as could be . . . God might not have seen any-thing. And if God hadn't seen, she might still avoid rolling down the hill into hell.

The child looked hopefully at the ceiling of the coal cellar. The light-bulb was broken, the cellar dark: how was it any different from night? She wished she could find a way to climb over the clouds and ask God whether He had seen what had happened in the cellar. She wished she knew whether God had seen.

*

As she entered the kitchen through the back door, she heard grandmother's voice. The children and neighbors were looking for her—in the yards, on the street, under the crimson car, at the Faraway Butcher. The game of hide-and-seek had ended a long time ago, and her absence was making everyone anxious.

She went in the bathroom. Rinsed her mouth. Removed her dress. Rinsed her mouth. Lathered the loofah. Rinsed her mouth. Scrubbed her body. Rinsed her mouth. Shampooed her hair. Rinsed her mouth. Dried her hair. Rinsed her mouth. Dried her body with a towel. Rinsed her mouth. Put on clean underwear. Rinsed her mouth. Took down her suitcase from the top of the armoire. Rinsed her mouth. Removed her favorite pair of shorts from the suitcase. Rinsed her mouth. Found a matching T-shirt. Rinsed her mouth. Put on one of the hats. Rinsed her mouth. Took a sugar cookie. Rinsed her mouth. Opened the door. Grandmother was standing in the doorway.

When her grandmother saw her—after spending hours frantically searching the neighborhood, wondering what she would tell the child's parents if she were lost for good—the old woman couldn't control herself. She slapped her across the face. The child got up from the floor. She stepped on the cookie she had dropped. She went to the bathroom. Rinsed her mouth.

*

"If you keep eating like this, you'll get fat. Then no one will think you're pretty. Do you want everyone to call you fatso?"

Without his glasses, the doctor had to squint when he looked at the child. The child looked back at him with an enigmatic smile.

*

She rinsed her mouth. She entered the living room.

All the neighborhood women were there. Young and old, they sat everywhere, piled on armchairs and floor cushions, even perching on one another's laps. They were waiting as if in mourning for the death of an unknown person, a death they couldn't taste. The child looked at them intently. She looked at them and envisioned sacks of potatoes, barrels of pickles, bunches of onions, baskets of fruit, boxes of chocolate, and jars of hazelnut cream. She was so hungry that her eyes began to devour the women's glances, gnaw at the grapes printed on the vinyl tablecloth. She was still hungry, terribly hungry. She couldn't get rid of the terrible taste in her mouth. She was desperate to erase it.

Grandmother had nothing prepared, and the child's urgent hunger fixed its lusterless eyes on the walls of the house. The house was the color of salted green almonds; it might taste just as good. But before hunger could sink its teeth into the walls, one of the neighbors rushed to her house and returned with a big pot of rice pilaf.

Tom and Jerry sparred on television; the rice pilaf steamed in the pot.

(The mouse was hungry.) She was hungry. (His eyes fell on the bowl of milk.) She pulled the pot toward her. (But the cat was sleeping beside it.) She removed the lid. (The cat's eyelids fluttered.) The pot was full. (The mouse inched toward the bowl.)

"May I have another plate?"

(The mouse gulped down the milk.) She was eating fast. (The cat's eyes opened wide.) The plate was wiped clean. (The cat pounced.) She stuck her hand into the pot. (The mouse dashed away.) The rice had nowhere to escape. (The chase began.) She scooped up rice, handful after handful. (The cat and mouse gasped for air.) She was out of breath. (The chase continued.) The more she ate, the hungrier she felt.

(The mouse fell into the bowl of milk.) She leaned into the pot. (He drank the milk to keep from drowning.) She ate handful after handful. (He grew so bloated that air bubbles rose from his mouth.) Her stomach began to ache. (The mouse began to rise like a balloon.) She felt heavy. (The cat caught the mouse by the tail.) Still, she couldn't stop. (Together, they rose into the sky.) She could see the bottom of the pot. (The sky was full of white clouds.) The bottom of the pot was pitch black.

*

"Let's see if you like my new glasses. My wife chose them."

The young doctor put them on and smiled. The glasses had tinted lenses with rectangular ebony frames. When he wore them, his blue eyes were concealed. The child frowned. She didn't want to talk to eyes she couldn't see. She didn't speak.

She never spoke again.

*

The stomach is a fairyland. For forty days and forty nights, its banquet tables are heaped with delicacies—rare bird's milk in gold chalices, pungent stews in ornate cauldrons. Rivers of wine stream through its valleys, healing honey trickles from its mountain peaks. It knows no hunger, this land of corpulent satisfaction.

The stomach is a fairyland. On the forty-first day it turns to ashes. A dragon spews fire at its gate, leaving not a grain of wheat nor a drop of water behind. Its bounty is blighted by droughts, its dark forests teem with witches who brew plagues in their cauldrons. It knows no satisfaction, this land of gnawing hunger.

The stomach is a fairyland. Like every fairyland, it is trapped in the mirror of its beguiling gaze.

*

Childhood's garden tastes of sour cherries. The memory of it stains her holiday best.

It is possible to forget everything. But when memories feel the cold of winter—dark despite its unfathomable whiteness—they awaken and lead back down to the coal cellar. The coal is made of memories; it burns quickly. Blood courses into memory's veins, and thick smoke scorches her eyes, purging them with tears. Coal dust flies across her skin, etching clear lines like clouds in the night sky, silver filaments drawn and drawn across the darkness.

Childhood's garden tastes of sour cherries. The flavor of it sets her teeth on edge.

It is not possible to forget everything. The eyes can forget what they see, but having been seen is another matter altogether. Witnesses alter the balance. Their every glance is an accusation, their existence defies letting go.

That's why she could never again count to three. She had put One on one side, Two on the other. Between them she was tugged, tugged endlessly, worn away in an impervious calculation.

Translated from the Turkish by Aron R. Aji

The Bed in Amsterdam

JOHN VIGNAUX SMYTH

If at times banal, our love is brutal
Enough to fulfill your prescription
Of perfection, almost to the letter:
All moves must be fast and violent, petals
Must be raped or shat upon;
The bed in Amsterdam, its many covers
Soaked in blood, incarnates the scene.
I am gutted. You are mad. Your fatal
Lust is cerebral, leading half the time
To suicide, half the time to murder,
Or their simulacra, well knowing that pain
Is all the worse, not being physical
But parastatic, projected by your
Body, not there, ecstatic, ill, infernal.

I

You're i, imaginary, complex, root
Of minus one. Your lack of identity
Is not one. You are the apex, third party,
Or point, of a triangle whose other
Points are real as hell. They constitute
A relation, a double determination,
Not a quantity: you will fight her
And win, in the mirror. The mirror world
Is real too, too real: it depicts right
And left inverted, inverted and cold
As the glass phallus you write of and dream
Of warming, owned by someone else it seems—
You sent the phallus to us both—for me:
Imaginary maybe, but here to stay.

Landscape, with Hungry Gulls

LANCE LARSEN

If I said burial, if I said a lovely morning
    to prepare the body, who would I startle?
Not this pair of teenage girls in matching swimsuits
    making a mound of their brother.
And not the boy himself, laid out like a cadaver
    on rye, who volunteered for interment.

In the language of skin, he knows that sand rhymes
    with patience, and that patience worketh
a blue sky dotted with gulls, if only he remains
    still enough. And he does, his face a cameo
dusted with sparkling grains. Meanwhile, my son
    brings me offerings he has dug up—

a jawbone, a pair of vertebrae, ribs like planks, three teeth.
    At my feet, an ancient horse assembles.
A lesson in calcification? A beginner's oracle kit?
    If the seagulls canvassing the beach
are questions, then the pelican riding the dihedral breeze
    above the buoys is an admonition, but to what?

The sisters are at work again, making a giant
    Shasta daisy of their brother's face,
six pieces of popcorn per petal, his eyes blinking.
    Now they scatter leftover kernels across the mound
like sextons scattering lime. To my left,
    ankle-deep in shallows, my son catches minnows.

No, not minnows, damselfly larvae,
    which swim like minnows but have six legs.
He places them in a moat, so they can swim freely.
    Soon enough they will climb this castle wall.
Soon enough they will shed their syntax and leave
    one language for another, like a good translation.

The sisters have moved farther down the beach
     in hopes that the seagulls will gently
nibble their brother. So many motives. Theirs: to dress
     a body in the sands of is as though tomorrow isn't.
His: to taste the world, mouth to beak.
     The gulls draw closer, to peck at his heart.

I am trying to pretend the body is only an idea.
     I watch the pelican. I have to keep reminding myself.
A pelican is not a pterodactyl with feathers.
     A pelican is not doing moral reconnaissance.
A pelican does not know my name.
     I close my eyes long enough to drift up and up.

Poor man, napping there, far below, who looks
     and smells like me, but is stuck in a beach chair.
Quick, someone teach him to bank and hover.
     And this horse my son is decorating the moat with,
broken into pieces so small and various and eloquent—
     why do I worry whether it has enough to eat?

HARUN FAROCKI

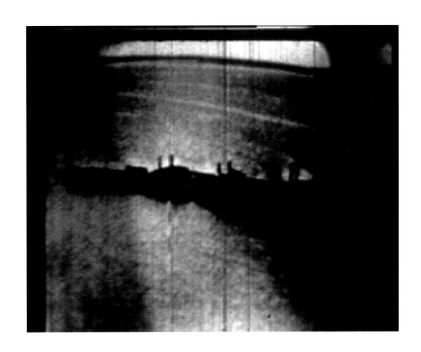

TOP: Still from *Eye/Machine II*, 2002. Image transferred from a German Hs 293 D missile to a TV monitor, 1942.

BOTTOM: Still from *Eye/Machine I*, 2001. Image from the Gulf War, 1991.

Still from Eye/Machine I, 2001.

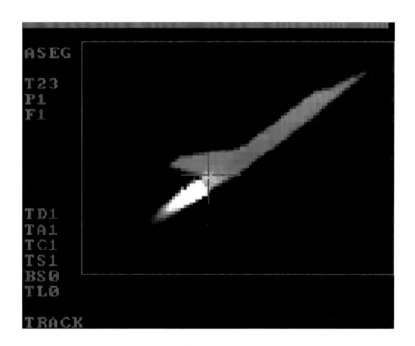

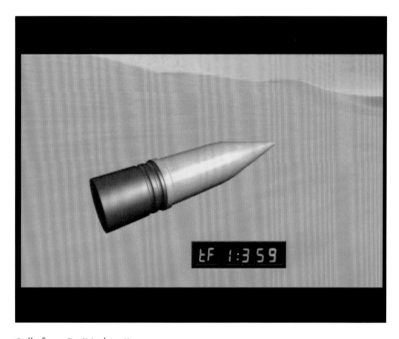

Stills from Eye/Machine II, 2002.

Stills from Eye/Machine III, 2003.

Harun Farocki

As early as 1942, scientists in Germany had succeeded in installing a television camera in a remote-control weapon. But it wasn't until the Gulf War, almost fifty years later, that missiles could actually be guided with the help of electronic images obtained from "suicide cameras" placed in their tips. Though many died in that war, there are never any people to be seen in the images released by the allied military forces. The human scale is missing, and so the enemy is distanced.

In the civil sector, robots are fitted with camera-eyes to survey operations in the workplace. Labor done with human hands and eyes is being transferred to poor countries, just as wars are being transferred to poor countries.

Two years ago I began making films using sequences of images from laboratories, archives, and factories to document the uses and effects of these smart technologies.

Eye/Machine I addresses the concept of autonomous systems. These systems adapt their performance in response to the data they receive, rather than repeating a task the same way each time. Imagine a war fought by autonomous machines—a war without soldiers, like a factory without workers.

Eye/Machine II addresses the concept of "battlefields by numbers." War has always fueled technological innovation, and today high-tech wars are simulated far more often than they are fought. Will the wars of the future require real battlefields, or will they be waged only on virtual plains?

Eye/Machine III, to be completed this year, will address the concept of operational images. These images do not describe an operation but rather are an integral part of it. The cruise missiles developed in the '80s by NATO nations contained image banks of idealized tactical landscapes—hills, plains, cities, factories. When the missiles flew over an actual landscape they recorded real images, and an algorithm compared those pictures to the stored geographical data. The montage that resulted—a juxtaposition of the purity of ideal war combined with the impurity of real conflict—transforms recognition into representation.

H.F.

Translated from the German by Daniel Slager

CHRIS BURDEN

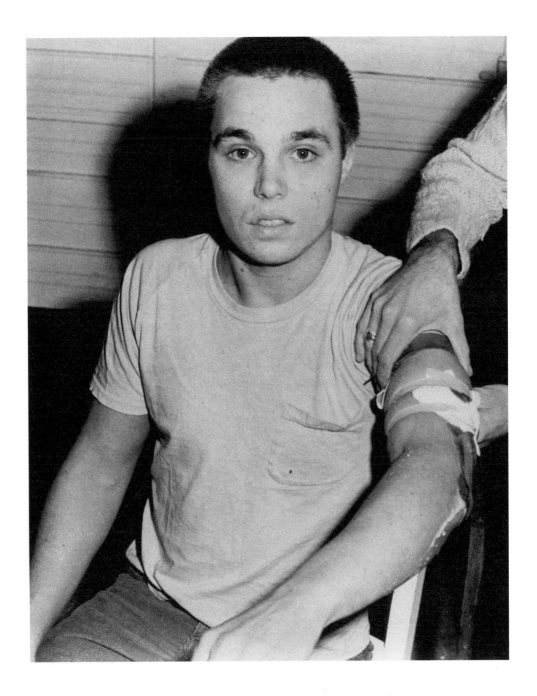

Shoot, November 19, 1971. F Space, Los Angeles.
"At 7:45 P.M. I was shot in the left arm by a friend. The bullet was a
copper jacket 22 long rifle. My friend was standing about fifteen
feet from me."

747, January 5, 1973. Los Angeles.
"At about 8:00 A.M. at a beach near the Los Angeles International
Airport, I fired several shots with a pistol at a Boeing 747."

Through the Night Softly, September 12, 1973. Main Street, Los Angeles.
"Holding my hands behind my back, I crawled through fifty feet of
broken glass. There were very few spectators, most of them passersby.
This piece was documented with a 16 mm film."

Doorway to Heaven, November 15, 1973. Venice, California.
"At 6:00 P.M. I stood in the doorway of my studio facing the Venice
boardwalk. A few spectators watched as I pushed two live electric
wires into my chest. The wires crossed and exploded, burning me
but saving me from electrocution."

Chris Burden

From 1971 to 1982, California-based artist Chris Burden made works that put himself and sometimes his audiences in physical danger. He had himself shut up in a school locker for five days straight. He had a friend shoot him in the arm at close range with a .22 rifle. When a radio interviewer invited him to give examples of his work, he pulled a knife on her and threatened to kill her if the station stopped live transmission. He blocked a lane of traffic with his body, lying under a tarp marked by two flares. Near an airport he fired a pistol at a Boeing 747 passing overhead. He dragged himself through fifty feet of broken glass on L.A.'s Main Street, and bought ten seconds of advertising time so he could air his filmed documentation of the performance on television. He pushed two live electric wires into his chest in Venice, California. For two minutes, he lay crucified to the back of a Volkswagen Beetle that had been pushed onto the California Speedway. For five minutes in Chicago, he tried to breathe water. In Basel, he was kicked down a flight of stairs. In Graz, he lay under a sink of burning alcohol that splashed onto his body. In Calgary, he showed a video of himself starting a fire at the foot of a gallery stairway, challenging the viewers inside to figure out whether it was a live or taped broadcast.

Although the number of people who actually saw Burden's performances was small in comparison to the number who heard about them, the artist's documentation of his work—and the care he took in selecting iconic images to represent each event—emphasized both the role of the witness in moments of violence and the artifacts and evidence that preserve such moments. In the 1980s, however, Burden stopped performing like a martyr, daredevil, terrorist, activist, and holy fool; like many artists of his generation, which came of age during the Vietnam War, he turned to a fundamentally safer practice. The sculpture installations he now produces address American policy and commodity culture, and they involve a different kind of risk: working against expectation is—for any artist—to go out on a limb that is fragile to begin with. But it's the radical violence of his early art that is thrown into relief by recent events, and this leads one to wonder what new dangers artists, including Burden, might risk, or provoke.

INGRID SCHAFFNER

from Feuillets d'Hypnos: Notes on the French Resistance

RENÉ CHAR

After serving for a year in the French army during World War II, the poet René Char returned to the mountain village of Céreste and joined the Resistance. The following excerpts are taken from his wartime notebook, Feuillets d'Hypnos, which was first published in France in 1946.

This war will drag on beyond any platonic armistice. Political concepts will go on being sewn, after a show of argument on both sides, amid the upheavals and under cover of a hypocrisy sure of its rights. Don't smile. Put aside skepticism and resignation and prepare your mortal soul to confront, within these walls, demons that have the cold-blooded genius of microbes.

*

The moment the instinct for survival gives way to the instinct for possession, reasonable human beings lose all sense of their probable life span and day-to-day equilibrium. They grow hostile to small chills in the atmosphere and acquiesce without further ado to whatever evil and deceit might require of them. Under a maleficent hailstorm their miserable condition simply crumbles away.

*

I think of that army of deserters, hungry for dictatorship, whom those who survive the Faustian algebra of these times will perhaps see back in power in this mindless country.

*

Archduke confides to me that it was on joining the Resistance that he found himself. Prior to that, he had been an actor in his life, mocking and suspicious. Insincerity was poisoning him. Little by little, he was being overcome by a barren sadness. Today, he loves, spends out, commits himself, goes naked, provokes. I think very highly of this alchemist.

*

Revolution and counterrevolution are putting on their masks, preparing themselves for combat once again.

Short-lived candor! After the combat of eagles comes the combat of octopi. The genius of man, who thinks he has discovered truths that are all-encompassing, turns truths that kill into truths that *authorize* one to kill. The show put on by these backward-looking visionaries, fighting at the front of an armor-plated and exhausted universe! While the collective neuroses grow ever more pronounced in the eye of myth and symbol, psychic man tortures life, without feeling, it would seem, the slightest remorse. The hideous flower, the *hand-drawn* flower, revolves its black petals in the mad flesh of the sun. Where is the source? Where the remedy? When will the economy finally change its ways?

*

Between the two rifle shots that would decide his fate, he had time to call a fly "Madame."

*

Over and against *whatever's out there*: a Colt .45 with its promise of sunrise!

*

Having the Mistral blowing didn't help matters. With every hour that passed my fears increased, with little reassurance to be had from the presence of Mutt watching the road for passing convoys that might stop to launch an attack. The first container exploded as it struck the ground. Driven on by the wind, the fire spread to the woods and had soon made a blot on the horizon.

The plane altered course slightly and came in for a second run. The cylinders swinging from their multicolored silks got scattered over an enormous area. We battled for hours in an infernal glare, splitting up into three groups: one lot fighting the fire, doing what they could with axes and spades; a second lot gone off in search of stray arms and explosives and bringing them to where the truck was waiting; a third providing us with cover. From the tops of pines, panicking squirrels leaped like tiny comets into the blaze.

As for the enemy, we just managed to avoid him. Dawn crept up on us before he did.

(Beware of anecdotes. They're like railway stations where the station-master loathes the signalman!)

*

The quality of those in the Resistance is not, alas, everywhere the same. For every Joseph Fontaine, who has the rectitude and tenor of a plowman's furrow, for every François Cuzin, Claude Dechevannes, André Grillet, Marius Bardouin, Gabriel Besson, Doctor Jean Roux, or Roger Chaudon converting the granary at Oraison into a castle perilous, how many elusive charlatans there are, more concerned with enjoying themselves than with producing. You can be sure that, come the Liberation, these cockerels of the void will be ringing in our ears. . . .

*

I see man ruined by political perversion, confusing action and atonement, and naming conquest his own annihilation.

*

Night, swift as a boomerang carved from our bones, and whistling, whistling. . . .

*

In action, be primitive; in foresight, a strategist.

*

What matters most in certain situations is mastering one's euphoria in time.

*

I thank whatever lucky star has allowed us to have the poachers of Provence fighting on our side. The knowledge these primitives have of the forest, their gift for calculation and their keen flair no matter what the weather—I'd be surprised if a failing were to come about from that quarter. I shall see to it that they are given shoes fit for gods!

*

The poet, guardian of the countless faces of life.

*

LS, thank you for ManHole Durance 12. It goes into operation from tonight. Make sure the young team assigned to the field doesn't get into the habit of appearing too often on the streets of Duranceville. Girls and cafés dangerous for more than a minute. But don't pull too tightly on the reins, I don't want a squealer in the team. No contacts outside the network. Put a stop to bragging. Check all intelligence against two sources. Allow for fifty percent fanciful in most cases. Teach your men to be attentive, to give an exact report, to set down the arithmetic of a given situation. Bring together rumors and synthesize. Drop-off point and letter-box with the Friend of the Wheat. Waffen operation possible, foreigners' camp at Les Mées, with overflow onto Jews and Resistance. Spanish Republicans in real danger. Urgent you warn them. For yourself, avoid combat. ManHole sacred. In the event of an alert, disperse. Other than to rescue captured comrade, never let the enemy know you exist. Intercept suspects. I leave it to you to judge. The camp will never be revealed. The camp doesn't exist, only charcoal kilns that don't give off smoke. No washing hung out when the planes come over, and all men under trees or in the scrub. No one will come to see you on my behalf, apart from the Friend of the Wheat and the Swimmer. With the men in your team be strict and considerate. Friendship muffles discipline. When working, always do a few kilos more than everyone else, without taking pride in the fact. Eat and smoke conspicuously less than they do. Don't favor one person over another. Tolerate only spontaneous, gratuitous lies. Don't let them call across to one another. Let them keep their bodies and their bedding clean. Let them learn to sing quietly and not to whistle tunes that stick in the head, to tell the truth exactly as it presents itself. At night, they should keep to the side of the path. Suggest precautions, but allow them the merit of discovering them for themselves. Rivalry excellent. Oppose monotonous habits and encourage the ones you don't want dying out too soon. Last but not least, love the people *they* love, at the same moment as them. Add, don't divide. All well here. Affectionately. HYPNOS.

*

The plane flies low. The invisible pilots jettison their night garden, then activate a brief light tucked in under the wing of the plane to notify us that it's over. All that remains is to gather up the scattered treasure. So it is with the poet. . . .

*

The flight path of a poem. Its presence should be felt by all.

*

He reminded me of a dead partridge, the poor invalid who, after being stripped of the few rags he possessed, was murdered by the militia at Vachères, who accused him of harboring "partisans." Before finishing him off, the gangsters enjoyed themselves at great length with a girl who was part of the expedition. With one eye torn out and his chest staved in, the innocent man took in this hell AND THEIR LAUGHTER.

(We have captured the girl.)

*

Eternity is hardly any longer than life.

*

I aimed at the lieutenant and Bloodspat the colonel. The flowering gorse concealed us behind its flamboyant yellow vapor. Jean and Robert threw the grenades. The little enemy column immediately beat a retreat. With the exception of the machine gunner, but he didn't have time to become dangerous: his belly exploded. We used the two cars to make our getaway. The colonel's briefcase was full of interest.

*

The baker hadn't even had time to unlock the iron curtain on his shop before the village was under siege, gagged, hypnotized, unable to make the slightest move. Two companies of SS and a detachment of militia had it pinned down under the muzzle of their machine guns and mortars. Then the ordeal began.

The inhabitants were thrown out of their houses and told to assemble in the main square. Keys to be left in their doors. An old man, hard of hearing, who did not respond quickly enough to the order, saw the four walls and roof of his barn blown to bits by a bomb. I had been up since four o'clock. Marcelle had come up to my shutters and whispered the alert. I realized at once that it would be pointless to try to break through the roadblocks and get out to the countryside. I quickly changed lodgings. The empty house where I took shelter would allow me, if worse came to worst, to put up an effective armed resistance. I could follow from behind the yellowed curtains of my window the nervous comings and goings of the occupying forces. Not one of my men was present in the village. I took comfort in the thought. A few miles from there, they would be following my instructions and lying low. I could hear blows being delivered, punctuated by cursing. The SS had caught a young mason, on his way home after emptying his traps. His fright made him an obvious target for their tortures. A voice leaned, screaming, over the swollen body: "Where is he? Take us to him," followed by silence. A shower of kicks and rifle butts. An insane rage took hold of me, banishing my distress. Sweat poured from my hands as I clutched my revolver, rejoicing in its pent-up powers. I calculated that the poor creature would remain silent for five minutes more, then, inevitably, would speak. I felt ashamed wanting him to die before the time was up. Then, issuing from every street, came a flood of women, children, and old men, making their way to the assembly point according to an *organized plan*. Taking their time, they hurried forward, literally streaming over the SS and paralyzing them "in all sincerity." The mason was left for dead. Furious, the patrol pushed its way through the crowd and marched off. With infinite prudence now, anxious, kind eyes glanced in my direction, passing like beams of light over my window. I partially revealed myself and my pale face broke into a smile. I was bound to these people by a thousand threads of trust, not one of which was to break.

I loved my fellow men fiercely that day, far beyond the call of sacrifice.

*

We are like those frogs who, in the austerity of the marshes at night, call to but cannot see one another, bending the fatal arc of the universe to their cry of love.

*

Horrible day! I witnessed, some hundred yards away, the execution of B. I had only to squeeze the trigger of my submachine gun and he could have been saved! We were on the high ground overlooking Céreste, the bushes bursting with weapons, and at least equal in number to the SS. They didn't know we were there. To the eyes all around me, begging me for the signal to open fire, I replied with a shake of the head. . . . The June sun sent a polar chill through my bones.

He seemed unaware of his executioners as he fell, and so light that the slightest breath of wind would have lifted him from the ground.

I didn't give the signal because the village had *at all costs* to be spared. What is a village? A village like any other? Perhaps *he* knew, at that final instant?

*

A time of raging mountains and fantastic friendship.

*

Roger was delighted at having become in the eyes of his young wife the husband-who-was-hiding-god.

Today, I passed the field of sunflowers, the sight of which so inspired him. The heads of these wonderful, insipid flowers were weighed down with drought. It was a few yards from there that his blood was spilled, at the foot of an ancient mulberry tree as deaf to the world as its bark is thick.

*

My arm is in plaster and causing me some pain. Dear Doctor Tall-Fellow has made a marvelous job of it, despite the swelling. Luck that my subconscious guided my fall in quite the way it did. Otherwise, the grenade I was holding, with its pin out, stood a very good chance of exploding. Luck that the *feldgendarmes* heard nothing (they had left the engine of their truck running). Luck that I didn't pass out with my head cracked like a flowerpot. . . . My comrades congratulate me on my presence of mind. I have difficulty persuading them that no credit is due me. It all went on outside me. After a thirty-foot fall, I felt like a basket of dislocated bones. Fortunately, there was almost nothing of the kind.

*

The silence of morning. The apprehension of color. The luck of the sparrow hawk.

*

So close is the affinity between the cuckoo and the furtive creatures we have become that whenever that bird—which you hardly ever see and, even when you do catch sight of one, is always dressed in anonymous gray—lets out its heartrending song, a long shudder goes through us in response.

*

For a heritage to be truly great, the hand of the deceased must be invisible.

*

Our dog, Ketty, takes as much pleasure as we do in gathering up the parachute drops. She goes briskly from one to the other without barking, knowing exactly what is required. Once the work is over, she stretches out, happy, on the dune formed by the parachutes and falls asleep.

*

Are we doomed to be only the beginnings of truth?

*

I see hope—the riverbed in which tomorrow's waters will run—drying up in the gestures of those all around me. The faces I love are wasting away in the nets of waiting, which eats into them like acid. How little help we receive, how little encouragement! The sea and its shores are an obvious step forward, but have been sealed off by the enemy. They are at the back of everyone's mind, the mold for a substance comprised, in equal measure, of the rumor of despair and the certainty of resurrection.

*

So unreceptive has our sleep become that even the briefest of dreams cannot come galloping through to refresh it. The prospect of dying is drowned out by an inundation of the Absolute so all-engulfing that merely to think of it is to lose any desire for life, which we call upon, which we implore. Once again, we must love one another well, must breathe more deeply than the executioner's lungs.

*

This man around whom my sympathy is sure to revolve for a while counts because his eagerness to serve coincides with a whole halo of auspicious circumstances and with the plans I have for him. Let us work together while there is still time, before whatever it is that brings us together turns unaccountably to hostility.

All of a sudden, you remember you have a face. The features that shape that face weren't always racked with grief. Drawn to its varied landscape, creatures gifted with kindness would appear. Nor was it only castaways who succumbed, exhausted, to its spell. The loneliness of lovers could breathe freely there. Look. Your mirror is now a fire. Little by little, you remember your age (which had been struck from the calendar), that surplus of existence which, by working at it, you will turn into a bridge. Step back inside the mirror. Arid it may be, yet at least its fruitfulness has not run dry.

Translated from the French by Mark Hutchinson

This selection includes the journal entries numbered 7, 8, 20, 30, 37, 42, 50, 53, 65, 69, 71, 72, 78, 79, 83, 87, 97, 98, 99, 110, 121, 128, 129, 138, 142, 146, 149, 152, 159, 166, 167, 186, 192, 193, 196, and 219.

ALREADY BEEN IN A LAKE OF FIRE:
NOTEBOOK VOLUME 38

A document by Fadl Fakhouri from the Atlas Group Archive
The Atlas Group / Walid Raad

Created by Walid Raad in 1999, the Atlas Group is a project whose goal is to research and record the contemporary history of Lebanon. The group has recovered and produced a number of artifacts pertaining to the Lebanese wars of 1975 to 1991, including notebooks, films, videotapes, and photographs. These are preserved in the foundation's archive, located in New York City and Beirut, and are organized in three categories: Type A (authored), Type FD (found), and Type AGP (Atlas Group Productions).

Some of the documents, stories, and individuals Raad presents with this project are real in that they exist in the historical world; others are imaginary in that the artist has conceived and produced them. But they are all informed by research in audio, visual, and print archives in Lebanon and elsewhere. In this sense, the Atlas Group project operates between the terms of the false binary of fiction and nonfiction.

The images in this portfolio come from the Fadl Fakhouri dossier, classified as Type A. Dr. Fakhouri was—according to the Atlas Group—the foremost historian of the Lebanese civil wars until his death in 1993, and he bequeathed 226 notebooks and two short films to the foundation. *Already Been in a Lake of Fire: Notebook Volume 38* contains 145 cutout photographs of cars. Each page shows a vehicle that was used as a car bomb during the civil wars—replicating the exact make, model, and color—and each picture is accompanied by text in Arabic specifying the date, time, and magnitude of the explosion.

HUSSEIN MEHDI

ف ٢٠٠ / ٢٨

RECORD

already been in a lake of fire

APPENDIX:

كل صورة من صور الـ ١٤٥
سيارة الواردة في هذا
الكشف تمثل سيارة
استعملت كسيارة ناسفة
بين سنوات ١٩٧٥ و ١٩٩٠.

التطابق بين الصور وما
تمثله كمي : من الماركة
الى اللون الى سنة الصنع.

Appendix:

This notebook contains 145 cutout
photographs of cars.

They correspond to the exact make,
model, and color of every car that was used
as a car bomb between 1975 and 1990.

Nissan
4WD
White
May 23, 1985
14:00
Beirut
Kills 55
Injures 174
300 kg of TNT
Hexogen
500 meter perimeter
Burns 35 cars

№ 55

DATSUN

٥/٢٣/٨٥

سيارة محشوة ٥٥ كيلو و ١٧٤ جريحاً في منطقة عين التينة لدى انفجارها
تحطم أوضاع الدشم غير دائرة قطرها حوالي ٢٥٠ متراً كما
حطم الحي العسكري بزنة المتفجرة ...؟ كيلوغرام مادة
Hexogen ... تسبب ... قوم ريش امطولنات.

№ 56

٦/١٤/٨٥

انفجرت سيارة مفخخة في منطقة الشياح
بعد انها قتلت صاحبها في اقتسام المركز
٢١ حزيران مما قتل ما نحو ٥٦ + ٧ واصابت ٣٩ مصاب
سيارة من اللحاد الحزين امى في مرسادية وزنة العبوة بـ ٣٥ كيلوغرام
الـ؟ المخزنة موضوع حبوب مخزنيان هابون ١٢٠ ملم ... في
٢٨٢ وصفت الشرح اخذان العبوة غوش بـ كيلوغرام من العادات
Hexogen وصعه

BMW
2002
Gray
June 14, 1985
19:55
Beirut
Kills 7
Injures 39
30 kg or 200 kg of TNT
Two 120 mm shells or Hexogen

№ 61   № 62

Volvo
Silver
August 20, 1985
12:22
Beirut
Kills 56

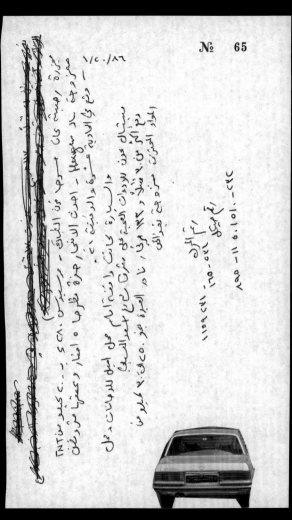

Honda
Civic
Blue
February 23, 1986
9:55
Beirut
Kills 4

The document *Already Been in a Lake of Fire: Notebook Volume 38* is part of an ongoing Atlas Group investigation into the events, experiences, and public and private discourses surrounding the use of car bombs in the Lebanese wars of 1975–91. With this project, the Atlas Group examines multiple dimensions of the wars— social, political, economic, military, technological, psychological, and epistemic— as expressed in what is believed and articulated with regard to the 245 car bombs that were detonated in Lebanon during this period.

This project is not an attempt to place blame or generalize suffering. Not all of the Lebanese people sustained physical or psychological harm from car bomb explosions, nor did all militias and armies use car bombs to terrorize, destroy, or kill. What our work demonstrates is that the detonation of a car bomb is not only an act of violence, but also produces a discourse that directly and indirectly affects individuals, families, and communities. We have found that the car bomb is both a cause and a consequence of the ongoing political, military, economic, and criminal conflicts that have defined most aspects of life in Lebanon for the past thirty years. The history of these car bomb explosions doubles as a history of how the wars were physically and psychically experienced, and how those who lived through such events speak about and assimilate their experiences.

THE ATLAS GROUP / WALID RAAD

from "The Memory of the City"

ELIAS KHOURY

A city and its myths are inextricably linked: What is Jerusalem if not the "mythical" center of the world? What is Alexandria without its Greek and Levantine myths? Can it be experienced without Cavafy or Durrell? What about New York? Rome? Paris? What is real about a place and what spawned from stories and histories?

Cities are invisible stories, and stories are invisible cities, to borrow Italo Calvino's words. Which is why I find talking about Beirut such a difficult task. Should I tell its history or should I unravel its myths? And what if those myths are still in the process of being generated today? Should I use Roland Barthes's mythological approach or should I dig deeper under the archaeological foundations of the city's historical memory?

Beirut today can be understood both as a mythological prototype of the city torn by civil war, disheveled by death, dismembered by destruction, and as a former Roman and Phoenician city, a city with a past built on ruins of the past. The two perspectives are not altogether different: in ancient history Beirut was demolished by seven earthquakes; in recent times, it has been razed by the seven major wars that punctuated its civil war. The city remains unstable, if temporarily sedated by the peace pact signed in 1989—which is, in itself, a myth the city may smother at birth.

(Grand Street 54, Fall 1995)

The Oven Man

ROBIN ROBERTSON

The house re-inflates
its skin of heat:

tightens it up
to the screen door,

frames creaking
like a boat at anchor.

The burners cut out
before the roof lifts.

The house rustles
and ticks, and clicks off.

During all this commotion
I am inside, in expansive mood,

relaxing
like a Sunday roast

in my juices,
my puddle of blood.

The Larches of
Zernikow

These lines of larch were planted
by children, here among the pines
and firs in 1938, they think, or '39.
Even if you walked beneath them now
in October, you would never know
that for these two weeks
the yellow gold of these hundred trees
would be branding the forest canopy
far above you,
blazing a swastika
visible from the moon.

At Kaikoura

I have driven through the mountains
in a turquoise jeep, to eat here
under these hills that come down to the sea:
a bowl of green-lipped mussels, each
exactly the size of my own mouth,
two local crayfish and a bottle
of cold South Island wine.
There are dolphins in the bay
and sperm whales out beyond the shelf,
trawling for squid. The sun is folded
into the water. I am far from home,
remembering how to live, remembering
I have no home.

Sorrows

An over-filled glass:
I take my head
in my hands,
careful not to spill.

*

Without a real death in my life
I had to make my own.

Now I build models of my father
out of smoke and light.

*

He was uncomfortable,
so I asked the nurse
if we could lift him higher.
He died an hour later.
Usually happens, she explained,
after you move them.
Forgive me, I say, at his feet,
through a mouthful of nails.

*

In his shirt-sleeves and flannels
I remember him:

a stitch in his side
from the long run home.

*

The dam he built
in the stream is finally broken:
cold Highland water
rushing to the sea.

To the Island

The fog rolling in toward San Michele
is folding round and over the lampposts
that are all that remain of some drowned street
and now guide the vaporetti
and the funeral barge with its black plumes
across the lagoon in a shawl of rain
to the cypresses of San Michele.

The Melancholy of Departure, 1914

(oil on canvas, Giorgio de Chirico)

RYAN G. VAN CLEAVE

Death slithers over cranberry walls
like a dark water serpent in the Garden
of Desire—you can see it, inhuman eyes
ojos demasiados inhumanos, among the nettles,
the cracks, the web of dried river-veins.

Pittura Metafisica needs a hero, a Theseus
and his golden club—the shivering foam
of legend—to break the skull of Cubism,
its daily hatefulness, those geometric fangs
that bite deep, quick, slathered black with poison.

Still, the deep channel sky tugs with a gravity
all its own, *la gravedad de la totalidad abrasadora*,
a shattering purity that bemoans the loss of myth,
the pull of vanishing coastline, time oozing
like a cut stem, its silent pain its own response.

Famous (Almost)

Up until the hearse hauls him away,
    my brother will seek fame, a moment
    of drinking oolong from the glitzy cups
    of Madonna's pointy bra, an hour of bloodying
himself before a suckling, gurgling, mooing
    crowd, a single day whose cross section is pork-
    white, pulpy, and sweet without question.
    Sure, he's right—music is the epidermis of the soul
and a pulsing bass drum and chunka-chunka raunch
    of a balls-out Les Paul you feel in your teeth,
    the subcutaneous fat, the pit cavities of your bones.
    But what slaps the glasses off his face
is the definition of roar, the rise and fall
    of a crowd's one voice, how it lowers the rope
    of his life into a rich, dark well once more.
    I visited him last week, the smell of bourbon
rank in the carpet, cigarette butts spearing
    the soil of a dead potted fern. Beneath the bed
    the ashes of his old bandmate, the Speedball King,
    cooling in a Nike box. My brother put on old
Iggy Pop vinyls, and we listened, the clogged
    roar through pop-crackle speakers pushing us apart,
    bringing us back in, like debris caught in a wave.

Glorious Days

AKIRA YOSHIMURA

They floated up and down the river, following the ebb and flow of the tide. Some floated alone, others were bunched together like rafts. Back and forth in front of the fur factory where we worked on the banks of the Sumida River, they came and went like so many aquatic commuters. We began seeing them a month ago, a few days after the villages downriver went up in flames. Their motion varied: some drifted down the center of the river, some traveled slowly along the quiet banks, while others, run aground on exposed shoals of mud, barely moved at all.

As far as we knew, there was no plan to retrieve them.

Unlike the burned corpses that lay contorted on the scorched earth, which were disposed of within a few days, these bodies were left to drift freely, perhaps to allow the bereaved a chance to identify them—though surely they no longer had families to speak of. Most of the passersby who looked down from the bridge gave them only a disinterested glance before moving on, and the few boats and barges that crossed the river made no effort to avoid them. They bobbed in the ripples of the boats' wake with the rest of the flotsam—charred basins and lattice doors, planks from wooden foot-bridges. The oil and fat processing plant on the opposite bank was a ruin of rusted iron frames, spelter, and tiles. The plant had burned down three months earlier during a daytime air raid; its remains pushed up like a natural ridge in the river. On windy days you could see white foam on the waves near it, but ebb tide showed deposits of blackened zinc. The bodies that trafficked to and fro across the river already seemed like a natural part of that polluted environment. Clothing, even exposed flesh, was stained by the filthy water that bled into everything it touched.

We stared at the bodies in frightened silence from the window in the factory lounge. We could easily imagine the circumstances of their deaths. Pursued by flames, they had plunged into the river, trying to escape the fierce heat. But the intense combustion had deprived the air of oxygen, and they died from asphyxiation. Their flesh and clothes bore no traces of charring; they weren't as ghastly as the carbonized bodies lying on the road. Those we had gotten used to, but the corpses in the river, still so lifelike, pressed their humanity on us.

Around noon, one particular group always happened to float right below our window. Perhaps some adhesive force was operating at the water's surface, or the bodies were caught up in the same current, but they seemed to be linked by an invisible bond. Creeping along the surface, surrounded on three sides by rotting driftwood, they clustered together like a school of fish trapped in a pen. The man in the iron helmet with a portable cashbox strapped to his back, the white-haired old man whose bare heels poked whitely out of the river, the young woman hoisting her near-to-bursting buttocks above the waterline, the woman in culottes whose baby was slipping from its harness— a party of five, four adults and a child, all with their faces thrust down into the water. We knew rigor mortis had set in, for their postures always remained the same.

Their visits tended to coincide with our lunch hour, when we gathered in the lounge, and I began to wonder if they weren't passing by at that time in order to be seen by us, because they liked human contact. They seemed like tamed carp approaching the shore. When we left the lounge to return to work, they'd leave the driftwood enclosure, slowly reentering the current.

Of course, I was disturbed by the fact that they were left exposed, those pitiful figures wreathed in flame by an American bomb. They drifted back and forth before our eyes when they should have been respectfully buried. But we lacked the will to reach out to them, and the village lacked the will to accommodate them. Besides, we were all busy. The American army was fast approaching the mainland, their bombers and carrier planes made frequent trips to replenish ammunition. We had to keep up production of *anything* that might contribute to the war effort. The dead were just the dead. They had ceased being productive; they were objects as useless as charred ruins. The living had neither time nor effort to waste in disposing of them. We could only gaze at them uneasily, until we began to feel a kind of doleful intimacy.

One day it was discovered that a fresh corpse had joined the group. It was a young man roughly our age wearing a student's uniform, face upturned and head wedged uncomfortably between the thighs of the old man with the protruding soles. The Kōtō district had gone up in flames three days before, and since then many more bodies had joined the drifting throng. This student was one of them: the color of his uniform and the flesh on his face were terribly fresh, setting him apart from the bodies saturated by filthy water. After silently observing him, we began to talk about Ukai and Kiyogawa. Neither of them had shown up that day, nor had they come to work the day before. They lived in the most densely populated area of the Kōtō district, which had almost certainly been incinerated. We realized that both of them had probably died.

The afternoon bell rang, and we silently dispersed to our work stations. It occurred to me that of the two friends it was Ukai who would have managed to escape, if anyone could. Ukai was clever and quick-witted and had drawn up an elaborate escape plan in case his house caught fire. The plan included a detailed air-raid map, which elicited amazement and admiration when he brought it to the factory. He had estimated a number of points likely to be hit and had classified them according to wind direction, with the probable corresponding air-raid routes complexly rendered like a traffic grid in various hues of cotton thread. Smiling and stroking the sparse hair on his chin, Ukai explained the protocol for clambering over the cul-de-sac wall and fleeing over the rooftops.

"Even my doddering neighbors will get out in no time!" he laughed.

Compared to Ukai, Kiyogawa was in considerably more danger. Nicknamed "Silkworm," the diminutive Kiyogawa was as delicate and slow as his namesake. On his narrow shoulders he carried the burden of a life essentially different from ours: in addition to caring for his aged mother, he was also, however inadequately, a husband. To be a husband at our age— we were seventeen—was unnatural, but in Kiyogawa's case it was just another necessity brought about by the war. According to Ukai, Kiyogawa's mother foresaw mortal danger for her only son, who might soon be sent to the front lines, and had pushed Kiyogawa to marry so that he could taste life as a man and perpetuate the family's bloodline.

Not that we didn't feel as if we too were growing up in fits and starts. Like most seventeen-year-olds, some of us were stuck in boyhood, but the war had dragged us into an adult world. As the head of a household, Kiyogawa was all the more endangered. It would have taken an additional effort for him to escape the flames while also shepherding his old mother and his wife.

I tried to recall his face, but it appeared to me only as an ashen image in an obituary notice.

*

Two or three days passed, and neither Ukai nor Kiyogawa showed up. We put on our heavy uniforms and continued working.

Our mobilized factory had been designated for army use, and the supervising officer periodically showed up for inspection rounds. But none of us was satisfied with our responsibilities. On the contrary, we resented them. We tanned and processed animal furs used in cold-weather gear—flight suits and the like—at the Northern Front, but the fact that we weren't making arms, that our labor had no direct impact on the war, bothered us to no end. On top of that, our wooden building was a far cry from the modern world, and its workers were mostly elderly. The factory had the silent, dismal feel of a primordial marsh. Only the faintest light crept in from a small window, and as soon as we set foot inside, our bodies were enveloped by the moist smell of animals and chemicals.

In our workroom there were four large wooden vats, where the pelts were cured in a chemical solvent. Goats, sheep, dogs, rabbits, cats, weasels, flying squirrels—the pelts differed from day to day, and we learned to tell the species apart by the smells they emitted. To tan the underside, we would pull a heavy, sodden pelt out of the vat, catch it with a hook, and spread it out on a washboard-like stand. Then, with a long, iron blade like a double-handled kitchen knife, we scraped away the hardened bands of white and yellowish fat, fine blood vessels, and strips of meat. Once inspected to insure that all the fat had been removed, the pelts were pitched into a deep vat of chromium alum to soak slowly, their fur swaying in the green solvent. Occasionally we splashed liquid onto the concrete floor, which was grooved like the grid of a go board. Fluid and fat deposits would collect in the furrows, gleaming dully, along with congealed strips of peeled-off flesh.

That day, just as I began the final preparation of two furs, the air-raid siren sounded. We undid the rubber aprons from around our necks and filed out of the workroom, stepping carefully across the slippery floor. We had become accustomed to air raids, convinced that they posed no threat to us— even if the bomber routes veered over our heads, even if they dropped their bombs. We'd stand outside, not overly concerned by the alarm. We'd gaze up at the B-29s, their fuselages glinting like mica, enveloped in flashes of anti-aircraft fire; the glittering Japanese interceptors, like delicate strips of tin, engaging and withdrawing; and the whiteness of a parachute opening in the clear sky like the crown of a dandelion.

This time, as the outlines of vapor trails began to fade, a friend tapped me on the shoulder and pointed to a slightly built man in rubber boots who was approaching the factory. He wore neither student uniform nor cap, but as he drew nearer, slope-shouldered and swaying back and forth with a pigeon-toed gait, we recognized Kiyogawa.

"Silkworm, it's Silkworm!"

The words erupted simultaneously from our mouths, and we surrounded him, each of us fighting to be the closest.

"We were worried! Are you all right?" we cried, slapping him on the back.

Kiyogawa looked around, blinking repeatedly. His eyes were unusually bloodshot, and he appeared close to tears.

"How are your wife and mother?"

Kiyogawa just nodded. Lowering his face as from a glare, he said hoarsely, "The smoke's really gotten to my eyes," and he wiped his bulging red eyes slowly with his handkerchief. He'd fled toward the ocean, chased by flames, and had escaped death by pouring water over his head in a boat moored on a mud shoal. His clothes had burned. He'd seen water in a roadside barrel suddenly evaporate—that was how fierce the heat had been.

"Do you know if Ukai made it? He hasn't come back."

Kiyogawa's thin brow furrowed. And again he rubbed his bloodshot eyes with his handkerchief. We kept our mouths shut as if rebuffed.

"He's fine! He's not the dying type!" one of us said, attempting to shake off the gloom.

We spent the hours until nightfall feverishly continuing our work. The only one to take a break was Kiyogawa. Mucus welled up ceaselessly in his eyes, and he'd go into the corner of the workroom to wash them with a handkerchief soaked in a cloudy white liquid. As he gently touched his eyes, a haggard shadow spread darkly across his face.

*

Night raids became more frequent, and since my home was in a crowded area of Tokyo, I figured it was just a matter of time before it burned down. My little brother and I buried the family album and our books in a hole we dug in the yard and placed a rucksack and trunk stuffed full of items we intended to salvage under the front steps. Less than a hundred yards from our house was a cemetery overgrown with luxuriant foliage. If we could make our way there, we would be able to escape the flames consuming the row houses; even if the fire spread to that sea of greenery, we were quite confident that we could dodge the flames, weaving in and out among the gravestones where we'd played since childhood. After Mother died, Father had gone to live with a woman he'd long been involved with, so my brother and I did as we pleased. Living alone lightened our spirits; there was no one to get in our way.

"The stink from that factory has pretty much sunk in, hasn't it?"

Teasing me, my brother laid his futon out on the opposite side of the room. The odor of chemicals and pelts emanating from my body was admittedly intolerable. But on the other hand, the smell of machine oil wafted thickly from his school uniform. My brother's detail was the Itabashi arsenal, where he worked day and night shifts. Whenever he opened his mouth, it was to talk about secret weapons. He looked down on me for working at the fur factory, though I was two grades his senior.

"I'm sure tanning hides is important and all, but couldn't you make yourself more useful burying those bodies floating in the river?" he said.

I could hear the sarcastic tone in his voice, but I too kept thinking about those bodies. Yes, we should have pulled them out of the water and buried them—but once buried, they would be forever cut off from human sight, and their neglected bones would deteriorate, and eventually vanish. As long as they floated on the surface, they would retain something close to their original form, and there was at least a slight chance that they might be identified by relatives and retrieved. So the person who tried to help might turn out to be, from the perspective of the corpse, a nuisance. Which isn't to say, of course, that leaving them in the river to float indefinitely was a preferable alternative.

One day when we gathered in the lounge for lunch, we noticed a group of soldiers pulling a large wagon along the riverbank. Stopping just below our window, they put on white masks and gloves and began dipping long hooks into the water to snare the corpses. We crowded around to watch as the bodies were vigorously hauled onto the bank, one by one.

They looked completely different out of the water. They were bloated; their clothes were taut, unable to contain the flesh, and their exposed limbs were as thick as well-nourished lotus roots—they looked like neglected sculptures. In the motions of the soldiers' hooks I sensed a familiarity with handling corpses. These bodies were nothing more than objects to them. We backed away from the window, not wanting to see the quickly arcing hooks, the blackened corpse of the woman with the baby still fastened on her back. I covered my mouth and, tearing down the stairs, vomited behind the building.

The next day, we approached the window ledge and fearfully peered down at the water. A large boat manned by soldiers and laden with cargo approached from downriver, its diesel engine echoing. The cargo, wrapped in straw mats, was unloaded onto the bank. Soon after, the wagon we'd seen the day before came back along the river road. The rolled-up mats with their strange protuberances were loaded carelessly into the wagon by the soldiers, who then disappeared down the road behind the factory.

The boat returned every two or three days. We realized by now that the bank below our window had been designated as an unloading zone for corpses, indicating that a suitable burial ground had been found near the factory. We closed the window, recoiling from the stench of death. Some of us fled the lounge altogether and spread our meager lunches on the factory floor.

A week or so after the boat first appeared, our old schoolmaster showed up at the factory and announced that, at the army's request, we were ordered to assist in the work of digging holes for the interment of victims. We were by no means required to touch the bodies, he added, just to dig the holes. The schoolmaster averted his eyes as he gave us this assignment, and we remained silent on hearing it. A year ago, when our class had been divided up among factories, we'd been stuck with the filthy, trivial detail of tanning hides, and now we had to suffer the further indignity of helping to dispose of drowned bodies.

A soldier arrived at the factory that afternoon, divided us into three groups, then took the leader of each group out through the gates to see the burial ground, a large vacant lot beyond the factory. We were informed that to expedite the disposal of bodies, several of them would be thrown together into a single hole, and therefore each hole would have to be at least twelve feet wide and six feet deep.

The next morning, we saw the first group off as they departed, shouldering shovels and scowling. When they returned that evening, exhausted and smeared with dirt, we learned that a total of nineteen bodies had been delivered in two groups, one in the morning and one in the afternoon, divided among three holes, and buried. Just as the schoolmaster had promised, the soldiers handled the bodies, and our team had only to dig the holes to accommodate them, then fill the holes in. But some students had had to stop working on account of the sight and stink of the corpses, and it seemed as if not much progress had been made.

My group started off the next day. On my way out of the house, I clipped a branch of peach blossoms blooming in the yard and wrapped it in newspaper. As I trudged down the road toward the factory, I began to feel self-conscious about the flowers and resolved to toss them into the bushes, but I soon saw that I wasn't the only one who'd thought of it. Some people even carried bundles of incense. We gathered outside the factory as though we were preparing to lay ashes to rest.

The vacant lot was surrounded by a marshy field of lotus flowers, and each time the wind blew, the petals rippled together, receding like the crests of waves. In one corner near the road, mounds of earth marked by rough wooden stakes indicated the holes in which corpses had been placed by the previous day's team. It reminded me of a ravaged beach piled with debris after a storm—like a place to abandon the dead rather than lay them to rest.

"If we don't get started, the corpses'll be here!"

We set our flowers and incense by the roadside, shuffled onto the lot, and thrust our shovels into the ground. The earth was soft, but weeds had spread vigorously, and the shovels' blades grated against them. Beneath the red topsoil was a layer of greenish clay, and we took turns in the holes tossing up the heavy earth.

As we finished our second hour on the job, we heard a voice call out, "They're here! They're here!" Three soldiers wearing white masks approached through the lotus field, pulling a large wagon. They stripped off the straw mats that covered its load, revealing a pile of corpses tangled together, arms and legs akimbo. A soldier with two stars on his collar searched through the clothing and bags of the deceased. He took a brush out of the inkhorn hanging from his waist and wrote names on a piece of scrap lumber, then signaled to another soldier, who snagged each body with a hook and tossed them one by one into a hole. The bodies vanished, their limbs outstretched. When the wagon was empty, the soldiers pulled it over to the roadside and threw in the straw mats.

"All right, kids, we're counting on you!" the two-starred soldier shouted, pulling his mask down. A smile spread across his face, mocking us as we stood rigid in fear.

The soldiers receded through the lotus fields, chatting. They wore swords on their hips, but they were scrawny men, past middle age.

"Well, let's do it," one of us said, feigning resolve, and covered his nose with a handkerchief. We all likewise firmly fastened our handkerchiefs and picked up our shovels. Some distance away, my classmates began scooping up dirt and tossing it in, but before long two of them, pale-faced, stopped working and hunched down in the weeds. I continued shoveling, driven by an impulse to hide the bodies from view as quickly as possible. I could imagine their sodden faces gazing up bleary-eyed at the sky.

Once the dirt was piled high over the hole, we tamped it down with our shovels and then stuck in the piece of scrap lumber the soldiers had left behind. Only three full names were recorded; for the remaining two, below a list of identifying marks, the words "male, unknown" and "female, unknown" were clumsily written. One classmate picked up the flowers we'd left on the side of the road. The rest of us lit sticks of incense, poking one into each mound. Then, slowly, we returned to our shovels.

*

The wagon came once or twice a day without fail, laden with corpses. We kept digging so that the number of holes would keep up with the number of bodies. Soon we had holes to spare.

"Are there a lot of bodies left?" a classmate asked the two-starred soldier.

"Oh yes. There aren't many in this part of the river, but downstream they're packed in. So many you can barely pull them out!" he said, grinning.

"Well then, this site alone won't be enough, will it?"

"Did you think this was the only place? There are more than ten lots where they're being buried. The wagons bring them in the middle of the night—so people won't have to see them." The soldier spoke in a businesslike tone, jotting down a corpse's identifying features in his notebook.

It dawned on us that our job wouldn't end until the lot was filled with holes. And since the holes we had dug so far covered only a fifth of the lot, it would take at least two more months to finish. But burial duty was still preferable to tanning hides at the factory. It involved soldiers directly, even if they were only auxiliary troops.

*

"We're helping the army bury the drowned bodies," I told my brother.
His reply fell short of my expectations.
"Tanning, burying—you've had nothing but weird jobs," he laughed.

*

We fell into a routine. If we dug continuously all morning, we could spend the afternoon relaxing. After a few weeks, half the site was filled with graves. New shoots came up from the dry grass, making the lot appear a little more like an actual cemetery.

The flow of bodies didn't diminish. Night raids became a regular occurrence, and each morning brought fresh corpses mixed with the old. We thought of them as mysteriously unburned objects endlessly spat out by the fire. By now I had lost my sense of purpose in burying the dead. There were plenty of dead women with babies on their backs, plenty of children; tossing dirt over their faces had become a purely mechanical gesture. On the battlefield, bodies were abandoned to rot away in piles. The war had marched over their deaths and moved on. But even as the decisive mainland battle became imminent, our strength was inexplicably wasted in returning these decomposing bodies to the earth. Didn't the soldiers who pulled the wagon day after day need to return to more active duty?

When I arrived at the factory one morning, I noticed pieces of broken glass and galvanized roof tiles scattered all over the grounds. Two buildings were on the verge of collapse. The factory operations disrupted, we answered roll call and walked out the gate with the other workers toward the lot. We were intercepted by two soldiers brandishing bayonets. Peering around the crowd that had gathered, we encountered a drastically changed scene.

Where the lotus flowers had once swayed in the wind, there were pock-marked depressions alongside high banks of freshly upturned earth. Between the ridges we saw chunks of metal shimmering in the sunlight. The undamaged tail of a plane with American markings stuck out of the field like an enormous figurehead.

The onlookers who lived in the neighborhood told us how, the night before, a B-29 straggling behind its formation had glided downward in a gentle arc and impaled itself in the earth. The four-man crew bailed out by parachute: one got caught on high-tension wires and was electrocuted, another landed in the river and hadn't been found, and the remaining two had been captured and taken away.

I searched for our graveyard in the changed landscape but couldn't make out the grave markers among the dirt and wreckage. If those markers had been destroyed, there would no longer be a way to distinguish among the dead. Any chance of the remains being restored to relatives would be lost, and the bodies would simply disintegrate in the earth. But we should have known from the beginning that there was no intention of transferring the remains to relatives. The corpses had been thrown haphazardly into holes in the first place. Most likely the army's plan was simply to hide them from view so as not to disturb public sentiment—the same result as if the burial site were erased or forgotten.

A month's work digging graves for the dead, and it might as well never have happened. Dejected, I headed back toward the factory with my class-mates, down the lotus-field road.

*

Four nights later, an incendiary bomb fell on my neighborhood.

I hoisted the rucksack I'd packed and, carrying a futon on my head, headed for the high ground of Yanaka cemetery. I climbed the stone steps, crossed the viaduct supporting the railroad tracks, and entered the cemetery. All around me people streamed down the road leading to the shrine and onto the narrow path winding through the gravestones beyond. The cherry blossoms were in full bloom. They stretched along both sides of the road, blanketing it with white petals.

I sat down at the base of a gravestone near the shrine and watched the ceaseless flow of evacuees—families carting away their earthly possessions, half-naked people clutching at singed scraps of clothing. I watched as they were swallowed up into the dim grounds of the cemetery.

The night sky was dyed vermilion, its reflection lighting the road. Above the treetops the not-quite-full moon hung like a bloodied egg yolk. And as though to block out even that light, B-29s skimmed past at low altitudes like huge green flashing fish.

How long until it was over, until the stream of people stopped, the thunder of bombs faded?

I stood up and left by the road. I could sense frightened people hiding in the bushes and among the gravestones, but not another soul walked on the road. The sky grew bright, and I began to hear a rumbling sound, like waves crashing on the shore. I slipped under some bushes and emerged at the edge of the cemetery to witness the cataclysmic spectacle unfolding before me.

Voluminous flames raged across my field of vision and surged at my feet like a terrible, angry sea. They whirled together in a vortex of yellow and vermilion, sparks flying violently overhead. My visual nerves, starved for light in the blackouts, were drawn to the fire's splendor. I lost the sensation of my feet touching the ground. I was caught up in the deep rumbling of the flames, the hallucination of being drawn into the midst of that sea of fire. Facing those flames I experienced a peculiar kind of solitude.

At last the reddish night sky began to lighten. As far as the eye could see, crackling flames extended like the bonfires of an enormous platoon camped on a plain at night.

I descended the cemetery slope and crossed the viaduct. I saw abandoned houses ablaze, crackling as if they were about to explode. No one was visible but a single old man squatting with a cane in the train station plaza. At the foot of the viaduct, a fallen telegraph pole was burning. I held out my hands to the fire.

"Brother!"

I spun around.

My little brother was back from night duty at the arsenal. He stood there with his sooty face. "What're you doing, just looking at the fire?"

In his bloodshot eyes glimmered the hint of a smile.

"It's cold!" I said. "You just got back from the factory?"

"It burned down. Nippori village is burning too, they say, so I walked back along the railroad tracks. The house?"

"Gone."

He nodded slightly and gazed at the city spread out before him, the color of smoldering coals. Then, squaring his narrow shoulders, he followed my example and held his hands to the flames spitting from the telegraph pole.

"If the arsenal's burned down, you can always come with me to the fur factory," I joked.

"Forget it!" he laughed.

I shrugged my shoulders and stuck out my tongue. My brother was in high spirits. I could understand why. He was thinking that the house we couldn't leave, even during weeks of air raids, the house that had become a heavy, detestable burden, had had the grace to burn down.

Strangely at peace, I gazed with my brother at the flames engulfing the blazing pole.

Translated from the Japanese by Keith Leslie Johnson

Contributors

Born in Imir, Turkey, **ARON R. AJI** is a professor of literature at Butler University, Indianapolis. His translations of works by Turkish authors Bilge Karasu, Latife Tekin, and Murathan Mungan have appeared in previous issues of Grand Street. He has completed translations of two of Bilge Karasu's books: a novel, Death in Troy, which was published by City Lights in 2002, and a collection of short fiction, The Garden of Migrant Cats, forthcoming from New Directions in fall 2003.

JORGE LUIS ARZOLA was born in Cuba in 1966, where he lives. He has published three collections of stories in Spanish, the third of which, La bandada infinita (The endless flock; Colección Premio, 2000) was awarded the Alejo Carpentier prize, the most prestigious award in Cuban literature. His work has been translated into French, German, and English and has appeared in a number of magazines and anthologies, including The Voice of the Turtle (Grove, 1998), a volume of contemporary Cuban fiction. Arzola completed his first novel while in residence at the German Academic Exchange Service in Berlin and is now at work on his second. This issue of Grand Street features two stories from his books Prisionero en el círculo del horizonte (Prisoner in the horizon's circle; Ediciones Avila, 2000) and La bandada infinita.

Walid Raad, founder of the **ATLAS GROUP**, was born in Chbanieh, Lebanon, in 1967 and was raised in predominantly Christian East Beirut. His critical essays have been published in Public Culture, Rethinking Marxism, and Third Text, and his media works have been shown at the Ayloul Festival, Beirut (2000); the Whitney Biennial, New York (2002); Documenta 11, Kassel, Germany (2002); the Fundació Antoni Tàpies, Barcelona, Spain (2002); and numerous other exhibitions in Europe, the Middle East, and North America. Raad is also a member of the Arab Image Foundation (Beirut/New York), a nonprofit organization that promotes photography in the Middle East and North Africa by locating, collecting, and preserving

the region's photographic heritage. He currently lives and works in New York, where he is an assistant professor at Cooper Union's School of Art.

AIDAS BAREIKIS was born in Vilnius, Lithuania, in 1967 and graduated from the Vilnius Art Academy in 1993. A recipient of a Soros Foundation grant and a Fulbright scholarship, Bareikis will represent Lithuania at the Venice Biennale this year. He lives and works in New York City.

BRUCE BEASLEY's fourth and latest collection of poems is Signs and Abominations (Wesleyan University Press, 2000). He teaches in the English department at Western Washington University, Bellingham.

NATHANIEL BELLOWS's poems have appeared in the New Republic, the Paris Review, Ploughshares, Southwest Review, Witness, and the Yale Review. He lives in New York.

WALLACE BERMAN was born on Staten Island, New York, in 1926. In 1955, he started Semina magazine, publishing writings by poets such as Michael McClure, Philip Lamantia, and David Meltzer, as well as Berman's own artwork and poetry. He had solo shows at the Ferus Gallery, Los Angeles, in 1957 and at the Los Angeles County Museum of Art and the Jewish Museum in New York in 1968. Retrospectives of his work have been presented by the Whitney Museum of American Art, New York (1978); the Otis Art Institute, Los Angeles (1978); the Institute of Contemporary Art, Amsterdam (1992–93); and L.A. Louver, Venice, California (1997). Berman's art has recently been on view in the group shows "Beat Culture and the New America, 1950–1965" at the Whitney Museum (1995), and "Sunshine and Noir: Art in L.A., 1960–1997," a traveling exhibition originating at the Louisiana Museum of Art, Humlebaek, Denmark, in 1997. Berman died in Topanga, California, in 1976.

CHRIS BURDEN was born in Boston, Massachusetts, in 1946. Recent exhibitions of his work include solo shows at the Austrian Museum of Applied Arts, Vienna (1996), the Tate Gallery, London (1999), and the Arts Club of Chicago (2001), and he participated in the 1999 Venice Biennale and the "Inaugural Exhibition" at the Baltic Center for Contemporary Art, Newcastle, England (2002). He lives and works in Topanga, California.

VIJA CELMINS was born in Riga, Latvia, in 1938 and emigrated to the United States in 1949. Recent surveys of her work include a 1993–94 retrospective organized by the Institute of Contemporary Art, Philadelphia, that traveled to the Walker Art Center (Minneapolis), the Whitney Museum of American Art (New York), and the Museum of Contemporary Art (Los Angeles); and a European retrospective that traveled to London, Madrid, and Frankfurt in 1996–97. In fall 2002 "The Prints of Vija Celmins" was exhibited at the Metropolitan Museum of Art, New York. Celmins received a MacArthur Fellowship in 1997.

RENÉ CHAR was born in 1907 at L'Isle-sur-Sorgue, France, and began publishing poetry in 1928. He was stationed with the French army in Alsace at the beginning of World War II and had joined the resistance movement by 1942. After the Liberation in 1944, Char's poems reappeared in print, and his wartime notebook Feuillets d'Hypnos was published in 1946 by Gallimard. Numerous editions of his poems and other writings appeared in the decades following the war, often in collaboration with artists and composers such as Georges Braque, Alberto Giacometti, Nicolas de Staël, and Pierre Boulez. Char died in 1988.

BRUCE CONNER was born in McPherson, Kansas, in 1933 and received a B.F.A. from the University of Nebraska, Lincoln, in 1956. "2002 BC: The Bruce Conner Story Part II," an exhibition of Conner's assemblages, drawings, collages, prints, photograms, and films opened at the Walker Art Center in Minneapolis in 1999 and traveled to the Modern Art Museum of Fort Worth, the M.H. de Young Memorial Museum in San Francisco, and the Museum of Contemporary Art in Los Angeles. His most recent solo show, "The Dennis Hopper One Man Show Vol. II," was held in 2003 at the Susan Inglett Gallery, New York.

MARGARET JULL COSTA was born in 1949 in Richmond, just outside London, and currently lives in Leicester, England. She has been a professional translator since 1987 and has translated works by many Spanish, Portuguese, and Latin American writers. Her awards include the 1992 Portuguese Translation Prize for her rendering of Fernando Pessoa's The Book of Disquiet; the translator's portion of the 1997 International IMPAC Dublin Literary Award for Javier Marías's A Heart So White; and the 2000 Weidenfeld Translation Prize for José Saramago's All the Names. She is currently translating Cousin Bazilio by the nineteenth-century Portuguese novelist Eça de Queiroz.

MIKE DAVIS was born in Fontana, California, in 1946 and is the author, most recently, of Dead Cities (New Press, 2002). A MacArthur Fellow, he teaches history and nonfiction writing at the University of California, Irvine. He has recently completed a history of sex, power, and scandal in San Diego as well as a young adult science-adventure novel.

RICHARD DOVE was born in 1954 in Bath and currently lives in Munich. An English poet, translator, and critic, he has been writing mainly in German since moving to the Federal Republic in 1987. Among his publications are two books of poems—Farbfleck auf einem Mondrian-Bild (St. Ingbert: Edition Thaleia, 2002) and Aus einem früheren Leben. Gedichte Englisch/Deutsch (Lyrikedition, 2000)— as well as translations from the German including two collections of poetry by Michael Krüger: Diderot's Cat (Carcanet, 1993) and At Night, Beneath Trees (George Braziller, 1998).

SUSAN EMERLING is a writer living in Los Angeles. Her fiction and nonfiction have appeared in the Los Angeles Times, Salon, and Faultline, among other publications. She wrote "Drinking, Drugging and Smoking in America: The Pursuit of Happiness," a two-hour documentary directed by Robert Zemeckis that premiered on Showtime in September 1999.

HARUN FAROCKI was born in Neutitschein, Germany, in 1944 and studied drama, journalism, and applied social studies in Berlin. He has lectured in Hamburg, Munich, Düsseldorf, and Stuttgart, and currently lectures at the Hochschule der Künste in Berlin. Until 1984, Farocki was also active as editor and writer of the influential German film periodical Filmkritik. He has made more than eighty films and was honored with a retrospective at the 14th Singapore International Film Festival in 2001. His films, videos, and installations have recently appeared at the Frankfurter Kunstverein; the Museum of Modern Art, New York; the Stedelijk Museum voor Actuele Kunst, Ghent; and the Museum Boijmans van Beuningen, Rotterdam.

JAMEY GAMBRELL writes on Russian art and culture and has translated works by Tatyana Tolstaya and Joseph Brodsky, among others. Her translation of Marina Tsvetaeva's Earthly Signs: Moscow Diaries, 1917–1922 (Yale University Press) was published in 2002. For this issue she has translated a new story by Vladimir Sorokin.

Born in Dresden in 1962, **DURS GRÜNBEIN** is the author of six volumes of poetry and a collection of essays and has received many literary awards, including the 1995 Georg Büchner Prize. The poems that appear in this issue of Grand Street come from Grünbein's first collection, Grauzone morgens (Suhrkamp, 1988). Grünbein has lived in Berlin since 1985.

HOWARD HALLE is a senior editor at Time Out New York.

BRIAN HENRY edits Verse magazine and teaches English at the University of Georgia, Athens. His first book, Astronaut (Arc Publications, 2000), was shortlisted for the Forward Prize for Best First Collection. He has two volumes of poetry forthcoming: Graft (New Issues Press, 2003) and American Incident (Salt Publishing, 2004). His poems have appeared in the Paris Review, American Poetry Review, and TriQuarterly.

MICHAEL HOFMANN's latest publication is Behind the Lines: Pieces on Writing and Pictures, a collection of essays and reviews. His translation of Franz Kafka's Amerika:

The Man Who Disappeared was published in 2002 by New Directions. He is currently translating a selection of Durs Grünbein's poems into English. Hofmann lives in London and teaches part-time in the English Department at the University of Florida, Gainesville.

MARK HUTCHINSON was born in London in 1957, where he founded and edited the review Straight Lines (1977–83). His translations of René Char have recently appeared in Selected Poems of René Char (New Directions, 1992), Three Poems (1994), Lascaux (1998), and 20th-Century French Poems (Faber, 2002). He has contributed to a number of magazines and journals, including the New York Times Book Review, Poetry Review, the Threepenny Review, the Times Literary Supplement, and is currently working on a selection of French translations of Hugh MacDiarmid's poetry (in collaboration with Antoine Joccottet) and a volume of Char's poems. He has lived in France since 1981.

KEITH LESLIE JOHNSON was born in Ojai, California, in 1974 and lived in Japan from 1993–95. He is currently a Presidential Fellow and Ph.D. candidate at Boston University. His translation of Haruki Murakami's "Three German Fantasies" appeared in the Review of Contemporary Fiction (summer 2002).

CRAIG KALPAKJIAN's work has been exhibited in a number of group exhibitions, including "Bitstreams" at the Whitney Museum of American Art, New York (2001); "01 01 01: Art in Technological Times" at the San Francisco Museum of Modern Art (2001); "Out of Sight: Fictional Architectural Spaces" at the New Museum of Contemporary Art, New York (2002); and "Contemporary Photographs" at the Metropolitan Museum of Art, New York (2002).

A. L. KENNEDY was born in Dundee, Scotland, in 1965 and lives in Glasgow. She is the author of three novels, four short-story collections, and two nonfiction books. Kennedy has received numerous prizes including the Somerset Maugham Award, the Encore Award, and the Saltire Scottish Book of the Year Award, and was named one of Britain's most original young novelists by Granta in 1993 and 2003. Appearing in this issue of Grand Street is a short story from Indelible Acts, to be published in the United States by Knopf in summer 2003.

ELIAS KHOURY was born in Beirut in 1948. He is the author of several novels, four of which—Little Mountain, Gates of the City, The Journey of the Little Gandhi (all University of Minnesota Press), and The Kingdom of Strangers (Arkansas University Press)—have been translated into English. An English translation of The Gate of the Sun, which won the Palestine Award in 1998, will be published next year by Seven Stories. Khoury is editor-in-chief of the literary supplement of An-Nahar, Beirut's principal newspaper, and currently a visiting professor of Arabic and comparative literature at New York University.

ISABELLA KIRKLAND was born in Old Lyme, Connecticut, in 1954 and studied at the San Francisco Art Institute. She is currently researching the subjects of her next three paintings: species that have become extinct since 1800; species that have been brought back from the brink of extinction; and species new to Western science. She lives in Sausalito, California.

MICHAEL KRÜGER was born in 1943 near Leipzig and now lives in Munich. He is the editor and publisher of the literary magazine Akzente, as well as the author of the volume of poems At Night, Beneath Trees (George Braziller, 1998) and the novel The Man in the Tower (George Braziller, 1993). A translation of his book The Celloplayer (Harcourt) is forthcoming in 2004.

RACHEL KUSHNER was born in Eugene, Oregon, in 1968. She is a contributing editor to Bomb magazine and has written on contemporary art for Artforum, Bookforum, Art and Text, and Cabinet. She has recently written on Roman Signer's work for the catalogue accompanying his 2003 solo exhibition at the Shisheido Gallery, Tokyo. Kushner, who lives in New York, is currently working on a novel about Americans living in pre-revolutionary Cuba.

DEBORAH LANDAU's poems have appeared in numerous literary magazines, including Columbia, Crab Orchard Review, Barrow Street, Prairie Schooner, and Gulf Coast. She was nominated for a Pushcart Prize in 1999, and her manuscript "Orchidelirium" was a 2002 National Poetry Series finalist. She teaches creative writing and literature at the New School in New York City.

LANCE LARSEN's first collection, Erasable Walls (New Issues Press), was published in 1998, and his poems have appeared in the Paris Review, Threepenny Review, the New Republic, and Kenyon Review, among other publications. He currently teaches literature at Brigham Young University.

The **LOS ANGELES FINE ARTS SQUAD** was founded by artists Terry Schoonhoven and Victor Henderson, who began their collaboration in 1969 with Brooks Street Painting, a mural on the back wall of Henderson's studio in Venice, California. They were joined briefly by Jim Frazen and Leonard Koren, who were students of Schoonhoven's. The Squad disbanded in 1974, and most of the group's work is now either badly damaged or completely gone.

ATI MAIER was born in Munich, Germany, in 1962. Her work has been included in many group exhibitions throughout Europe and the United States, most recently in "Drawing on Landscape" at Philadelphia's Gallery Joe. She lives in Brooklyn, New York.

THOMAS MEDIODIA is the assistant editor of lacanian ink and the Wooster Press.

ALICE OSWALD's second volume of poetry, Dart (Faber, 2002), was awarded this year's T. S. Eliot prize for the best collection of poetry published in the UK and Ireland. She received the 1996 Forward Prize for Best First Collection for The Thing in the Gap-Stone Stile (Oxford University Press). She lives in Devon, England.

EDUARDO PAOLOZZI was born in 1924 in Edinburgh and studied at the Edinburgh College of Art and the Slade School of Fine Art in London. Solo exhibitions of his work have been held at the Museum of Modern Art, New York; the Scottish National Gallery of Art, Edinburgh; the Stedelijk Museum, Amsterdam; the Tate Gallery, London; and the Ludwig Museum, Cologne, among other venues. Recent public commissions include stained glass windows for St. Mary's Episcopal Cathedral, Palmerston Place, Edinburgh (2002). The Dean Gallery, housing a reconstruction of Paolozzi's studio and a portion of the artist's archive, opened in 1999 in Edinburgh. Paolozzi, who was knighted in 1989, is currently professor emeritus at the Royal College of Art in London.

NEO RAUCH was born in Leipzig, East Germany, in 1960. A traveling exhibition of Rauch's work originated at the Museum Galerie für Zeitgenössische Kunst, Leipzig, in 2000, and a solo exhibition of his paintings was held in 2002 at the Bonnefantenmuseum, Maastricht, Holland, where he received the Vincent Van Gogh Award for Contemporary Art.

ROBIN ROBERTSON is from the northeast coast of Scotland. His book of poems A Painted Field won a number of British prizes, including the 1997 Forward Prize for Best First Collection and the Consignia/Saltire Scottish First Book of the Year Award, and was subsequently published in the U.S. by Harcourt and in Italy by Guanda. His poetry appears regularly in the London Review of Books and the New Yorker, and he is represented in many anthologies. His second collection, Slow Air, is due out from Harcourt this April.

JAMES ROSENQUIST was born in Grand Forks, North Dakota, and studied art at the University of Minnesota and at the Art Students League in New York. He has exhibited widely in the United States and Europe, and surveys of his work have been held at the National Gallery of Canada, Ottawa (1968); the Whitney Museum of American Art, New York, and the Museum of Contemporary Art, Chicago (1972); and the National Museum of American Art, Smithsonian Institution, Washington, D.C. (1986), among other venues. A retrospective of Rosenquist's work, curated by Grand Street art editor Walter Hopps, will open in May 2003 at the Menil Collection and at the Museum of Fine Arts in Houston, Texas. It will travel to the Solomon R. Guggenheim Museum, New York, in fall 2003.

SABINE RUSS is a German art critic and curator based in New York. She has published numerous articles on con-temporary art and contributed to exhibition catalogues for shows in Europe and the United States. Among her recent writings is a fictional text for a catalogue of Ati Maier's paintings, published in fall 2002 by Dogenhaus Galerie, Leipzig, and Pierogi, New York.

INGRID SCHAFFNER is a writer and curator based in New York, and a senior curator at the Institute of Contemporary Art, University of Pennsylvania, Philadelphia. As an independent curator, Schaffner has organized numerous exhibitions, including "Julien Levy: Portrait of an Art Gallery" at the Equitable Gallery, New York (1998), and "Gloria: Another Look at Feminist Art of the 1970s," a traveling exhibition co-curated with Catherine Morris originating at White Columns, New York (2002). Her writings have appeared in numerous publications, including Artforum, Arts, Frieze, Art on Paper, and Parkett, and her most recent book is Salvador Dalí's Dream of Venus: The Surrealist Funhouse at the 1939 World's Fair (Princeton Architectural Press, 2002).

ELIF SHAFAK is the author of four novels that are celebrated in her native Turkey. Her first, Pinhan, published when she was twenty-seven, received the Mevlana Prize for work in mystical literature. Her third, Mahrem (The sacred; Metis), won the 2000 Turkish Novel Award, the country's most prestigious literary honor. An excerpt from that novel appears in this issue of Grand Street. Shafak is in residence this year at the Five College Program in Women's Studies, Amherst, Massachusetts.

ROMAN SIGNER was born in Appenzell, Switzerland, in 1938. His work has been exhibited in galleries and museums throughout Europe and the United States, and was featured in the 1976 Venice Biennale and Documenta 8, Kassel, Germany (1987). A solo exhibition of his work opened in February 2003 at the Shiseido Gallery, Tokyo. Signer lives and works in St. Gallen, Switzerland.

DANIEL SLAGER is an editor at Harcourt and a contributing editor to Grand Street. His translations from the German of works by writers Durs Grünbein, Felicitas Hoppe, and Terézia Mora have appeared in recent issues of Grand Street.

JOHN VIGNAUX SMYTH is the author of two books, A Question of Eros (University Press of Florida, 1986) and The Habit of Lying (Duke University Press, 2002). He divides the year between Oregon and his home in Scotland.

VLADIMIR SOROKIN was born in 1955 in the Moscow region. In 1977, he graduated from the Oil and Gas Institute with a degree in mechanical engineering, but he never worked as an engineer. Sorokin has written ten plays, five screenplays, and six novels, the latest of which, Ice, was short-listed for the 2002 Russian Booker Prize. He is currently working on a libretto for the Bolshoi Opera. Sorokin made his English-language debut in Grand Street 48 with "A Month in Dachau," and his new story "Hiroshima" appears in this issue. He lives in Moscow.

KYOKO UCHIDA's work has appeared in Grand Street, the Georgia Review, and Black Warrior Review, among other journals, and is forthcoming in Prairie Schooner. She currently works as a translator and bilingual editor in Washington, D.C.

RYAN G. VAN CLEAVE's most recent books are a volume of poems, Say Hello (Pecan Grove Press, 2001), and the anthology American Diaspora: Poetry of Displacement (University of Iowa Press, 2001), which he co-edited.

WILLIAM T. VOLLMANN is the author of eight novels, three collections of stories, and two nonfiction works. Vollmann's writing has appeared in the New Yorker, Esquire, and Granta, and he is a frequent contributor to Grand Street. His new nonfiction book, Rising Up and Rising Down, parts of which were featured in Grand Street 65, will be published in summer 2003 by McSweeney's.

ALAN WARNER was born in Argyll, Scotland, in 1964. His first novel, Morvern Callar (Anchor Books, 1997), was excerpted in Grand Street 57; a film version, directed by Lynne Ramsay, was released in winter 2002. These Demented Lands (Anchor Books) won the 1998 Encore Award for second novels, and The Sopranos (Harvest Books, 2000) is also set to be filmed. This issue of Grand Street features an excerpt from Warner's fourth and latest novel, The Man Who Walks, published in Britain by Jonathan Cape in 2002. Warner was recently named one of Britain's most original young novelists by Granta.

AKIRA YOSHIMURA, an acclaimed author in his native Japan, was born in 1927 in Tokyo. Winner of the 1966 Dazai Osamu Prize, awarded annually for an outstanding short story by a new writer, he has since published a number of novels, short stories, and nonfiction works, including Battleship Musashi: The Making and Sinking of the World's Biggest Battleship (Kodansha International, 1999), for which he received the Kikuchi Kan Prize. His translated books include On Parole and Shipwrecks (both Harvest Books, 2000), and One Man's Justice (Harcourt, 2001). This issue of Grand Street includes a new translation of Yoshimura's story "Glorious Days," which will be included in a collection of stories forthcoming from Harcourt.

Grand Street would like to thank:
MORGAN ENTREKIN, SHARON GALLAGHER, PAUL HASSETT, MICHAEL KAZMAREK, AVERY LOZADA, ALLISON SMITH, MÜGE GÜRSOY SÖKMEN

This issue of Grand Street is dedicated to the memory of
SIGVARD BERNADOTTE (1907–2002)
IRENE DIAMOND (1911–2003)
CHARLES HENRI FORD (1908–2002)
FRANCES FRALIN (1932–2003)
FREDERIC D. GRAB (1935–2002)
KENNETH KOCH (1925–2002)
INGE MORATH (1923–2002)
WILLIAM PHILLIPS (1907–2002)
LARRY RIVERS (1923–2002)
DR. SIEGFRIED UNSELD (1924–2002)
LEW WASSERMAN (1915–2002)
and
COLIN DE LAND (1955–2003)
for whom we cared deeply

Illustrations

Front cover Neo Rauch, *Hatz (Chase)*, 2002. Oil on canvas, 82 11/16 x 98 7/16". Copyright © 2003 Artists Rights Society (ARS), New York/VG Bild-Kunst, Bonn. Courtesy of the artist and David Zwirner, New York/Galerie EIGEN + ART, Berlin. Photo credit: Uwe Walter, Berlin.

Back cover Neo Rauch, *Sturmnacht (Stormy night)*, 2000. Oil on canvas, 78 3/4 x 118 1/8". Copyright © 2003 Artists Rights Society (ARS), New York/VG Bild-Kunst, Bonn. Courtesy of the artist and David Zwirner, NewYork/Galerie EIGEN + ART, Berlin.

p. 6 Woodcut by Eduardo Paolozzi. Title and date appear with image. 22 7/16 x 14 15/16". Copyright © 2003 Artists Rights Society (ARS), New York/DACS, London. Courtesy of the artist and the Paolozzi Archive, Scottish National Gallery of Modern Art.

pp. 41–44 Four paintings by James Rosenquist. Titles and dates appear with images. **p. 41** Oil and sand on canvas with burnt wood and found objects (paintbrush and wooden carving), 100 x 93 1/2". Photo credit: Peter Foe. **p. 42** Oil on canvas with attached Plexiglas sheet, 108 x 96". **p. 43** Oil on canvas, 102 x 72". **p. 44** Oil on linen with attached metal springs, 96 x 69 x 5". All images © James Rosenquist/Licensed by VAGA, New York. Courtesy of the artist.

pp. 57–60 Installation by Aidas Bareikis. Title and date appear with images. Mixed media installation, dimensions variable. Courtesy of the artist and Leo Koenig, Inc., New York.

p. 69 Collage by Wallace Berman. Title and date appear with image. Verifax collage, negative image, 8 1/4 x 10 1/2". Collection of Nicole Klagsbrun Gallery, New York. Courtesy of the Wallace Berman Estate.

p. 74 Photograph by Craig Kalpakjian. Title and date appear with image. Giclée print mounted on Plexiglas, 58 x 72 1/4". Edition of six. Copyright © Craig Kalpakjian. Courtesy of the artist and Andrea Rosen Gallery, New York.

pp. 93–96 Four paintings by Isabella Kirkland. Titles and dates appear with images. All works oil and alkyd paint on canvas, except **p. 94** oil and alkyd paint on panel. **p. 93** 36 x 48". **p. 94** 48 x 36". **p. 95** 48 x 36". **p. 96** 36 x 48". All images courtesy of the artist and Feature, Inc., New York.

p. 102 Mural by the Los Angeles Fine Arts Squad. Title and date appear with image. Enamel on stucco, 42 x 65'. Photograph copyright © Terry Schoonhoven. Courtesy of Sheila Schoonhoven.

pp. 104 and 122 Two works by Vija Celmins. Titles and dates appear with images. p. 104 Drypoint aquatint, 23 7/8 x 19 3/8". Edition of forty-eight. p. 122 Plastic, wood, canvas, and oil paint, diameter 8 1/2". Both images courtesy of the artist and McKee Gallery, New York.

pp. 109–112 Four paintings by Ati Maier. Titles and dates appear with images. All works colored ink and woodstain on paper. p. 109 7 1/2 x 22 1/2". p. 110 7 x 27". p. 111 24 x 24". p. 112 16 x 28". All images courtesy of the artist and Pierogi, New York.

pp. 117–120 Four paintings by Neo Rauch. Titles and dates appear with images. p. 117 Oil on canvas, 78 3/4 x 118 1/8". p. 118 Oil on canvas, 98 7/16 x 78 3/4". p. 119 Oil on canvas, 98 7/16 x 70 7/8". p. 120 Oil on canvas, 82 11/16 x 98 7/16". All images copyright © 2003 Artists Rights Society (ARS), New York/VG Bild-Kunst, Bonn. Courtesy of the artist and David Zwirner, New York/Galerie EIGEN + ART, Berlin. p. 118 Photo credit: Uwe Walter, Berlin.

pp. 156–160 Five works by Roman Signer. Titles and dates appear with images. p. 156 Video stills: Tomasz Rogowiec. p. 157 Photos: Emil Grubenmann. p. 158 Video stills: Aleksandra Signer. p. 159 Film stills: Peter Liechti. p. 160 Photos: Stefan Rohner. All images courtesy of the artist and Galerie Hauser & Wirth, Zurich.

p. 163 Drawing by Bruce Conner. Title and date appear with image. Ink on paper, 20 3/8 x 17 1/2". Courtesy of the artist and Michael Kohn Gallery, Los Angeles.

pp. 193–196 Seven stills from three color videos by Harun Farocki. Titles and dates appear with images. pp. 193 (bottom) and 194 Two stills from Eye/Machine I, 24 minutes. pp. 193 (top) and 195 Three stills from Eye/Machine II, 15 minutes. Photo credit p. 193 (top): Peenemünde. p. 196 Two stills from Eye/Machine III. All images courtesy of the artist and Greene Naftali Gallery, New York.

pp. 199–202 Four performances by Chris Burden. Titles, dates, and descriptions appear with images. p. 199 Photo credit: Alfred Lutjeans. p. 200 Photo credit: Terry McDonnell. pp. 201 and 202 Photo credit: Charles Hill. All images courtesy of the artist.

pp. 217–220 Eight digital color prints by the Atlas Group/Walid Raad. Titles and dates appear with images. Original notebook dimensions: 9 x 6 1/2". All images courtesy of the artist.

Back Issues

To place an order, visit our website at WWW.GRANDSTREET.COM or send name, address, issue number(s), and quantity to

GRAND STREET, Back Issues
214 Sullivan Street, #6C
New York, NY 10012

Back issues are $18 each ($25 overseas and Canada) including postage and handling, payable by check or money order in U.S. dollars.

For more information, call 877-533-2944.

For complete tables of contents and selections from the Grand Street archive, visit WWW.GRANDSTREET.COM

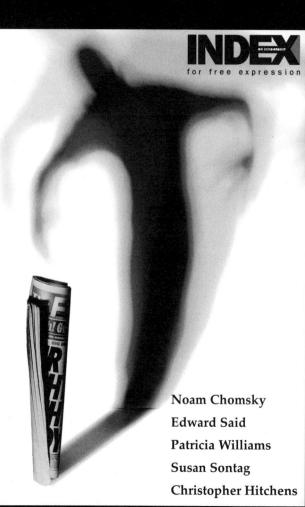

"QUITE SIMPLY, THE MOST IMPRESSIVE LITERARY MAGAZINE OF ITS TIME." *

The Group
Pictures from Previous Lives

WE'D LIKE TO INTRODUCE YOU TO <u>GRANTA</u> MAGAZINE.

If you don't know it yet, you've probably read about it. The current issue ('The Group,' shown here) was the *Observer*'s Book Of The Week, last week. The *Economist* recommended the Spring 2002 issue ('What We Think Of America') to "anyone who is distressed by the gap in comprehension that is threatening to open up between Americans and their non-American friends" (which now reads like an understatement). 'Music,' before that, was described in the *Observer* as "Granta at its luminous best." (And you might have seen articles in the press recently about our forthcoming Spring issue, 'BEST OF YOUNG BRITISH NOVELISTS.')

SO WHAT IS <u>GRANTA</u>, EXACTLY?

It's a quarterly paperback magazine (big—at least 256 pages, and illustrated) which publishes the most intelligent and engaging new fiction, reportage, memoir, argument and photography that we can commission, inspire or find. Often the issues are based on a theme, which is why each issue has a title, like a book.

An anthology, in other words?

No. *Granta* is a magazine—alive to the present. It is produced in book format because writing this good deserves nothing less. It also deserves to be widely read, which is why we are inviting you to try *Granta*—at absolutely no risk—with this:

FREE ISSUE OFFER. *You'll receive:*

➤ **FREE:** 'The Group,' the latest issue ($12.95 in bookshops), with short stories by **JOYCE CAROL OATES** and **PAUL THEROUX; CHRISTOPHER BARKER** (son of the poets George Barker and Elizabeth Smart) on *la vie Bohème* in Essex; **C. J. DRIVER** on the lost friendships of South Africa. Plus **LUKE HARDING** in Afghanistan, and more.

➤ **WITH A ONE-YEAR SUBSCRIPTION:** four more quarterly paperback issues (starting with 'Best of Young British Novelists' in Spring), worth $14.95 each, for $24.95. **IN ALL YOU SAVE $47 (65%) OFF THE BOOKSHOP PRICE.**

➤ **AND A FULL MONEY BACK GUARANTEE.** If *Granta* doesn't absorb, engage, entertain, provoke and move you, simply cancel your subscription, and we will refund you for the remaining issues.

* The Daily Telegraph

INTRODUCTORY TRIAL OFFER—SAVE $47 (65%) ✂

○ **YES:** I'd like to try *Granta* for $24.95. I'll get the latest issue, 'The Group,' FREE, with a trial subscription (four more quarterly paperback issues of at least 256 pages each, worth $14.95 each, starting with the forthcoming Spring issue, 'Best of Young British Novelists'). In all, I save $47 (65%) off the bookshop price. I can cancel the subscription at any time, for any reason, and will receive a refund for the unsent issues.

Name/Address: _____

City/State/Zip code: _____

NS03C17G0

Payment** by ○ Check payable to Granta (US dollars drawn on US bank)   ○ Visa, MasterCard, AmEx.

Card no: __ __ __ __ __ __ __ __ __ __ __ __ __ __ __ __   Expires: __ __ / __ __   Signed: _____

** Rates outside US and UK: Canada $36.95/$49.95 CDN, Mexico/S. America $33.70, Rest of World $45.45. Credit cards will be charged at US dollar rates shown. Please allow 4-6 weeks for delivery of your first issue.

➡ **FOR FASTER SERVICE,** fax this order form to: (601) 353-0176. Or return to: Granta, PO Box 23152, Jackson, MS 39225-3152.

This offer expires June 30, 2003.

PATRICK MCGRATH

In *The Designated Mourner*, there is a sense that the liberal intelligentsia may be impotent, irresponsible, hypothetical, but at the same time, when they go, everything of value goes with them.

BOMB

WALLACE SHAWN

My dear fellow, you've summarized my work so beautifully that I don't need to say any more or write any more.

FENCE

WILL ALEXANDER
ELIZABETH
ALEXANDER
BRUCE ANDREWS
DAVID ANTIN
RAE ARMANTROUT
JOHN ASHBERY
CAL BEDIENT
CHARLES
BERNSTEIN
MICHAEL
BURKARD
LEE ANN BROWN
ANNE CARSON
HELENE CIXOUS
NORMA COLE
GILLIAN CONOLEY
CLARK COOLIDGE
ROBERT COOVER
MAHMOUD
DARWISH
MARK DOTY
CORNELIUS EADY
RUSSELL EDSON
KENWARD
ELMSLIE
THALIA FIELD
NICK FLYNN
AMY GERSTLER

PETER GIZZI
JORIE GRAHAM
ALLEN GROSSMAN
BRENDA HILLMAN
FANNY HOWE
CHRISTINE HUME
DEVIN JOHNSTON
CLAUDIA KEELAN
WELDON KEES
KENNETH KOCH
PAUL LaFARGE
ANN LAUTERBACH
SAM LIPSYTE
JACKSON
MacLOW
PAUL
MALISZEWSKI
BEN MARCUS
RICK MOODY
JANE MILLER
SUSAN MITCHELL
LAURA MULLEN
HARRYETTE
MULLEN
EILEEN MYLES
ALICE NOTLEY
GEOFFREY
NUTTER
G.E. PATTERSON
CLAUDIA RANKINE
DONALD REVELL

ADRIENNE RICH
LAURA RIDING
ELIZABETH
ROBINSON
MARY RUEFLE
MURIEL
RUKEYSER
TOMAS SALAMUN
YI SANG
LESLIE SCALAPINO
ELENI SIKELIANOS
JULIANA SPAHR
COLE SWENSEN
WALLACE
STEVENS
JANE UNRUE
JAMES TATE
SAM TRUITT
JEAN VALENTINE
KAREN VOLKMAN
ROSMARIE
WALDROP
MARJORIE WELISH
JOE WENDEROTH
SUSAN WHEELER
DARA WIER
C.D. WRIGHT
MARK
WUNDERLICH
KEVIN YOUNG
DEAN YOUNG

14 Fifth Avenue, #1A New York, NY 10011
www.fencemag.com/www.fencebooks.com

TIN HOUSE MAGAZINE & TIN HOUSE BOOKS PRESENT THE 1ST ANNUAL

TIN HOUSE
summer writers workshop

A ONE-WEEK WRITING INTENSIVE —

seminars, workshops, panels, and readings

○ ○ ○ ○

FICTION › NONFICTION › POETRY › FILM

FACULTY: Amy Bartlett › Charles D'Ambrosio › Percival Everett
F.X. Feeney › Judith Hall › Bruce Handy › Jeanne McCulloch
Oren Moverman › Chris Offutt › Whitney Otto › Peter Rock
Lynne Sampson › Elissa Schappell › Helen Schulman
Rob Spillman › Sallie Tisdale › Bill Wadsworth

SPECIAL GUESTS:
DOROTHY ALLISON, TODD HAYNES
DENIS JOHNSON, MIRANDA JULY
RICK MOODY, JOY HARRIS
AMY WILLIAMS

REED COLLEGE › PORTLAND, OREGON

JULY 12 – JULY 19 : 2003

SCHOLARSHIPS AVAILABLE. *Space is limited. Application deadline: May 1st, 2003*
For more information and application guidelines: www.tinhouse.com or call 503 219-0622

locus novus
a synthesis of text and image

www.locusnovus.com

Chinua Achebe
Meena Alexander
Dorothy Allison
Kwame Anthony Appiah
James Atlas
Russell Banks
Peter Carey
Anne Carson
Sandra Cisneros

Maureen Howard
Richard Howard
Denis Johnson
William Kennedy
Tony Kushner
Arthur Miller
Lorrie Moore
Joyce Carol Oates
Tim O'Brien

PEN

A M E R I C A

A Journal for Writers and Readers

$10 single copy
$18 one year
$32 two years
www.pen.org/journal/
AmEx, MasterCard, Visa

PEN America #A13GS
568 Broadway, Suite 401
New York, NY 10012-3224

Stanley Crouch
Michael Cunningham
Lydia Davis
Thulani Davis
Umberto Eco
Lynn Emanuel
Rosario Ferré
Carolyn Forché
Paula Fox
Ian Frazier
Mary Gaitskill
William H. Gass
Amitav Ghosh
Francisco Goldman
Nadine Gordimer
Mary Gordon
Jessica Hagedorn
Amy Hempel
Bob Holman

Grace Paley
Suzan-Lori Parks
Willie Perdomo
Marilynne Robinson
Salman Rushdie
Edward Said
Sonia Sanchez
Simon Schama
Frederick Seidel
Elaine Showalter
Charles Simic
Susan Sontag
William T. Vollmann
Anne Waldman
John Edgar Wideman
C. K. Williams
Jeanette Winterson
James Wood
C. D. Wright